When a White Horse Is Not a Horse

Ethan James Kaplan

When a White Horse Is Not a Horse

Ethan James Kaplan

Published by Unsolicited Press
www.unsolicitedpress.com

Copyright © 2019 Ethan James Kaplan
All Rights Reserved.
First Edition Paperback.

Cover Art: Ashwin Anandani
Editor: Chandler S. White
Editor: S.R. Stewart

For information, contact the publisher at info@unsolicitedpress.com

Unsolicited Press Books are distributed to the trade by Ingram.
Printed in the United States of America.
ISBN: 978-1-947021-68-6

Table of Contents

Truth becomes fiction when the fiction's true,

Real becomes unreal where the unreal's real

- Cao Xueqin ("Dream of the Red Chamber")

2014 / Chapter 1: A Rough Landing

Julian was twenty-six thousand feet in the air when he first saw Hong Kong in the distance. He pressed his face against the window and stared out, watching the city lights cut through the clouds. It was midnight local time but still 4:00pm back in London—a full twenty hours since he'd last seen the sun. His brain was screaming silently at the continued darkness, refusing to sleep but rejecting reality. The city below looked like an illuminated blur.

Flying was a special sort of hell for Julian. The thought of it alone caused his heart to quiver incessantly and made the hairs on his arms rise in protest. He knew that it was the safest form of travel, but every time the jets flared on and the nose of the plane tilted up into the sky, his brain shut off, and his gut took over, screaming "This is not natural. Humans are *not* supposed to fly." His chest would pound so forcefully that the anxiety pills he took for his daily panic attacks might as well have been candy for all the good they did. Even when fatigue took hold and his eyes rolled backward into his skull, a new fear would always take hold and jolt him back awake. He felt like the plane was going to fall out of the sky midflight and drop into the ocean or that there would be an air pressure leak causing everyone onboard to be strangled by hypoxia, the plane sailing on autopilot for hours until it finally ran out of fuel.

"It's beautiful, isn't it?" said the girl on his right, a pudgy Chinese woman with a round face and sunken lidless eyes. She had a weathered sleep mask strapped to her forehead and a red London School of Economics hoodie draped over her lap.

"I don't know," Julian replied as he ironed out a fierce itch on his thigh. The blue-and-white-striped pajamas he wore were made of some kind of synthetic polyester seemingly designed to cause contact dermatitis. A bit of revenge from the assembly lines in Guangdong, which Julian could see just across the water. He leaned back against the undersized pillow that came free with his Economy Basic seat, scarcely able to discern a difference between the island and the mainland. "It's hard to tell from up here. Everything looks pretty much the same from this height."

"No *way*," the girl gasped, offended by the supposition. She reached over Julian's seat and pointed out the window toward a pale blue light in the haze. "Look down there."

"At what? The smog?"

The girl shook her head emphatically, causing her bun to come loose and morph into a slender ponytail. "No," she said. "You have to look through it."

Julian squinted his eyes, and the anemic skyline came into focus. Each tower gave off its own faint aura of color; blots of blue, red, and gold dotted the iridescent fog, blending into each other like watercolor fireworks. Julian struggled to make out the lettering on the side of one tower. "Pana . . . Panasonic?"

"That's right," the girl said. "And Bank of America, HSBC . . . Hong Kong is the only place that advertises *in* its skyline. Even from up here, you can't escape."

"Well, that's unnerving."

"Actually, I kind of like it," she said. "This city doesn't lie. It doesn't try to hide anything. It is what it is."

"I guess," Julian sighed. The longer he stared, the thicker the fog grew, until even the outlines of the buildings melted away into a pale rainbow cloud.

"So, what's with the outfit?" the girl asked, stretching her arms high above her head. "You a narcoleptic or something?"

"No."

"Well, you look like you got some quality shut-eye at least."

"Not even a wink."

She grimaced at the thought. "Yeesh. Then what'd you *do* the whole flight?"

"Read half a Murakami novel. Watched a bunch of old Raymond Lau films."

"Twelve hours of Raymond Lau? Sounds like a real nightmare."

"He's not so bad. Sure, he hams it up a little, and the special effects really haven't aged well. But I've seen his films a thousand times already. It's hard to explain, but they feel like home. The good guys win, the bad guys lose—just like it should be."

"But they're not realistic. Half the time, you can even see the wires."

"I don't watch movies for realism," Julian said. "I watch them to get away."

"I get it. Sometimes the dream is more interesting than reality."

"Not for me. My life is interesting enough as is."

"Puh-lease. A *gweilo* steps into Chinese airspace for all of five minutes and now he thinks he's Marco Polo. What, are you here to teach English or something? Or just to shave off a little bit of gold like everyone else?"

Julian again pressed his face to the window, the cold glass sending a shiver down his gaunt, stubbled cheek. The air inside the cabin was so arid that his lips cracked at the corners, and he had worse cottonmouth than the first time he ripped a bong in A-Level. His instincts told him not to say anything, but he was so tired and drugged that candor got the better of him.

"I'm here to find a monk."

The girl looked skeptical. "A monk?"

Julian nodded. "That's right. He friended me on Facebook last year, just a few weeks after my mom died."

"A monk on Facebook. Never heard of that."

"Every day he sent me these little proverbs and stories. Excerpts of the Lotus, Diamond, and Heart Sutras. At first, I thought he was reading off fortune cookies or something . . ."

"What's a fortune cookie?"

". . . but then," Julian said, reaching into his bag and producing a small envelope with a blue HK Post airmail sticker on its top right corner, "he sent me this." He opened the envelope and removed a sheet of yellow lined paper, folded in thirds. The girl unfurled the letter, revealing a handwritten poem scribbled in faded black ink:

> *A white horse from Hong Kong,*
> *holding debts from yesterday.*
> *Have you ever heard the song*
> *of the ox who ran astray?*
> *(Ask for Shih-yin at Man Mo Temple)*

"So he's a poet," the girl said. "And not a very good one."

"A white horse from Hong Kong," Julian repeated. "I was born in Hong Kong in 1978, the Year of the Horse. And I'm a debt collector . . . or I was one, at least."

"You're from Hong Kong?"

"I was born there," he explained, "but I haven't lived there in a long time. My mum took me away when I was six years old."

"Couldn't take the heat anymore?"

"No," he said. "Divorce. My father was working there as a police inspector. But one night he didn't come home from work, and no one's heard from him since. My mum said he fell in love with a whore."

"That does tend to happen."

"He was born in 1949, the Year of the Ox."

The girl scratched her chin, then examined the letter again. "Interesting."

"*Very* interesting," Julian said, staring wistfully at the clouds below. Outside, there was a pitter-patter of raindrops on the wing.

"Do you know anyone else in Hong Kong? Besides this monk, I mean."

"No."

"Do you speak any Cantonese?"

"No."

She leaned in. "Do you have money?"

Julian shook his head resoundingly. "I spent what was left of my savings on this flight. I don't even have a return ticket."

"*Aiyyya*," the girl groaned. "You *gweilos* do have a flair for the romantic." She scratched her ear and emitted a deep sigh. "Alright, I'll help you out."

Julian raised an eyebrow. "You will?"

"If I don't, you'll get eaten alive out there. And besides, now I want to know what happened too. The whole thing sounds like an action movie."

"Like a Raymond Lau film," Julian said. "That's what I thought too."

The girl picked up her plush Pikachu backpack and unzipped the front pouch, pulling a handmade business card out from its plump belly. In the center of the pink latticed paper, which smelled vaguely of mulberry, the girl's name and information were emblazoned in sparkling golden gel ink:

FLORA KONG

Economist / Graphic Designer

+44 020 5464 9468

queenkong@lse.ac.uk

Julian took the card. "Flora," he said. "I like your name."

"Thank you," she replied proudly. "I picked it myself."

"I can tell."

"What's yours?"

"Julian," he said, handing her the last business card from his wallet. "Julian Kensington. My mum picked that one."

"I can tell."

There was a crash of thunder outside, and the seatbelt sign flashed on. The rain was getting heavier, causing the already unsteady plane to gyrate. A voice came on over the PA: "Cabin crew, please be seated for landing." Then it buzzed again. "*Gei cong fuk mou jyun zeon bei gong lok.*"

The plane shook violently as it descended, the flashes of lightning outside growing increasingly bright. Chills dotted by pangs of terror descended on Julian like raging thundersnow. He reached for his backpack and the prescription bottle inside, but the bag had burrowed too far beneath the seat in front of him, the descent of the plane having shifted it forward, and he couldn't quite reach it with his seatbelt fastened. Safety or the illusion of safety; it was a difficult choice.

"Relax," Flora said. "This is just a light drizzle. Wait till you see the typhoons, the black rain . . ."

Julian gulped as the plane slipped beneath the clouds. The fog outside lifted somewhat, but he still couldn't see the landing strip through the diagonal sheets of rain. The wings tilted up and down uncontrollably, and Julian reflexively reached out for Flora's hand.

"There's nothing to worry about," she said. "Those are professionals up there."

"I know . . ."

"You've got to have faith."

The water below drew closer, and the buildings in the distance grew taller and taller with each passing second. Julian took a deep breath and braced himself, squeezing Flora's hand tight. He closed his eyes, and there was a violent jolt, followed by the sound of rubber scratching against concrete. The plane skidded to a halt.

A voice came on over the PA: "Welcome to Hong Kong International Airport."

Julian opened his eyes again and saw Flora looking over with a wide grin. "See?"

***

After a short bus ride and a trip on the underground train, Julian and Flora finally reached the immigration counter inside the terminal and parted ways. Julian stepped onto the snaking, seemingly endless line for foreigners, while Flora breezily passed through the gate for local residents with just a scan of her ID card and a thumbprint. Although it was nearly one o'clock in the morning, it seemed as though the entire UN Assembly had just arrived in Hong Kong simultaneously, and there was only one immigration officer stationed to admit them all. Julian looked over the crowded line and saw faces of every color—black, brown, white, tan—all waddling forward at a snail's pace, fuming in their native tongues.

The woman ahead of Julian wore a fully veiled *niqab* and was texting incessantly on her iPhone. Her mustached husband pushed their child in a pink stroller, using it for support as he kept his eyes closed. To Julian's immediate left, just beyond the velvet rope barrier, a tall Filipino woman powdered her face in a small pocket mirror, which had a horse etched on its ivory case. She was wearing a curly blonde wig and a pair of dark sunglasses and was either too blind or too oblivious to notice the line slowly inching ahead. Eventually, an old Chinese woman behind her gave up and simply lifted the rope over her head and motioned for all five of her children to dash underneath.

Julian, however, was not so daring. By the time he got through to baggage claim, nearly an hour had passed, and Julian's black roller bag was circling the carousel all on its own. He picked it up by its handle and darted straight towards the exit, through a red-lit tunnel lined with advertisements for Chanel N°5.

When he got outside, Julian felt like he was sucked into deep space. He labored to breathe in and out—the humidity was so thick that drops of sweat had already formed on his skin. A pale, yellow fog covered everything; Julian couldn't tell if it was pollution or a side effect of sleep deprivation. Whatever it was, he mucked through it, holding his breath for good measure, until he reached the empty taxi line and stepped into the first red-and-white cab available. He threw his luggage in the backseat and shut the door tight like a cabin lock.

"Hello," said the driver, who wore thick turtle-shell glasses and was missing several of his front teeth. He puffed on a cigarette as Julian haphazardly latched his seatbelt to the wrong buckle. "Where you going?"

The noxious, menthol-tinged fumes in the car lulled Julian into a stupor, and now that the ground beneath him had stopped moving, he felt the combined effects of the exhaustion and the sedatives. Groggily, he produced a small card from his wallet that the monk had sent him along with the letter. It bore an insignia of a jagged red stone, below which was an address: "Lucky Guest House, Block A 3M/F, Chungking Mansions."

"Lucky Guest House," he mumbled. "Chungking Mansions."

"*Huh?*" the driver shouted.

"Chungking Mansions. Like in the Wong Kar-Wai movie."

The driver scratched his head, apparently dumbfounded by the pale, pajama-clad *gweilo* in his backseat. Julian realized he was getting nowhere, both literally and figuratively. In frustration, he leaned forward and handed over the business card. The old man pushed his glasses up the bridge of his nose, staring down skeptically at the small piece of paper. He pursed his lips and nodded. "Ohh," he said. "*Chungking.*"

"What did I say?"

The driver shifted the car into gear, and the taxi sped forward into a brightly lit tunnel. As the fluorescent lights hit his eyes, Julian felt the cool air lulling him to sleep. He slumped back, and his eyes drooped closed.

***

After what felt like just a few moments, the driver tapped Julian on the shoulder to wake him up. "Hello," he said. "We're here."

Julian rubbed his eyes and looked out the window. Under a neon glare, tourists rushed up and down the block, weaving through insistent tailors and watch salesmen. The sheer number of lights and advertisements hanging off the sides of the buildings was overwhelming—it looked like a cross between a department store and a rave. Julian had seen this panorama of Nathan Road in films, but up close the lights were downright disorienting, especially in his hypnogogic state. The streets, freshly showered by the now slowing rain, practically glowed.

"How much is it?" Julian asked.

"One ninety," the driver said. "Uhh, two hundred."

Julian combed through his wallet, trying to make sense of the notes. He had exchanged his last £300 at Heathrow and was still confused by the assortment of colorful bills that he had received. They came not only in different sizes and shades, but even from different companies: Bank of China, Standard Chartered, HSBC. In this city, it seemed, the banks printed their own money. Julian picked out two red $100 bills from HSBC, each adorned with a majestic lion, and handed them to the driver. He unlatched the door and stepped outside.

As the car sped away, Julian looked up at the complex in front of him. It was hardly a mansion at all; above the patchwork of neon signs adorning the facade, an army of window air conditioners huffed in unison. Paint was peeling off the building's side, chipping off onto unsuspecting tourists. The faux-marble gate above Chungking was the only unlit sign on the whole block, buttressed by two flashing LED advertisements, gleaming WELLCOME and BONJOUR. It felt like stepping into the old world.

As he walked through the gate, he smelled a mix of cardamom and sandalwood wafting through the air, but he couldn't enjoy it for long. An army of hawkers caught his scent and massed around him, waving placards and brochures in Julian's face as they crushed him with their immense combined weight.

"Good massage," one said. "Very happy."

"Not interested," Julian replied.

"You want hashish?" another man whispered in his ear. "Pure Numidian."

"Please," Julian said, trying to fight his way in, "I just want to get through . . ."

Several hands clawed at him, pulling him in every direction. He felt like he was being drawn and quartered, utterly at the mercy of the swarm. Eventually, the hands let go when another tourist passed through the gate: a blonde-haired Swedish man rolling a red Lacoste bag behind him. A new wave of hawkers brushed past Julian, encircling the more auspicious prey.

As Julian wandered down the hallway, he heard a faint voice in the distance—a wailing woman, seemingly in pain. Instinctively, he moved towards it, passing a wall of tailors and run-down restaurants selling microwaved Saag Paneer and Chana Masala for one dollar a plate. Middle-aged Indian men stood in front of the stalls, eyeing Julian suspiciously as he passed by.

At the end of the hall, he discovered the source of the wailing: a DVD store called *Ruttonjee Video*, which was blaring a Hindi Pop song from a speaker above its door. Four young men were standing at the front window, glaring at the blurry TV monitors playing Bollywood films and softcore pornography inside the shop. *Maybe Flora's right*, Julian thought. *In this city, you are who you are. And no one cares.*

Eventually, he reached the two gunmetal grey elevators at the end of the hall, marked BLOCK A. As he stepped into the car on the right, it dipped slightly under his weight. Hesitantly, he pressed the 3M button, which was placed directly between the numbers three and five. The number four was conspicuously absent.

The elevator wobbled as it ascended at a glacial pace. A faded WANTED poster was stuck to the inside of the elevator door, depicting a composite sketch of an old bald man in sunglasses. "Wong Chiu-Wai," it read, "Wanted for robbery, rape, and jaywalking." The poster was browned at the edges and had been torn at several times.

The elevator doors opened abruptly, practically spitting him out, and Julian darted into the hallway with his luggage and pillow behind him, half expecting the whole contraption to free-fall down the shaft. Rusted pipes ran along the walls, and frayed wires and cobwebs dangled off the ceiling. The fluorescent lights above flickered on and off at random intervals, and a pentagon of dead cockroaches lay flattened on the grey tiled floor like an occult symbol. At the end of the hall and past a dozen shuttered shops stood a metal gate with the words LUCKY GUEST HOUSE pasted above the door. A pink neon foot hung to its right with a smiley face sputtering on and off in the center of its heel.

Julian had to duck his head just to get into the lobby. The reception area felt like a dollhouse, with a simple wooden counter taking up almost half of the whole space. There were two doors behind the counter, one marked ROOMS and the other marked LAVATORY, both written with red paint on uneven planks of plywood. Between the two doors, a jagged red stone was painted on the wall, in the middle of which wheezed a dusty old security camera, creaking as it turned. The whole lobby was swelteringly hot and smelled of mildew. A single fan stood in the corner, blowing out clouds of warm dust.

Behind the counter, a woman sat in front of what looked like a Cold War-era computer, reading from a red tome with three golden characters etched on its front: 红楼梦. She had shoulder length black hair and brown eyes the shade of fertile soil and was wearing a nearly translucent blue nightgown with a jade pendant strapped around her neck. There was a small pockmark on the right side of her forehead and a tiny mole just to the left of her nose, a bit like Marilyn Monroe.

"Hello," she said in a hollow voice. "Do you have a reservation?"

As the words hit his ears, Julian felt an indescribable rush from his skull down to his toes. He opened his mouth to answer but stopped abruptly, gawking at the woman's chest. The jade pendant that hung between her breasts gave off an eerie glow, like the first kindling of charcoal.

"Excuse me," the woman said. "Are you Mr. Kensington?"

Julian snapped out of his trance. "Yes," he said. "That's right."

"One moment, please." The old computer clacked and clanked furiously like an old typewriter, her two bulbous cheeks bouncing up and down slightly with each click. "Single room, three nights. Is that correct?"

"I think so," Julian answered without thinking, his eyes rolling so far backward he felt as if he could see his own brain. "Whatever you say." He would do anything now for a soft bed; he wanted nothing more than to pop another Xanax and drift off for half a day.

"It comes out to one hundred and sixty dollars per night, plus a ten percent service charge, for a total of five hundred and thirty dollars. Will you be paying cash or credit?"

"Cash," Julian said as he reached for his wallet. He pulled out two bills—one blue and one gold—and handed them to the woman. Her small hand was as delicate as salmon skin, and it had a similar slippery texture. Just as Julian's fingers brushed hers, she pulled her hand away and tucked the two notes into a drawer, plunking a purple note and a single heavy coin on the counter as change.

"Can I interest you in any *other* services?"

But before Julian could answer, the front door swung open again, slamming into the wall and knocking out a chunk of fresh paint. A fat man stormed through, with a black eyepatch over his right eye and twin phoenix tattoos running up both of his blubbery arms. He had three chins and per-haps four stomachs, and the stained tank top on his chest was stretched to its tensile limit. Julian didn't quite understand how he even fit through the door.

"K-King Chow," the hostess stammered, her voice shaking. "*Ngo mmji lei wi lei. Hai mmhai tong yat tiu lui?*"

The fat man glared menacingly at Julian. "*Li gor gweilo hai li dou jo mei?*"

The woman bowed in deference, her eyes peering down to the floor. "*Dui mmzi,*" she said contritely. "*Kui hai ha tsai.*"

"Excuse me," Julian chimed in, "but who is this exactly?"

"King Chow," the hostess whispered. "He's the owner of this establishment."

"Pleased to meet you," Julian said, dropping his backpack to the ground. He extended his hand in the fat man's direction.

King Chow took one look down at Julian's pallid face and jabbed him once straight in the forehead, sending him crashing to the floor. As he hit the concrete, a trail of blood seeped down over his heavy eyes.

For the first time all day, he was on solid ground.

1984 / Chapter 1: Hong Kong's Finest

It was eleven-thirty in the morning when a burst of static came on over Inspector Leung's police scanner. He sat in his small cubicle on the seventh floor of the police headquarters in Wan Chai, which faced Victoria Harbor and the Walled City of Kowloon far in the distance. Leung was wearing a white shirt, a loose-fitting red tie, and a pair of trousers held up by thick suspenders that looked more like seatbelts than fashion accessories—the standard uniform for inspectors in the *Criminal Investigations Department.*

"Ten-thirty-four," the radio buzzed. "Officers in . . . blood *everywhere!*"

Leung sipped his morning cup of tea, a heavily-caffeinated "Iron Buddha" blend that the higher-ups stocked for free in the break room, and calmly pressed the receiver.

"This is Leung," he said in a raspy, almost crackling voice, the result of smoking four packs a day for the last forty years. "What's your position?"

"I'm in Sai . . . Kung? No, Sai Wan." The static cut out.

Leung heard a high, faint noise in the background, like a bird chirping. "Who is this?" he asked.

"Lau," the voice responded, the chirping growing louder and louder behind him. "Raymond Lau." Now, unmistakably, he heard a laugh.

Inspector Leung stood up and turned around, peering over the side of his cubicle. His two partners, Inspectors Wong and Smithfield, were crouched around their radio, giggling like a pair of little girls.

"Get back to work," he said flatly.

"What work?" asked Inspector Wong, a rail-thin man and perhaps the best dressed in the whole department, with coiffed hair, a black leather jacket, and a pair of dark sunglasses that he never took off, even indoors—*especially* indoors. He was also the youngest inspector on the whole force and had been assigned to Leung's unit to benefit from the elder man's experience and poise—and so Leung could monitor his probation. Wong stood up and straightened his jacket.

"God," Smithfield said as he dusted off his fraying trousers and wiped the spittle from his bushy, caterpillar mustache. "That was funny."

"I thought we had you," Wong groaned as he slumped back down in his black chair, which leaked foam as he pressed against it. "What tipped you off?"

"Your voice," Leung said.

"What's wrong with my voice?"

"The tone was all wrong. You didn't sound like you were in danger."

"What, I had to panic more?"

Leung sipped his tea pensively. "No, that's not it. It's hard to explain, but when you see blood your whole demeanor changes. It's like time stops, but it also speeds up too. You think faster and slower at the same time."

"So I had to be calmer."

"No," Leung replied. It was pointless to bother. The experience couldn't be adequately expressed with words. "You'll see," he said simply.

"Well, I *hope* I see some action soon," Wong replied. His desk was littered with crumpled forms and loose pens, each one riddled with bite marks. "I swear to god, if I have to fill out another goddamn form . . ."

Smithfield looked over his shoulder and smirked. "Consider yourself lucky. Back in the old days, we used to see four, five cases a month. And believe me, they weren't pretty. You see one head bashed in with a cricket bat, you've seen enough."

Wong tapped his feet restlessly. "I don't know," he said. "That sounds fun to me."

"You're in the wrong city, then."

"No," Wong said, staring out the large window behind his desk. "I'm in the right city. Just at the wrong time." The crystal blue waters of Victoria Harbor were dotted with ferries and fishing trawlers sputtering out black exhaust. The squat, old buildings of Kowloon stood along the opposite shore, in stark contrast to the burgeoning superstructures running down the reclaimed coast of Hong Kong

Island. In the distance, Wong could see the outline of the soon-to-be demolished Walled City—the former home of the triads. He recalled the climactic scene of *A Symphony of Fists*—how Raymond Lau had soared off the top of those walls onto a pair of unsuspecting gangsters below. "We're cops, goddammit. And we're stuck in here doing nothing."

Smithfield scribbled a note onto the timesheet he was processing, then dotted all the i's in his previous sentence. "This looks like nothing to you?"

Wong sighed. "If I knew this job would be so boring, I would've gone to law school instead. At least then I could make some money . . ."

"You couldn't be a lawyer, Wong."

"Why not?"

"You don't have the patience. Or the brain, for that matter."

"*Diu lei!*" Wong shouted. He crumpled up one of the forms on his desk and threw it at his British counterpart. Smithfield dodged artfully, without even stopping his pen.

"I like you, kid, but you're going to drive yourself mental with that attitude."

"What's wrong with my attitude?" Wong asked as he threw another crumpled form, this time hitting Smithfield in the leg.

"Work is boring," Smithfield said. He stapled the timesheet to another piece of paper and placed it in the outbox on his desk. "That's the point. That's why they pay you to do it. If it was fun, people would do it for free."

Wong shook his head, then chugged what was left of the Coca-Cola on his desk. "Whatever," he said. "I need some air." He stood up and cracked his knuckles so loud it sounded like bubble wrap popping. Then he jumped over the cubicle wall and made for the break room on the other side of the floor.

"*Aiyyya*," Leung groaned. "He's exhausting."

"I like him," Smithfield said. "He keeps things interesting."

"This is the Criminal Investigations Department. Interesting means bad news for everyone. Interesting means people dying."

"He's just enthusiastic. Weren't you when you started out?"

Leung's eyes wandered to the wall of his cubicle on which two photographs were thumbtacked side by side. One was an autographed portrait of Bruce Lee in his classic black and yellow jumpsuit from *Game of Death*. It was perhaps Leung's most prized possession, something of a consolation prize for officers injured in the last real triad war. The other was a grainy sepia-tinged photograph of Leung's graduation ceremony at the police academy: Leung stood in a line with his fellow graduates, holding his new badge high in the air. He was a bit less wrinkled back then, but he wore the same black crewcut and the same vacant expression. "You've got to have passion to get into this line of work," he said. "But there's a difference between enthusiastic and impatient, and I don't think he gets it."

"Cut him some slack. He's new."

"He's going to get us *killed.* Or worse yet, he might kill us himself."

"Okay, now you're just being ridiculous."

"All it takes is one wrong move. It's a dangerous world out there . . ."

Smithfield raised an eyebrow. "Is it now? I hadn't noticed."

Leung looked at the one small stack of papers piled neatly beside his police scanner. "It's a slow season, I admit. But you have to stay diligent."

"In the last ten years, how much field work have we seen? Two cases a year? Three tops."

"Killers never go out of business. Sometimes they sleep, but they never go away."

"Well, they've been sleeping an awful long time. Hibernating, really."

"You're wrong," Leung said defiantly. He adjusted the knobs on his police scanner, ensuring it was at top volume, but nothing came through.

Smithfield sighed. "You know why I took this job, Leung?"

"I don't know," Leung replied, barely listening to his partner's voice. There was a crackle on the radio, followed by several barely audible words.

"Family . . ."

"Shh!" Leung blurted out, trying to hear the faint voice on the scanner.

". . . disturbance at . . . shooting location . . . Lau . . ."

"It's another prank," Smithfield said matter-of-factly. "I bet Wong called it in."

"No," Leung replied. "This is real." He pressed the red button on the receiver. "This is Leung. Give me a location."

"Jianghu Studios," a voice replied crisply, cutting through the static. "We have reports of a shooting. At least one deceased."

"Roger," Leung replied as he slipped on his brown overcoat. He stood up and took his snub-nose pistol and badge from the top drawer of the desk. "I'm on my way."

Smithfield swiveled around in his chair. "You don't want to wait for a confirmation? It could be a false lead."

"No," Leung said, his voice without a hint of doubt. "It's not."

2014 / Chapter 2: The Story of the Stone

Julian opened his eyes, shielding them from the light. He stood up and found himself at the lip of a wide riverbank in the middle of a forest. The water below was deep blue, filled with white and orange koi swimming against the current. In the distance, jagged limestone formations stretched upward, covered by green trees and moss. There were rice paddies in the hills, stacked one atop the other in a striated pattern like white temple steps. Julian cupped his hand and drank a few sips from the river. The fields around him were silent and serene.

A dewdrop dripped onto Julian's shoulder from a branch above him. He turned around and came face-to-face with its source: an enormous fig tree, at least ten times his height, with coiled bark running up and down its trunk like the hairs of a mop caught in a Salvador Dalí painting. Julian moved towards it in a daze. At the base of its trunk sat a wilted flower and a single grey stone with a poem etched on its side.

"Years ago," Julian read aloud. He didn't know how he could read the Chinese characters, but the words flowed from his mouth instinctually. "Empress Nü Wo created thirty-six thousand five hundred and one stones with which to repair the heavens. She used only thirty-six thousand five hundred."

When he looked away from the stone again, the flower was gone. Another drop fell from the branches above him, but this time it came from the eye of a small but beautiful woman now sitting in the tree. She had the same face as the guest house hostess and the same jade pendant around her neck. Only now, instead of a translucent nightgown, she was wearing a long purple dress with sleeves twice the length of her arms. Her jet-black hair floated in the wind.

"It's you," Julian said.

The woman smiled and opened her two slight lips, which were painted crimson. "*Thanks!*" she sang in a man's voice.

"Umm, you're welcome?"

"*Thanks! Thanks! Thanks! Monica!*"

"No," Julian said, trying in vain to block out the sound. "Not now . . ." He covered his ears, but her voice grew so loud he might as well have been using toilet paper for ear plugs. The sheer force jolted him awake.

Julian opened his eyes, now splayed across a tiny mattress in what was ostensibly a hotel room. He reached for his iPhone, which was still blaring Leslie Cheung's "Monica" at full volume.

"Hello?" Julian answered in a scratchy voice. His throat felt like it had been scraped with steel wool.

"Julian," a woman's voice responded. "Are you alright?"

"Yeah," Julian said. He rolled over and tried to sit up, but his muscles failed him. "Actually, I don't know. Who is this?"

"Flora," she replied. "Man, you don't sound too good."

"I don't feel too good either."

"What happened to you?"

"How to put this," Julian wondered aloud. "I got punched in the face."

Flora couldn't help but laugh. "Already?"

"It's not funny," Julian said. "I don't think I can even stand up."

"Where are you staying?"

"Chungking Mansions."

There was a moment of silence. "Well, what did you expect?"

Julian sighed. "You get what you pay for, I guess."

"Come on," Flora said. "If I'm going to take you to Man Mo Temple, we'll need to head out soon. I'm supposed to take my grandma shopping later."

"How pious of you."

"Let's meet up at the Star Ferry. We can take the scenic route to Hong Kong Island, then hop on the tram to Sheung Wan."

"Star Ferry? I'm not a big fan of boats."

"You don't like boats, you don't like planes. Is there anything you do like?"

"I like cars, just as long as I'm not driving them."

"What about trains?"

"I'm okay if they stay above ground. But the tubes are the absolute worst. I can't stand going from A to B with no hint of the in-between. It makes me want to puke."

"Well, unless you want to swim across the Harbor, I think you're stuck."

"Alright," Julian said. "The ferry it is then. But how do I get there?"

"Just make a left out of Chungking Mansions and follow the crowd to the Avenue of Stars. We can meet by the Bruce Lee statue."

"Hang a left to the Bruce Lee statue. Simple enough."

"I'll meet you there in a half hour. I'm bringing you a special treat."

"That sounds ominous," Julian said as the phone beeped off. Groaning mightily, he mustered all his strength and forced himself up. He slipped on his pair of white Converse sneakers and laced them one-by-one.

The room wasn't much bigger than a linen closet, and the only furniture was a small plywood end table and a cardboard box with a stained white towel folded inside. There was a TV mounted on the wall at the foot of the bed, playing a movie on its grainy, low resolution screen. Even through the static, though, Julian recognized it: *Canton Violence*, a Raymond Lau picture. A campy time-traveling mystery and a cheap homage to Jin Wong's *wuxia* novels. The film was at its climax: Raymond Lau confronting the Evil Ming Cult up on Bright Peak Mountain. The star actor dodged their spears artfully, jumping ten feet into the air, then dropped into a battle stance, flicking the corner of his mouth like Bruce Lee. "*Toiii!*" he screamed as he lunged at them fist-first.

Julian's forehead was throbbing; there was a welt the size of a cricket ball where King Chow had punched him, and his eyelids were so heavy it felt like there was a sandbag strapped to every lash. He never thought he'd be caught up so soon in such a frenzy of violence; he knew that the triads existed, but it's one thing to know something and another thing entirely for it to punch you in the face. There was no turning back now, Julian realized. There was no going back to his simple life of Excel documents and form emails. He was already on the shit list of a raging triad, and for all he knew he'd be done away with the moment he stepped out of this room. This prison. His pulse started to race, and he felt a violent, twisting pain in the left side of his chest, like a heart attack about to begin. The unmistakable sign of an oncoming panic attack. As he tied his shoes, he looked around the cloistered space, wondering where the hostess had deposited his backpack and luggage, desperate to quickly swallow another Xanax before the fit grew so severe that he'd be unable to move. He checked inside the cardboard box and looked under the bed, but there was no sign of them. Other than the clothes he came in with, the room was empty.

The violent twisting in his chest spread down his abdomen into a throbbing lump, like a cyst, above the left side of his pelvis. His clothes and guidebook he could care less about, but without his anxiety pills he was lost. His doctors were clear with him: He'd been taking these pills for so long that he did *not* want to miss a dose. Failing to taper off slowly could result in severe withdrawal, even seizures. With a frantic resolve, he dashed into the hallway, nearly knocking the door off its creaky frame, and slammed immediately into a tanned Filipino woman walking out of the door across the hall. She was wearing half-torn denim clothes with purple mascara dripping down the left side of her face.

"*Mmgoi,*" she barked in a hoarse voice. There was a pungent, almost sulfuric smell emanating from the room, and through the crack in the doorway Julian could see King Chow lying naked amidst a cloud of haze. The woman shut the door behind her and darted toward the exit, holding a pair of pink high heel shoes in her left hand.

Julian followed her into the hotel lobby where the hostess was sitting at the counter with her red tome in hand, studying its pages intently. She was dressed in a black T-shirt with the V-neck running halfway down her cleavage.

"G-good morning," Julian stammered, his new-found determination evaporating instantly as her gaze met his. He looked down abashedly, unable to even meet her eye.

"It's one o'clock."

"Um," he grunted, not knowing how to broach the uncomfortable subject. The girl was acting so blasé, Julian wondered if it might have been a dream, after all. "What are you, uh . . . reading there?" he asked. "It looks heavy."

"*Dream of the Red Chamber*," she replied. "It's a classic."

"Oh," Julian said. "I've never heard of it."

"Of course you haven't. It's a *Chinese* classic."

"Listen," he said, scratching the back of his head. "About last night . . ."

"You're welcome," the hostess said simply.

"You're welcome?"

"I checked you in after you fainted."

"I didn't faint," Julian insisted, his desperate energy returning to him all at once. "Your boss punched me in the face!"

"I didn't see anything."

"There's a security camera right there!" Julian exclaimed, pointing up at the logo on the wall. The creaky old device was blinking red but looking in another direction.

"You believe what you want to believe. It's a free country. Mostly."

"What about my bags?"

"What about them? As a rule, the hotel isn't liable for any items lost."

Julian was taken aback by the sheer crassness of her excuse. "What kind of scam are you running here?" he demanded. "You knock your customers out and rob them blind? I want my stuff back! I want my *medication!*"

"I told you already: I don't have it. If you need medicine, I'm happy to point you to the nearest dispensary."

"I don't have any money!" Julian seethed. He clutched his hand into a fist and slammed it on the counter. "You took all of it! You took everything! And if I don't get it back, I don't know what will happen."

The hostess closed her book. "Are you threatening me, Mr. Kensington? Do I need to call the manager? Because he can be a little cranky when he's disturbed. It's not wise to upset a Red Pole."

"A Red Pole?"

"A lieutenant of the Lucky Stone."

Julian's hand began to tremble, and instinctively he felt at the bulge seemingly growing above his waist. But he couldn't just give in. "If you don't give it back, I'll call the police."

"Oh, please do. And when you call, say hi to Inspector Cheung and Commissioner Li for me. They're old customers."

"*What?*" Julian blurted out in disbelief. "You're bluffing."

"That's how it is in this town: screw or be screwed. So get over it. Be glad I didn't take the rest of it while you slept."

"I'm sorry," Julian said, though he wasn't quite sure what he was apologizing for.

The hostess grimaced. "Don't look at me like that. *Gweilo* . . ."

***

Thirty minutes later, Julian arrived at the Avenue of Stars—a scenic boardwalk along the south end of the Kowloon peninsula. His pockets were lighter than they'd ever been, and he was no closer to finding his medication, but he was okay. Even calm. *To hell with my doctors*, he thought. Their only answers were more and more pills, which, of course, only they could prescribe, and stern warnings about ever trying to quit them. All they'd done was taken his anxiety—an addiction to negative thoughts, as his psychiatrist described it—and replaced it with an addiction more suitable to their interests. The problem had been compartmentalized, never solved. Yet, even as he understood this intellectually, the lump in his stomach was still there, and the pain only magnified as the chattering Cantonese voices around him seeped their way into his ears. *What am I doing here?* he asked himself bluntly. He was stuck alone in a foreign country, chasing the shadow of a father he'd never known.

The skyline of Hong Kong Island was clearly visible just across Victoria Harbor to the south: the protruding twin IFC buildings, one twice the height of the other, were the most prominent, just beside the triangular-paned Bank of China Tower, which looked like it had spilled out from a geometry textbook. In front of all three was Jardine House, once the tallest building in all of Asia, standing at a squat 52 floors with a diminutive hubris like that of Napoleon. Julian had read in his guidebook that it was once nicknamed "The House of a Thousand Arseholes," half for multitudinous circular windows and half for the colorful assortment of financial services professionals who worked inside. Further east, a greenish skyscraper stood alone, its golden spire piercing the clouds.

As Julian stood mesmerized by the skyline, Flora approached from behind, wearing a white DKNY T-shirt and a pink skirt that hung just over her knees. Her hair was tied up in two buns like Princess Leia, and there were at least eight or nine plastic bracelets strapped to each of her arms.

"That's Central Plaza," she said. "My brother Xavier works there."

"It looks ominous."

"Maybe in a certain light," she said, tilting her head slightly. "Here." She handed Julian a styrofoam bowl filled with black gelatin.

"Is this for me?"

"It's herbal jelly," she explained. "You'll feel better after you eat it."

Julian took one bite of the black substance and nearly spit it back out. It tasted like crushed rocks covered with corn syrup. "What the hell *is* this stuff?"

"It's made from turtle shells. You know how it is: Everything that tastes bad is good for you."

As Julian stared at the gelatinous goop, they started down the Avenue of Stars, passing over the handprints and autographs of all the seminal figures in the Hong Kong film industry: Chow Yun-fat, Leslie Cheung, Andy Lau, even Jet Li. They weaved through tourists snapping photographs of the brass and cement placards.

"Look!" Julian said, pointing one out. "There's Jackie Chan."

Flora grimaced and spat directly onto the handprint. "*Sei puk gai.*"

"I take it you're not a fan."

"Not just me," she said. "*No one* in Hong Kong likes Jackie Chan. He grew up in a mansion on Victoria Peak, and now that spoiled brat insults us all when we protest. He says democracy is the biggest joke in the world."

"Huh," Julian said, blithely unaware that his second favorite action star could ever be so reviled. "He makes good movies, though."

"That's true," she admitted. "I'll give him that."

"Look, Raymond Lau is right next to him." Julian knelt, placing his container of herbal jelly on the brick road. He placed his two palms onto the star actor's handprints and was surprised to discover that his own hands were nearly double their size. "Wow, he's really tiny."

"He's only five foot four," Flora said. "I don't understand your obsession with the guy. Sure, his movies made a lot of money, but there was nothing all that good about them. If you want comedy, there's Stephen Chow. If you want drama, there's Tony Leung or Maggie Cheung. And if you want action, well, just look." She turned over her shoulder, motioning with her thumb toward the bronze statue behind them, around which a crowd of tourists had gathered.

"Bruce Lee," Julian said, gaping at the chiseled statue of the star actor in a battle pose. His muscles were more intricately carved than Michelangelo's David; every vestige of fat had been literally chipped away. "To be honest," Julian admitted. "I never really saw the appeal."

"Of Bruce Lee?"

"I always thought he was more myth than reality. He died when he was most popular, so people made him into some kind of a legend."

"You're crazy," she replied. "His films were dumb, but he was the real deal."

"I heard he took steroids. Isn't that what killed him?"

"Depends on who you ask. Officially, he died from an adverse reaction to a painkiller . . ."

"Killed by a painkiller. So what does that make him?"

"... but if you believe the rumors, that was all just a cover story. Some people say he was poisoned by the triads."

"Why would they do that?"

"Because he refused to give them a cut of his films. The triads run half the studios in the city, or at least they used to when the industry was still doing well."

"Where's this from?" Julian asked. "Wikipedia?"

"Come on," she said. "*Everyone* knows that."

***

After the ferry was fastened to the dock and the captain gave them the all-clear, Julian and Flora stepped off the Star Ferry and shuffled along with the crowd towards the Wan Chai Convention Center, beside which stood the famous "Golden Bauhinia" statue. The Bauhinia—an orchid—was the symbol of Hong Kong, the same flower featured on the city's red-and-white flag. It was in front of this statue that Britain had lowered the Union Jack once and for all on this city—the last of its colonies. The place where the world's greatest empire finally reached its end. Julian could remember watching the ceremony on TV, his mom sitting beside him with a wine bottle in hand as a funeral-like silence hung in the air. Perhaps because Julian had no memory of the city—or because of the copious amounts of marijuana he smoked that summer between A-Level and university—he was comfortably numb watching the proceedings. The heavy accent of Chinese Supreme

Leader Jiang Zemin was the only part of it he could even remember.

Julian reached out to touch the statue that the tourists were all snapping photos of. He wondered if he would feel something, but when his fingers brushed the gilded exterior, there was no realization. It was cold.

While Julian stared up at the statue, a stream of spiky-headed and scantily-clad cosplayers exited through the front door of the convention center. A pink-haired Sakura and a blond Cloud Strife walked up to Julian with their iPhones out. Lurking behind them was an androgynous girl with cropped hair, wearing a pair of platform shoes and holding two fake pistols. The girl in the Sakura outfit handed her phone to Flora, bearing her yellow, crooked teeth in a forced smile that looked almost like a Chelsea Grin. "*Hor mm hor yi bong ngo de yengxiong?*" she asked in a high-pitched voice.

"*Momentai,*" Flora replied, taking the phone as the three characters crowded around Julian. Sakura and Cloud both smiled warmly, holding up peace signs, but the third girl scowled at the camera, holding one pistol to Julian's chin and the other to the side of her own head. "*Yet, yi, sam!*"

"*Chee-tsee!*" the characters replied in unison as the flash went off, leaving a purple blind spot in the center of Julian's vision.

"*Mmgoisai!*" Sakura gleamed as she took back the phone. She and Cloud giggled their way down the road, but the androgynous girl was expressionless, staring at the floor as she shuffled forward.

"What the hell was that about?" Julian asked. "Was that because of my clothes?"

"Maybe they confused you with some character from an anime. Or maybe they just wanted to take a photo with a *gweilo*. I've seen it before."

"What was wrong with that girl?" Julian asked as they continued down the road, passing by the base of Central Plaza. "Or was it a boy? She seemed awfully depressed."

"She was just in character. Some people stay like that for days."

"Like a method actor."

"Sort of. Except method actors are getting paid for it."

"So why do they do it then?"

Flora shrugged. "Some people would do anything to be someone else."

Julian wondered if he felt the same—if perhaps this whole trip was just a quixotic exercise in escapism. An apprehensive silence clouded their conversation as they followed a raised pedestrian bridge that led from Central Plaza down to the busy streets of Wan Chai. The sidewalks there were claustrophobically narrow, and the iron bars that lined the curbs made each street feel like its own little prison. An old woman was tiptoeing in front of Julian, using two large umbrellas in place of canes, but every time Julian tried to pass by her she shuffled to the same side, seeming to anticipate his every move. Eventually, he gave up and resigned himself to the slower pace. "But who was she supposed to be?" he asked finally.

"Lin Daiyu from *Red Stone*. It's a sci-fi manga adaptation of *Hung Lou Meng. Dream of the Red Chamber.*"

"*Dream of the Red Chamber*," Julian repeated, remembering the thick tome on the guest house counter. "I've heard of it."

"I'm sure you have. It's one of the four classics, along with *Romance of the Three Kingdoms*, *Water Margin*, and *Journey to the West.*"

"Have you read it?"

"No, but the manga is good. Lin Daiyu is the sickly, depressive beauty who falls in love with her cousin. She's the one he secretly wants but isn't supposed to have."

"Understandably."

"Because he's engaged to his other cousin."

"Uh-huh . . ."

"The whole thing is basically porn."

Julian scratched his chin. "I'll have to check it out sometime."

Soon, they reached the tram stop and joined a seemingly endless line running down the whole block. Above the road, a tangled mess of wires snaked between the billboards and glowing signs that jutted off the sides of the old buildings. Even above the ground, space was at a premium here.

A double-decker tram pulled up to the curb and rang its bell. The line shuffled forward at a rapid pace, filling up the entire streetcar. Somehow, everyone managed to fit in, albeit with little room to spare. As Julian and Flora stepped onboard, they pushed through the mass of bodies and went upstairs, miraculously finding two empty seats at the very front of the car. They sat down and leaned out the open window, taking in the cool breeze—the last remnants of the previous day's storm. For the first time since he'd come to Hong Kong, Julian felt like he could breathe. The old streetcar rumbled to a start and plodded forward at a walking pace as a cyclist biked leisurely along the tracks ahead of it, with two large canisters of Shell gasoline sitting in the bike's metal basket. "That looks safe," Julian thought aloud.

However, by the time the tram arrived at their station on a sloped road, the cyclist was nowhere in sight, having far outpaced the ancient trolley. Julian and Flora stumbled down the narrow staircase and paid on their way out, Flora swiping her phone case twice against the card reader for the equivalent of 0.2£.

"Stay close," Flora said. "It's easy to get lost here."

The sidewalks in Sheung Wan were somehow even narrower than those in Wan Chai and were seemingly devoid of any logic or planning. Some streets bisected each other diagonally; others stopped abruptly and curved around a slope. Julian struggled his way up the winding roads, the lactic acid building in his calves and thighs.

When they arrived at their destination, he was completely out of breath. His striped pajamas were soaked through and his hair was slicked back, dripping sweat onto the pavement. Flora, however, had scarcely broken a sweat.

"This is it," she said. "Man Mo Temple."

"This?" Julian replied. From outside, the temple was wholly unimpressive—it was just one story tall and appeared to be under heavy construction, with a latticed bamboo scaffold lining its facade. There was a white gate in front, topped with green-gabled tiles, but otherwise the exterior was bare.

"Alright," Flora said. "I think you can take it from here."

"T-take it from here?" Julian stammered, his hands curling into tight fists. The sweat in his palms grew so slippery it felt like he'd popped a water balloon in each of them. "What are you talking about?"

"I'm saying I have to go. I'm not here to sightsee. I'm visiting family."

"I thought you wanted to hear the rest of the story."

"I do," she replied. "But my grandma wants me to take her shopping in Causeway Bay, so I have to get back before the stores close. We'll grab some dim sum in the morning, and you'll tell me the whole thing."

"Can't you take your grandma shopping tomorrow? We're already here."

"No can do. Tomorrow she plays Mahjong with her old schoolmates. And the day after is July first, the anniversary of the handover. With all the protests, half the island will be closed."

Julian glared furtively at the temple doors, on which two angry gods were emblazoned carrying halberds and spears. "Is it safe to go in by myself?"

"You'll be fine," Flora insisted. "This is the safest city in the world."

"Tell that to the left side of my face," Julian muttered under his breath. Waving goodbye to Flora, he skirted around a pile of bamboo sticks lying on the street and passed through the gate into the temple courtyard. Burning embers from the nearby furnace floated through the air like fireflies. Worshippers shoveled in notes of white and gold paper, and one even threw in a toy car and a fake iPhone. A monk clad in an orange robe sat cross-legged on a stool by one of the three entrances into the temple. As Julian passed through the double door, he could see that the elder friar was dozing off, a thin trail of drool hanging off his chin.

Once inside, Julian's eyes began to water from the smoke. Spirals of incense hung off the ceiling, dripping ash onto the unsuspecting worshippers below. The temple was made up of golds and reds. Colorful idols were scattered all throughout the room, but two golden gods were featured most prominently at the very back. The painted tiles on the walls each depicted some ancient story: On one, a man lay on ice to melt it and catch the carp swimming underneath. On another, a woman carved the skin off her own leg and threw it into a stew for her ailing mother. Julian was fascinated by them all, his eyes darting back and forth so rapidly that the ornate paintings and carvings all blended together into one fine blur. His mouth hung open as he craned his neck around, gawking at the intricacies of the artwork, which must have required the same care and skill as the ceiling of the Sistine Chapel. Yet, no one else seemed to pay them any mind; the other temple-goers were lost in their own ceremonies, and without anyone to guide him their meaning simply eluded him. They were pretty, yes, but that was all.

Near the entrance, an old woman sat behind a counter, selling bundles of incense, red candles, and the same white and gold notes that the worshippers had been throwing into the furnace. There were no signs of any fake cars or phones.

"Excuse me," Julian said as he approached the counter. "I'm looking for a man named Shih-yin."

"*Momentai*," the woman replied. She reached below the counter and pulled out a tin can filled with long wooden sticks. Each was painted blue and had a number between one and ninety-nine engraved on its wide end. She set the can down on the counter and handed Julian two red stones in the shape of crescent moons.

"I don't understand," Julian said, confused by the procedure. But the woman was silent, simply pointing to one of the golden idols at the back of the room.

Julian took the items and stepped forward, approaching a mustached god. Various offerings were laid out on the altar—fruits, vegetables, and bottles of water, wine, and Coca-Cola. Someone had even left a styrofoam container of rice and roasted pork with a box of Pocky beside it for dessert. A bald monk lit several red candles on a nearby table. His fingers were crusted with dry wax.

"This is Man Cheong," he explained. "The God of Literature." The monk's face was dark and leathered, but the skin around his eyes was of a lighter hue, like a panda in reverse. "Are you a student?"

"No," Julian said. "Not for a long time."

The monk placed one final candle into the sconce. "A smart man is always a student. To understand a problem is to solve it. To ignore a problem . . . some would call that being an adult." He smirked. "What's your problem?"

"My problem," Julian said. "Where to even begin?"

"At the start, of course."

"I guess I'm here to find my father."

"Is that right? Well, that's a noble cause."

"I'm glad I have your approval."

"Most who come in here are schoolchildren praying for higher grades. A waste of time, if you ask me."

"Better off studying at home."

"Smart," the monk said. "Why pray when you can work?"

Julian raised an eyebrow. "You're pretty cynical for a monk."

"It's Hollywood Road," he replied. "It's all bullshit here."

Julian laughed at the monk's blunt honesty. "So what are you doing here then?"

"What are *you* doing here?" the monk asked plainly. "Me, I know a good story when I see one." He pointed to the other golden idol at the back of the room: a fierce-looking god with a bushy black beard. "This is Mo Tai," the monk said. "Or Kwan Yu, the God of War. He was a famous general a long time ago, but most people only know him from novels and films. He was one of the most popular characters from *Romance of the Three Kingdoms*, one of the four Chinese classics. So now people like to offer him their prayers."

"People pray to a character from a book?"

"You could say the same of Jesus Christ."

"It's just weird to me. Almost like praying to Hamlet."

"Some people do that too, in their own way."

"I guess you're right."

"These days, he's the resident god of gangsters. And policemen, for that matter."

"Strange bedfellows."

"Not so strange," the monk said. "Long ago, the locals came to him to settle their petty disputes. The monks would give each person a piece of paper with a gruesome punishment written on it, like being cut in half with a saw or explosive dysentery . . ."

"Lovely."

"The monks would cut off a chicken's head, let its blood drip onto the paper, and then they threw everything into the fire. The paper and the chicken too."

"And how did that solve anything?"

"Simple. If the punishments came true, that person was guilty. Judgment and retribution go together. Two for one."

"And the chicken?"

"The monks ate it for dinner."

"Economical."

"Exactly. No one takes responsibility, no one takes blame, and yet everyone leaves and the dispute is settled. The people leave it to the gods."

"I guess that's one way to handle it."

"Sometimes the only way."

Julian looked down at the tin can full of sticks. "Is that what this is for?"

The monk nodded. "First, you tell Man Cheong your name, your age, and your question. Then you shake the can until a stick comes out. That stick is your fortune."

"Alright," Julian said. "That seems easy enough." He closed his eyes and did as the monk instructed: *Julian Kensington*, he thought to himself as he stared at the golden, mustached idol. *35 years old, from London by way of Hong Kong. When my father was my age, he disappeared off the face of the Earth. What happened to him?*

He opened his eyes again and shook the can back and forth, rattling the sticks inside until one started creeping out. As it slid out of the rim of the can, Julian noticed one errant stick with a green tip instead of a blue one.

"What are you doing?" the monk asked.

"Shaking it, just like you told me."

"You haven't listened to a word I said."

Julian stopped just as a blue-tipped stick fell out onto the floor. Number eighty-four. "What do you mean?" he asked.

"Which fortune do you want?"

"I don't know . . ." He looked again into the can. "The green one, I guess."

"Then take it."

Julian picked out the green stick, which had the number ninety-seven etched on its wide end. Then, he picked up the two crescent stones. "Now what do I do with these?"

"You roll them," the monk replied. "If they lie face up, that's an open mouth. If they lie face down, that's a closed mouth. It tells you if the fortune you've chosen is true. Two open mouths is happy. Two closed mouths is sad."

"So I want two open mouths then?"

"No. Two open mouths is *too* happy, which is itself a delusion. You want one open, one closed. Balance."

Julian rolled the stones, but they both landed face down. "Sad," he said. "So now I pick again?"

"It's up to you."

Julian stopped, his hand hovering above the stones on the floor.

"Be careful," the monk said. "The students come to Man Cheong for knowledge. But once you know, you can never go back."

"So ignorance is bliss then?"

"No," the monk replied. "But it can be useful."

Julian shook his head and steeled himself. His heart was beating through his chest, but he couldn't turn back now. "I didn't come all the way here just to bury my head." He reached down and turned one of the two stones over.

"Good," the monk said. "You understand."

"But what do I do now?"

"Now I give you your fortune."

1984 / Chapter 2: Mise-en-Scène

Inspector Leung sat in the passenger seat of his partner's Mercedes Benz as it sped through the Aberdeen Tunnel at 120 kilometers per hour. Inspector Wong was splayed across the backseat, drumming on his right leg to the beat of Leslie Cheung's "Monica," which creaked from the car's wobbly speakers. As they exited the tunnel, Leung could see the commercial vessels and fishing trawlers anchored by Aberdeen Harbor. An orange haze clouded the fresh morning air.

"*Thanks! Thanks! Thanks! Thanks! Monica!*" Wong sang out in a crackly, almost prepubescent voice. He leaned forward, sticking his head between his two older partners. "You think he'll be there?" he asked.

Smithfield raised an eyebrow. "Who, Leslie Cheung?"

"No," Wong said, unable to contain his excitement. "*Raymond Lau.* Jianghu Studios is where he makes all his films."

Leung shook his head in disgust. Just hearing the name sent a cold shiver down his spine. "Raymond Lau," he scoffed. "He's a comedian, not a martial artist."

"That's his genius," Wong said. "He mixes action and comedy. Tragedy and romance."

"*Romance?* He's supposed to be an action star!"

"What's wrong with a little romance?"

Leung pressed his forehead against the window, staring through the smog into the harbor, where several cargo ships were being loaded and unloaded. He could make out the outline of a sampan through the haze, but, as soon as he saw it, he blinked and the outline was gone. "Real police work isn't so glamorous," he said.

"We should get an autograph," Wong suggested.

"Wong," Leung snapped. "Be professional."

"I'm just saying . . . when else will we get the chance? This is Raymond Lau we're talking about. *The* Raymond Lau."

"He's right," Smithfield said. "That thing could be worth money someday. And I need a down payment on a new car."

"What's wrong with this one?" Wong asked.

"It's a bit shabby, don't you think?"

"We're not here to collect autographs," Leung said tersely. "We're inspectors. Someone *died*, and it's our job to find out how."

Wong sighed. "Yeah, I guess you're right."

"Besides," Leung said. "It's not like he's Bruce Lee or anything."

"That's true," Smithfield agreed. "Bruce Lee *was* the best."

"*Aiyyya*," Wong groaned. "You old timers are all the same. Bruce Lee this, Bruce Lee that. He was in what, like three good films?"

Leung rolled his eyes. He knew it was inevitable that new stars would rise and styles would change, but it bothered him to see how quickly a true artist had fallen out of fashion. Bruce Lee had turned his body into a temple—had synthesized disparate styles from the East and West and turned them into a form all his own. "Maybe you're just too young to remember."

"No, I remember. I saw *Fist of Fury*. The dialogue was terrible, the plot was a joke . . ."

"It wasn't about those things," Leung said. "It was about the choreography, the dance . . . the moral lessons."

"Give me a break," Wong said. "You old geezers have a selective memory."

"And you kids have horrible taste."

"You know," Smithfield added, "my son loves Raymond Lau too. Especially that last film, *City of Devils*. I bought him a fake gun and badge for Christmas. He keeps trying to arrest our poodle."

"See, he gets it!" Wong exclaimed.

Smithfield laughed. "He's five years old."

Soon, the car arrived at Jianghu Studios, which was nestled at the base of a hill halfway between Aberdeen and Shek O. The compound looked more like a warehouse than the home of a major motion picture—like an airport hangar that had been dropped at random in the mountains. The facade was covered with soot, and the chartreuse paint was chipping away in several places, revealing sheet metal below. Inspector Smithfield drove his car past the conspicuously empty security booth and parked it in a handicapped spot by the entrance.

"*This* is Jianghu Studios?" Wong asked skeptically.

"It must be," Smithfield replied. "This is the address they gave me."

"This can't be right," Leung said. "I've been here before."

Smithfield raised an eyebrow. "You have?"

"And so have you. This was the Cock-Brand Fireworks Factory, remember?"

"Is that right?" Smithfield said curtly. "I barely recognized it."

"How can you not?" Leung asked. "The last time we left here, they carried us out on stretchers."

"Some people have shorter memories than others," Smithfield said. "And besides, there's no use dwelling on the past. We have a job to do." He patted his partner on the shoulder and the three inspectors stepped out of the car.

Inspector Leung observed a string of trailers at the other end of the parking lot. Several black sedans and SUVs were parked in front of them, surrounded by men in black suits and sunglasses sweltering in the midday heat. "Who are they?" Leung wondered aloud.

The leader of the bunch was a burly, bald-headed man with a birthmark on his forehead in the shape of South America. He looked like Gorbachev in sunglasses. As the three inspectors eyed him from across the lot, he barked orders to the others and knocked on the door of a nearby trailer. After a few moments, a skinny, peevish-looking man stepped out, dressed in a purple buttoned-down shirt. The man's hairline had receded in such a way that it formed a large "M" on his forehead.

"Holy shit," Wong said. "That's Charlie Yip!"

"Who's Charlie Yip?" Leung asked.

"He's Raymond Lau's personal director!"

"Gentlemen," the director said as he approached, accompanied by the bald-headed man. "Thank you all for getting here so quickly. Needless to say, we're all quite shaken up."

Wong was too excited to speak, so Leung made all the introductions. "Inspector Leung," he said. "Kevin Leung. And these are Inspectors Smithfield and Wong."

"Charlie Yip," the director replied, shaking the hand of the senior inspector. "And this is our chief of security, Colm O'Callaghan."

The burly man nodded but said nothing, eyeing the inspectors closely. He looked familiar, but Leung couldn't quite put his finger on where he'd seen him before.

"What happened?" Leung asked. "Is the shooter still here?"

"In a sense," Yip replied. "I can show you, if you like."

"Mr. Yip," Smithfield said tersely, reaching for the snub nose pistol in his shoulder holster. "You misunderstood my partner's question. He's asking if we have anything to be worried about."

The director smiled. "I assure you, gentlemen. It's perfectly safe."

"And how do you know that?" Leung asked.

"Because he killed himself," the director said, pulling the front door open.

The interior of the building was just as shabby—the ground was made of hard concrete and there were holes in the ceiling through which light shone onto the broken rafters. The only sign of a film shoot were the two sets built at opposite ends of the room—one of an imperial-era mansion and the other of a department in a police station. The latter so closely resembled his own office on the seventh floor of the Wan Chai HQ that Leung was disturbed by the surreal verisimilitude. It was perfect—*too* perfect—like taking a step right over the edge of the uncanny valley. The only difference was that here the air conditioning actually worked.

As the three inspectors passed through the police station set, Leung looked down at one of the oak desks, which was covered in fake documents. One was an old printing bill for the studio, dated February 1981. Another said the word "filler" over and over, bearing an illegible signature on a line at the bottom of the page. There were several small cuts in the desk, but Leung couldn't tell if they formed a pattern or were just natural defects in the grain.

The closer they drew toward the other end of the room, the deeper the stench of death burrowed into their nostrils. The change in scenery was jarring; it was as if they'd stepped out of their office and straight into the Qing Dynasty. Coiling dragons ran along the top of each wall with lit oil lanterns hanging from their claws. At the center of the room, three potted plants stood in front of a triptych screen that depicted a woman in a flaming chariot hurtling off the top of a cliff. Two bonsais were placed at the edges and a single Mandarin tree sat in the middle, stretching nearly to the dragons overhead. A spiral staircase encircled the whole room, and a body lay at its base with a .357 magnum still dangling from its fingers. The dead man was lying supine in a pool of his own blood, wearing a blue embroidered dress that was quickly turning purple. A demonic mask lay off to the side, perhaps a meter away, surrounded by hundreds of white shards.

"What exactly happened?" Smithfield asked, opening up his three-ringed notepad.

"There was a fight on camera last night," Yip replied, turning away from the body.

"That's normal for an action picture," Leung said.

"Only this one wasn't part of the script. We had a short scene planned: Raymond, playing Wong Fei-Hung, was supposed to encounter the ghosts of his dead ancestors and knock them both out with two fierce kicks. But after he delivered the blows, one of the ghosts didn't stay down. He fought back."

Wong guffawed. "He challenged *Raymond Lau* to a fight?"

"Not really a fight," the director said. "More like a thrashing."

Leung smirked. "I'm sure it was. Raymond Lau couldn't beat a screaming toddler in a fight, let alone a real martial artist."

"No," the director said, staring at the woman in the flaming chariot. "Sure, Raymond was startled at first. But once he realized what was happening, he ended it pretty quickly. He can be quite violent, when the situation allows."

"I find that very hard to believe," Leung said. "Who was this actor exactly?"

"His name was Eddie. Eddie Yang."

"Have you worked with him before?"

"Nobody has. I think we hired him as a favor for one of the producers. He said he was a dockworker or something."

"A dockworker?" Leung wondered aloud. "What the hell was he doing here?"

"Just like Raymond Lau," Wong chimed in. "I heard that he worked in Aberdeen before he got famous."

"That's right," Yip replied, scratching his neck. "You know your history."

"I don't understand," Smithfield said. "Why pick a fight with the cameras rolling? What was he trying to accomplish?"

"Honor," Yip replied. "It's not that unusual in this line of work. If you want more screen time, you have to prove that you're the better fighter. Bruce Lee used to fend off challenges every day."

"And no one ever beat him," Leung boasted proudly.

"You don't become an action star by accident," Yip said. "There's always a good reason. But usually you have to fight your way up the ranks. The extras fight the stunt doubles. The stunt doubles fight the actors. And only then do you take on a major star. So, of course we were all a bit surprised when it started, especially with the cameras rolling. But these things happen on set, and if he didn't want to get hurt, he shouldn't have picked a fight with Raymond."

"So he lost the fight," Smithfield said. "But when did he kill himself?"

"I'm not sure," Yip replied. "We found him here this morning, just before the morning shoot. Raymond and I were the first ones in the room. You know," he said, his voice quaking. "It's easy to write this stuff, but it's not so easy to see it firsthand."

"It's hard the first time," Leung said. "But you get used to it."

"Where is Raymond?" Wong asked. "We, uh, need to question him, I'm sure. He *was* a firsthand witness."

"I hate to say this," Leung said, "but you're right."

"He's not here," Yip replied tersely.

"Not here?" Leung asked, his eyebrow shooting upward. "What do you mean he's not here?"

"He's on a plane to China," the director explained.

"*China*?" Leung exclaimed.

"That's right," Yip said. "This whole film is part of a major co-production with a small mainland studio, and he had to head back immediately to keep on schedule. It's much cheaper to shoot there these days . . . and, of course, far more realistic. Most of this film is set in Guangzhou, after all. He'll be there for the next five days."

Leung stepped forward. "You understand how this might sound *suspicious*. There was a shooting on set this morning, and the man who discovered the crime headed straight to the airport and out of the country."

"To be fair," Yip said, "it's not another country. At least as far as Beijing is concerned."

"If I didn't know any better," Leung said, "I might think that Raymond killed Eddie Yang himself."

Wong removed his sunglasses. "What, are you out of your mind?" he asked, his eyes bulging. "You think *Raymond Lau* murdered someone?"

Yip forced a smile. "I can see where you're coming from, Inspector Leung. Really, I can. I write enough mysteries that I can start to connect the dots myself. But Raymond's trip to Guangzhou has been planned for several months *and* cleared with the authorities. Given the political climate and Raymond's international stature, security guarantees from the police force were altogether necessary. Commissioner Dayne himself helped us arrange these matters. I'm sure he could clear up any misunderstandings here."

Leung scratched his chin. "Is that right?"

"I was supposed to be on that flight myself," Yip said, "but *someone* had to stay behind and deal with this mess."

Leung shook his head. "I don't care who he is," he said. "Leaving the scene of a crime is a serious offense. We'll need to get him back here immediately for a statement."

"But it's not a crime," Smithfield said as he scribbled yet another note in his notepad. "It's a suicide. And I'm sure if these men are telling the truth that there must be some kind of footage to back up their statements. The fight *did* happen on camera, yes?"

"Of course," O'Callaghan said, breaking his long silence. "I can take one of you gentlemen to the security office and recover any recordings we have."

"I'll go," Smithfield said without hesitation, shutting his notepad. "You two stay here and search for any other clues you can dig up."

"Alright," Leung said, "but be careful. Something doesn't add up."

"If I can take on the triads," Smithfield said with a grin, "I think I'll be alright. You boys take care of yourselves." He put two fingers to his forehead in a half-salute as he exited the room with the burly chief of security.

"Now," Yip said, "if you'll excuse me, I have another flight to catch. And if I miss it because of you, your commissioner will be quite upset."

"Alright," Leung replied. "Thank you for your assistance, Mr. Yip. We'll call you if we need anything else."

"Safe travels!" Wong exclaimed.

"Yes," Yip said coldly as he turned to exit the studio. "Ciao."

There was a long silence as the director walked away from them, his footsteps echoing in the distance. "So what do we do now?" Wong asked, ending the respite.

"What do you think?" Leung replied. "We're inspectors. We look for clues."

Leung walked onto the set of the mansion where Eddie Yang's corpse lay motionless. He picked up the mask and ran his hand along it. Blood and ceramic dust stuck to his fingers.

"You're not talking," Leung said, "but you're telling me a story." He looked around for the source of the shards, but the remaining plates and vases were all either unbroken or the wrong color. "What's the twist?" Leung wondered aloud.

"You find anything?" Wong asked.

Inspector Leung looked at the triptych screen beside him and pushed aside the plants to get a closer view. The right fold bore the character 恩 for "grace," and the left fold bore the character 力 for "power." But the center character was gone. In its place was a large hole near the bottom of the center fold, surrounded by a ring of either blood or red paint. *What's missing?* Leung thought.

"Look over here!" Wong called out. He was standing just beside the corpse, whose left arm was hanging onto the second step. Leung walked over, wading carefully through the rivers of blood. "There's something on his wrist," Wong said.

Leung could make out the trace of an image under the loose sleeve. "Any last words?" he asked. He reached out and pulled the sleeve further back, revealing a red blotch in the shape of a jagged stone.

"What is that?" Wong asked. "A tattoo or a birthmark?"

"Neither," Leung replied. "It's an omen."

"Follow me," the monk said, leading Julian through a hidden door in the temple courtyard. The two entered a nearly pitch-black room—the only light came from spirals of incense hanging from the ceiling, emanating scented smoke and dropping ashes onto the shadows below. "Keep close. And try not to get burned."

"Alright . . ."

"This temple used to be at the waterfront, you know."

"Is that right?" Julian replied, struggling to follow the old man's voice.

"Hollywood Road used to be the edge of Hong Kong, where the British made their first landing in the city. But now, with land reclamation, this temple and all its history is buried amidst malls and packed apartments. A litany of nightclubs and skyscrapers. . ."

"Don't forget the diamond shops."

"Exactly," the monk said. He found a switch and flipped on the lights, revealing a dusty old room with stacks of scrolls and books on chestnut wood bookshelves. A pink mattress sat in the corner of the library beside an unlit brass oil lamp, and at the very center of the room rested a round wooden table with a red, white, and blue shield engraved as a crest. The words TUNG WAH GROUP OF HOSPITALS were carved just beneath it.

"What is this place?" Julian asked.

"My home," the monk replied. He picked up a matchbook, which bore a crescent moon with a tear in its eye, then struck one of the matches and lit the burner. "And also where I come to study." He shook the match until the flame went out.

"Study what?" Julian asked.

"History," the monk said. He stood back up and approached one of the bookshelves, removing an oversized hardcover book from its racks. The title WATER MARGIN was etched in white on the book's hard black spine. The monk laid the tome down on the table with a hard thump and opened it, revealing its hidden treasure. The pages were carved out in the center, hiding a glass jar containing a ball of white goop. "You know," the monk said as he removed it, "this room was once the seat of government in Hong Kong."

"A temple was the seat of government?"

"That's right," the monk replied. He reached under the table, removing a slender black stick that looked like a cross between an oboe and a flute. "Of course, the British administered their own portion of old Victoria City from their palaces in Central, but the locals were left to fend for themselves. The colonial administration had no intention of making any of them into British subjects, so they allowed the

Tung Wah Hospital Board of Directors to adjudicate local matters in their stead."

"What does this have to do with my father?"

"Everything," the monk replied. He held out the obsidian stick, which had a coiling brass dragon running down its side, culminating in a deep bowl just a few centimeters from its end. Then, he opened the jar and removed the whole sphere of white goop, about the size of a small golf ball. "Do you know what this is?" he asked.

"I'm not sure," Julian said. "But I can't imagine it's good."

"Opium," the monk replied. "Your country's legacy. Two wars were fought over this drug, leading ultimately to the concession of Hong Kong. To many Chinese, it was after those defeats that the Qing emperors, colonists themselves from Manchuria, lost the Mandate of Heaven and had to be replaced. The beginning of a century of humiliation."

"I know the history," Julian said. "We studied this in Form 2."

"You studied what the textbooks told you. History is written by the victors, but what's just as important is what's left out. Even today, this substance holds power in this city. Secret wars fought between the triads have caused the deaths of thousands, and addiction has cost us countless more."

"Isn't opium brown?" Julian asked.

"This isn't just opium," the monk said, peeling off a thick white clump and stuffing it into the brass bowl. "It's a special blend developed by the Lucky Stone Triad in the 1980's, called Yulong. In English, it's called White Horse. It's cut with ketamine, MDMA, a sprinkle of DMT, and probably some kind of bonemeal to achieve the proper color. It gives it all a hallucinatory effect."

"I'm sure," Julian replied.

"It feels like sailing through time," the monk said. "And nostalgia is a powerful drug itself. The past is always insufficient, so we seek out a mythical one instead."

"And what are you going to do with it?"

"What do you think I'm going to do?" the monk asked rhetorically. He lay down on the mattress and held the pipe upside down over the flame, so that the open bowl rested just a millimeter from the fire.

"What kind of monk *are* you?"

"You know who I am already," he replied as his lips brushed against the end of the long pipe. "My name is Shih-yin."

The monk breathed in deep, and the fire ascended from the burner to meet the brass bowl. A chemical vapor began to fill the room like wafts of poison incense. Shih-yin dropped the pipe and rose to his feet, standing face-to-face with Julian.

"What are you doing?" Julian gasped. Smoke was escaping from the corner of the monk's mouth, and his eyes were so glassy it looked like he'd been crying. Julian held out his arms to keep the old man away, but it was no use. Shih-yin pushed them aside and pressed his lips against Julian's mouth, blowing in a cloud of noxious smoke.

"*Mmrph!*" Julian mumbled as he struggled in vain. He shut his eyelids, and the room went pitch black, save for a pinpoint of light in his periphery.

"You say the past is lost to you. You say when you close your eyes and think back, all you draw is a blank. But this is true for everyone. Memories aren't hardwired—they're a story we tell ourselves over and over. And the more we tell it, the more authentic it feels. Even the most ridiculous lies, if repeated often enough, can start to sound like reality."

Julian thought of his own mother—how she would rant at him with a wine bottle in hand, begging him not to abandon her. "Arthur," she would call him. "Arthur, no . . ."

"Knowledge is the first step," the monk said. "And, when applied well, it is the only one. In Confucian philosophy, the scholar is the highest class and the merchant is the lowest. The old man would have hated Hong Kong."

Julian slipped in and out of focus until even the single flicker of light disappeared from view. He couldn't tell if he was still awake or if he'd already slipped out of consciousness. Shih-yin's voice was real enough, but the darkness felt strangely transitory.

"In ancient times," the old monk said, "if you wanted to become a magistrate and join the nobility, you had to pass the Imperial Examination. And for many, this was the only path out of squalor—the only chance to make something of their lives. If you weren't a noble, your family history wasn't even recorded. Failure meant not only poverty, but erasure."

The light flickered back, and Julian found himself in a drab old classroom with dim fluorescent lighting. A mustached proctor was pacing back and forth at the head of the room, holding a long ruler. The desks were lined in columns and filled with pimple-faced teenagers in thick winter clothes. Half of them were biting their pencils, and the other half were chewing their nails.

"Where are you now?" Shih-yin asked.

"I'm at the police academy in London," Julian said. He reached out and picked up the test paper in front of him, but the questions were so far beyond him they might as well have been written in Chinese. "I'm taking a test," he said. "The paper exam."

"And why are you taking it?" Shih-yin asked.

"Because I always wanted to be a cop. I wanted to be like my father."

"Number three zero nine two!" the proctor shouted, holding the ruler high in the air. "Why the bloody hell are you talking? This is an exam!"

"Forget him," the old monk said. "He's not important."

"But he'll fail me."

"Kensington!" the proctor exclaimed.

"Memory," Shih-yin said, "is not a keyhole to the past. No matter how much that voice echoes in your head, it's just an illusion. It's only as imposing as you make it."

"Dammit, Kensington!" the proctor yelled again, only now his voice was high-pitched, like Mickey Mouse after inhaling helium. The other cadets in the classroom all laughed aloud. "What in the hell?" the proctor squeaked. "What the hell did you do?"

"Is the fear still there?" Shih-yin asked.

"No," Julian said as he looked again at the question sheet, which remained as impenetrable as before. "But I still don't know what to do."

Shih-yin laughed along with all the other students. "And this is just a single test," he said. "For the Imperial Exam, you had to know math, music, poetry, and more. But the worst part was the essay. The students called it 'Eight Legs.'"

"Like a spider," Julian said.

"Exactly. One for each of the eight sections they had to write. *Potai, tseuntai, heigong, heigu, zonggu, haogu, cheukgu,* and *daigit.* Each section had a strict form to follow, down to the phraseology and even the number of words and syllables. Only in *daigit*—the 'Big Knot'—was any form of creativity permitted, but most scholars discouraged it, preferring a strict adherence to the forms. After all, one missed beat could mean the end of your chances. An extra syllable and your whole family would be forgotten."

Julian looked down again, but the test had metamorphized into a blank paper scroll. Instead of a pencil, a long wooden inkbrush rested in Julian's right hand. "I don't remember this," he said, looking around the room. The other cadets were now dressed in black robes and were chewing on their brushes just as incessantly as they were chewing their pencils before. Each one was carefully drawing traditional Chinese characters on a scroll as a stern man in a purple dress sat motionless at the head of the classroom, watching in stone silence. Julian glanced over at the scroll of the young man next to him. His calligraphy was so masterful that Julian could only gaze in awe. Though he couldn't understand the characters, there was beauty in the writing—the thick lines and subtle strokes telling a story of their own. Julian pressed his own brush to the scroll, but when he tried to draw the same characters, his wrist wouldn't respond. Wet ink trailed down the page, seeping onto the wooden floorboards.

"You'll fail," Shih-yin commented.

"*Cheung-kee!*" the man at the head of the room shouted. His voice was so loud that all the other students froze. The proctor stood up deliberately, using the cane in his right hand for support. As he lurched toward Julian, the other examinees were silent, and their wrists were utterly still. The footsteps were the only sound in the whole room.

Beads of sweat formed on Julian's neck. "I'm sorry," he said contritely. "I shouldn't be here, I . . ." He held his hands out as the proctor lifted his cane high in the air.

"That same power works in reverse," Shih-yin said. "Just as we can change the past, the past can change us. Old fears return to the present."

"Please!" Julian pleaded.

"This is how we travel through time."

The proctor swung down, and the cane snapped across Julian's face, breaking in two.

The pain was real.

***

"Wake up," Shih-yin said.

After what felt like many days, Julian once again opened his eyes. He was back in the old study, splayed out across the pink mattress. It was blisteringly hot inside, and Julian's blue and white striped pajamas were already turning green and yellow from sweat. Shih-yin opened the blinds, but what little sunlight came in through the window was oppressively drab, choked of its luminescence.

"Get up," Shih-yin said. "You've been asleep for almost twenty hours."

Julian rubbed his eyes. "Twenty hours?"

"Yes," the monk replied. "It's one o'clock already."

"Why did you do that to me? I thought you were going to tell me about my father."

"I will," Shih-yin replied. "But first you need the proper context."

"Context for what?"

"For everything," Shih-yin said. "The boy beside you, the one whose work you admired. You know that he failed too."

"Why, because of me?"

"Perhaps you got him distracted. Or perhaps it was his destiny. His name was Hong Huoxiu, but he was later known as Hong Xiuquan, the Heavenly King of the Taiping Rebellion."

"I've never heard of him."

"Most haven't. And yet, that boy was responsible for the deaths of tens of millions. Almost as many as Hitler himself. After he failed that exam for a third time, he had a dream that he was the son of God and the younger brother of Jesus Christ."

"Humble, too."

"He attracted a sizable following, but when the Qing government tried to suppress him, he led a revolt of ethnic Chinese against their Manchurian overlords. He would have succeeded, too, if your country hadn't aided his enemies."

"What are you talking about? We beat the Qing Dynasty in the Opium Wars. We fought them off in the Boxer Rebellion. We never helped them."

"It's true that many in the West supported Hong Xiuquan's cause, at least at the outset. After all, the Taiping were at least nominally Christian and had shown admiration for some of your political and economic institutions. But there was a wrinkle."

"There always is."

"The Taiping would have banned the sale of opium. And they would have made all your unequal treaties with the Qing null and void. The treaty ports of Shanghai and Canton would no longer be open, and Hong Kong itself would have to be returned."

"Can't get in the way of business, can we?"

"No. But the dream that Hong Xiuquan fought for never died."

"Really? I don't see too many Christians around here."

"The dream to rid China of foreign invaders. The dream to take this and other cities back."

"I think you got it back twenty years ago."

"And how exactly did that happen?"

"Is this a trick question?" Julian asked. "We gave it back to you."

"We'll see," the monk said cryptically. "But I'm afraid you have your own examination first."

"Was I supposed to be taking notes?"

The monk crossed his arms. "You have an interview in one hour."

Julian raised an eyebrow. "An interview?"

Shih-yin handed Julian a business card with a horse's head for a logo. "You're meeting a man named Chester Dayne."

"White Horse Future Bullion," Julian read from the card. "Central Plaza, forty-ninth floor."

"Do you know where that is?"

"Sure," Julian said. "That's right by the convention center. But I don't understand—what exactly am I interviewing for?"

"A job, of course. If you live in this temple, you work."

"Since when do I live here?"

"You slept here, didn't you? I'm not running a charity. And besides, you don't want to leave a gap on your resume."

Julian stood up and stretched his arms. His whole body was numb, except for a searing pain across his cheek. "Did you hit me?" he asked.

"That's not important."

"I feel like I got dropkicked in the face."

"Listen, Julian. It was hard enough just to set up this meeting. I had to call in every last favor I had. So don't blow it, understand?"

"I'll try," Julian said, "but I still don't understand what I'm doing."

"That's for the best. The less you know, the better your chances."

***

An hour later, Julian had finally retraced his steps to Central Plaza. He wore a skinny leather jacket that was at least four sizes too small, along with a white dress shirt and a polka-dotted bowtie, all borrowed from the old monk. The massive skyscraper towered far above all the other buildings on Gloucester Road, spearing the grey overcast sky with its golden spire.

As he stepped inside the lobby, Julian gaped at its sheer splendor, starkly contrasting the dirty streets and whorehouses in the rest of Wan Chai. There were polished marble floors and oversized columns stretching four stories high, and artificial palm trees lined every corridor. Modernist oil paintings hung on the wall, most of which looked like they could have been made by children. One was just an entirely blank canvas, framed.

I don't get it, Julian thought.

All at once, the golden elevators rang open and a rush of businessmen poured out, filling the lobby like a swarm of bees. A skinny man with spiked hair and a black messenger bag on his shoulder bumped into Julian, nearly knocking him to the ground. "*Mmgoi!*" the man called out behind him, already halfway to the front door. However, before Julian could lodge a word of protest, he and all the businessmen were gone, and the lobby was deserted again, except for a pudgy woman standing under a palm tree. She wore a red and white buttoned-down shirt and a pair of Miu Miu sunglasses, with a lumpy black garbage bag in one hand and her cellphone in the other.

"Flora?" Julian blurted out.

"Oh," she said. "It's you."

"In the flesh. What are you doing here?"

"My brother's a headhunter," she explained. "I told you, he works upstairs."

"A *headhunter?*"

"Yeah, a recruiter. He had a little accident after lunch, so he asked me to bring him a change of clothes." She held up the garbage bag, which smelled ghastly.

"What size of suit is he?" Julian asked.

"Believe me," Flora said. "You don't want to touch these."

"Shit," Julian groaned. "I have an interview in fifteen minutes . . ."

Flora raised an eyebrow. "An interview?"

"For a job, I think. I'm not too sure of the details."

"What happened with the monk?" she asked. "I thought you were going to call me for breakfast this morning."

"Blame him," Julian said. "He's the one who set this whole thing up for me. Says I have to get this job before he'll tell me anything, but this tiny jacket of his is all I have to wear. I look ridiculous."

"Oh, relax. They'll hire you."

"How do you know that?"

"Just *look* at you."

Julian blushed. "You're saying I look good?"

"Not at all," she laughed. "But you're white."

***

Julian adjusted his bowtie in the mirror as the golden elevator ascended. He tried to psych himself up for the interview, to iron out the pangs of anxiety he normally felt whenever a situation got too stressful, but it was hard to feel much pressure when the situation made so little sense. Maybe that's what Shih-yin had planned.

When the elevator opened, Julian stood across from a stocky mustached man with nearly orange skin. He was wearing a navy-blue sports coat and beige khakis and was smiling with both his upper and lower teeth.

"Mr. Kensington!" he gushed effusively. "So nice to meet you. My name is Chester Dayne." They shook hands, but upon touching Dayne's palm a chill rose up Julian's arm and into his spine. It felt like grabbing an icepack.

"Likewise," Julian responded curtly.

"Strange," Dayne said. "You don't look like a Kensington to me." Though his eyes were baby blue, his pupils were gigantic, like two black holes pulling all of the color into the void.

"Um . . . well . . . that's my name."

"No matter," Dayne replied. "This way, please." He led Julian to the front desk, where an old woman with curly white hair was busy answering calls.

"White Horse Future Bullion," the receptionist said. "Please hold." The old woman hung up the phone, then repeated the procedure with the next caller.

"Come," Dayne said. "Before we start, there are some administrative matters we need to take care of." On the counter sat a stack of forms at least half a meter tall and a single ballpoint pen bearing the company's logo.

"What is all this?" Julian asked.

"Oh, legal matters," Dayne replied. "NDA, TPRIEOB . . ."

"What was that last one?"

"TPRIEOB," Dayne repeated. "Transfer of Property Rights in Event of Breach." He cleared his throat. "Purely for insurance purposes, of course."

"Right."

Dayne handed him the pen. "If you could just sign here and here . . ."

Julian hesitated for a moment, but there was no way he would read through all those forms. It was like the iTunes terms and conditions—he was probably selling his soul, but if that's what it cost to hear the rest of the song, he was willing to pay it. He signed on the dotted line.

"Wonderful," Dayne said, grinning widely. "Just grand."

"If I want to work here, don't I need a visa or something?"

"Oh, don't you worry about that. We have a close partnership with the immigration department." He pointed to a black tower out the window, which looked like a futuristic stalagmite with its roots planted deep in the artificial earth. A bespectacled Chinese man in a black suit waved back at them from behind the glass panel just opposite their own.

"I see," Julian said.

"Let me take you to one of our breakout rooms. We can talk there."

Dayne led Julian into the triangular office, which stretched across the whole forty-ninth floor. The space was open and modern—a large bullpen with no private rooms or cubicles, save for one or two glass-paneled meeting rooms at the far edge of the floor. Suited workers were packed into several long benches, typing away madly at dusty computers that looked like old NeXT Cubes. The only sound Julian could hear was the clattering of keys.

"As you can see," Dayne said, "we strive for openness and transparency here at White Horse. The open office plan allows us to maintain peak synergy while promoting healthy social connections. Within reason, of course."

"Of course."

"We insist that all of our employees work out in plain view like this. Even me." He pointed to a lacquered oak desk in the far back corner, sitting just in front of an imposing metal door. A golden nameplate sat prominently on the front of the desk, displaying CHESTER DAYNE THE FOURTH in bold capital letters. "You can see me, and I can certainly see you."

"What about that door in the back?"

"That's our CEO's office," Dayne said. "He's the leader of one of the most successful corporations in Hong Kong, so of course he has his own office. But he keeps a close eye on all of his employees." Dayne pointed to a video camera mounted on the ceiling beside the door.

Julian gulped. "He . . . uh, watches everything?"

"We're a family company. We stress a certain . . . *personal touch.*"

"I can see that."

"The video monitoring system also helps us eliminate timesheets by automatically clocking workers in and out. You are paid for each second you're in the office, and not a penny more."

"What time does the day start, then?"

"Eight o'clock," Dayne replied, "but I always say: if you're on time, you're late. And if you're ten minutes early, you're still late."

"And if you're actually late?"

"Then you're fired."

Julian winced. "Um . . . what time should I get here then?"

"Oh, eight o'clock is fine."

Julian scratched his head, but before he could make any further inquiries, Dayne had already started marching down another aisle. As Julian followed behind him, squeezing between a pair of thin benches, he could see that most of the workers were typing away madly at Microsoft Excel spreadsheets as their supervisor came through, their hands moving quicker the closer he approached. Some weren't even given their own spaces on the desk but were sitting cross-legged on the floor using tablet computers. One woman with a pixie cut sat in front of the glass meeting room at the corner of the office, sporting a navy pantsuit.

Mr. Dayne cleared his throat. "*Lei hai lidou zhou mei?*" he yelled violently in perfect Cantonese.

"*Dui mmzi,*" the woman replied meekly. "*Ngo yiwai lidou hai ngo ngam yat gek wai.*"

"*Yi geng mm hai la!*" Dayne commanded. "*Lei yee ga hai luk ling chat wai!*"

"*Luk ling chat wai,*" she repeated. "*Mmgoi sai!*" She nodded and scurried to the elevator, carrying her small tablet computer under her arms.

Dayne smiled warmly. "If you'll just come this way . . ."

Julian looked back at her, confused about the scene that had just unfolded in front of him. But Mr. Dayne put an arm on his shoulder and guided him toward the conference room. Through the glass, Julian could see a burly Chinese man dressed in a pinstriped suit with a skinny black tie. He looked more like a bouncer than an office worker; both his arms were nearly the size of Julian's waist. Julian could feel the fabric under his armpits moistening rapidly.

"Please," Dayne said, opening the door and taking a seat beside his massive counterpart. "Sit down. Make yourself comfortable."

His legs quaking, Julian lowered himself into a chair across the table from the two executives, keeping his eyes off of the larger man. "So . . . here we all are."

"This must be a dream come true for you," Dayne said.

Julian pulled at his collar, desperate to stanch the heat. "It certainly feels like it."

"So tell me: Why are you interested in a career at White Horse?"

"I'm not really sure, to be honest. I guess it's just the place to be right now."

"That's a bold position," Dayne said. "Maximizing flexibility. You see opportunity where it is, and you take it." He scribbled an approving message on his notepad, then flipped onto the next page. "Next," he continued. "If you were a fruit, which one would you be?"

"Is that a serious question?"

"Deathly serious."

Julian scratched his head. "I, uh . . ." He thought deeply but couldn't come up with anything interesting. "I don't know," he said. "A lime?"

"And why's that?"

"I'm sour, but healthy. And I go well with beer."

Dayne laughed. "He has a sense of humor too!" He nudged his counterpart in the ribs, but the brawny man didn't move an inch. "Favorite animal?" Dayne asked.

"Um, spiders?"

"Spiders?" Dayne replied, reeling at the thought. "Most people say dogs."

"I don't know. I guess I just like the idea of having eight legs."

"Alright. You seem *eminently* qualified, but . . ."

"I do?"

". . . I have one final question for you." Dayne cleared his throat, gazing intently in Julian's direction like a greyhound pointing out a duck in the bushes. The longer Julian stared into those two great abysses, the more the pressure built in his chest. He felt like he was on the plane again, one hand on the emergency exit as the jet entered a sudden tailspin. "Why do you think you're the best man for this position?" Dayne asked.

"W-well," Julian stammered, until he pushed the handle down in his mind and the cabin rapidly depressurized. All the baggage burst open and came pouring out in one great rush. "To be honest, I don't even know what the position is, or what your company even does. I was kind of just told to be here. Shih-yin sent me. You know, the old monk? Or at least I think he's a monk anyway, even though he doesn't act like one. But he didn't tell me anything about you. I mean . . . Future Bullion? What is that? Are you trading on currency futures or you trying to sell me a pot of gold? And what the hell do you want with someone like me?"

The room was silent.

"I like him," Dayne's counterpart said, breaking from his hibernation. "He has moxie."

"And poise," Dayne added. "He's a self-starter. A real entrepreneur." He held out his hand and stared unblinkingly into Julian's eyes, his two irises receding into expanses of darkness. "You're hired."

1984 / Chapter 3: A Short Leash

Inspector Leung sat across from the police commissioner, a fat, bespectacled man whose uniform was bursting at the seams. He had tanned skin, a bushy brown mustache, and wide, spongy cheeks. His eyes were the color of Victoria Harbor—blue, but with enough green and brown to make it all look dirty. The commissioner's office on the twenty-first floor was the largest and most opulent in the whole building, decorated with fine art from every continent. There was an impressionist painting on the wall behind him, two Zulu masks pasted to the front of his oaken desk, and portraits of the Queen, Prince, and governor hanging on the dark chestnut-stained walls. Marble busts of Winston Churchill and Lady Thatcher faced each other on opposite sides of the door. The only running theme throughout the artwork was that, in place of human heads, each piece featured a different breed of dog. A golden nameplate stood prominently at the front of the commissioner's desk, displaying CHESTER DAYNE THE THIRD in bold, capital letters.

"So," Dayne inquired in his typically ostentatious tone, "what news do you have from Jiangsu?"

"Jianghu," Leung corrected.

"Yes, well. Whatever it is."

The Churchill bust, a Schnauzer, seemed particularly out of place to Leung. He always thought of the late prime minister as more of a bulldog—one who bites and barks with equal measure. Leung pulled a cigarette from his coat pocket. "Do you mind?"

"Of course not. Go ahead."

Leung lit his cigarette and inhaled, blowing smoke in the direction of Queen Elizabeth the Terrier and Prince Charles the Shih Tzu. The billowing cloud seeped past the royal portraits toward a pair of framed photographs of a woman and a young boy, both with ghost white skin. The smoke obscured their faces.

"Where to even begin?" Leung wondered aloud. "We have a dead man with a Lucky Stone tattoo. Let's start with that."

"Good," the commissioner replied. "One less triad to deal with."

"Fewer," Leung corrected.

The commissioner wagged his finger in Leung's direction. "You're a basset hound, Leung. That's what you are."

"Whatever you say, sir. You're the expert on that."

Dayne leaned back in his chair, and it lifted onto its hind legs and wobbled under his weight. "What's the issue then? A two-bit criminal is dead. So what?"

"So how did a triad even get on set in the first place? And why would he kill himself right there in the studio? If he was mad at Raymond Lau or

Charlie Yip, why didn't he take his anger out on them? It doesn't make sense."

"Hah!" the commissioner laughed. "Not enough hugs in the triads these days."

"But what's more important is that Inspector Smithfield has gone missing too. He went off to find some security footage, but he never came back. The chief of security and Charlie Yip both disappeared as well."

"I put Charlie Yip on a plane to Beijing."

"I thought he was on his way to Guangzhou. And what about the chief of security? There was something off about him. I feel like I've seen him before."

"O'Callaghan? You probably have. He's a former cop, after all."

"Is that right?"

"What about the security footage, Leung? Was there any trace of it?"

"All missing. It's almost like there was some kind of an electrical failure."

"Strange."

"Extremely," Leung replied. "Smithfield's not the type to just run off. And if this O'Callaghan was really a cop, maybe they're both in trouble."

"From who?"

"Whom," Leung corrected again. "The triads. The Lucky Stone in particular."

The chief leaned forward, and his chair returned to the floor with a loud thud. He pressed the buzzer on his phone. "Linda, get me Inspector Woo."

"Inspector *Woo?*" Leung said. "What do we need him for?"

"He's my top man in the Triad Bureau. He's handled more of these cases than anyone on the force."

"That's because you never let us touch those anymore."

"You're a *homicide* inspector, Leung. And there's no murder here."

Leung pounded the desk, knocking over the commissioner's golden nameplate. "He's my partner!" Leung exclaimed. "This should be my case!"

"I admire your enthusiasm, but triad cases require a more . . . delicate approach. One false step can tip the balance. One wrong move can lead to war."

"There hasn't been a triad war in twelve years."

"But who's to say it will stay that way?"

"So we should just sit back and do *nothing?* If the triads are plotting something, we need to get out there and find the truth."

"Truth," the commissioner scoffed. "There are ten thousand truths out there, Leung. And the one I want is what we have right now: a low crime rate and triads who keep to themselves. That's what the governor wants. That's what Lady Thatcher wants. And if they're not happy, we lose our jobs."

"Is that all you care about? Your job?"

"It's what we *choose* to believe. That's what defines us."

"You're wrong, sir. There's only one truth."

The commissioner sighed. "There's no convincing a basset hound. But a Shiba Inu . . ." There were two sudden knocks on the door.

Inspector Woo walked into the office wearing his usual outré attire: a red Hawaiian shirt with printed white palm trees and a pair of white skinny jeans. Unlike Inspector Wong, whose choice of dress was a matter of style, Woo chose his outfit for professional reasons. He had to stay hidden among the triads he was supposed to infiltrate, and, in that world, sticking out was the best way to blend in. Of course, staying inconspicuous came easy to Inspector Woo; he was remarkably short and thin, perhaps five feet tall and a hundred pounds at most, though his jet-black hair was spiked enough to compensate. "You called?" he said in a gruff, baritone voice, belying his tiny stature. He was chomping loudly on a stick of gum.

"Yes," the commissioner replied. "What took you so long?"

"Sorry," Woo said as he slumped onto the red leather couch beneath the governor's portrait. "I was . . . indisposed."

Leung winced. "I don't even want to know."

The commissioner smiled and pointed to three wooden figurines on the front of his desk, beside the fallen nameplate: three dogs—the first covering his eyes, the second his ears, and the third his mouth. "See no evil, hear no evil, speak no evil. A mantra to live by."

"Or a recipe for ignorance," Leung thought aloud.

"Woo," the commissioner said, ignoring Leung's remark. "I want you to lead the investigation at Jianghu Studios. Inspector Smithfield has gone missing, and it sounds like the Lucky Stone might be involved."

"Don't worry," Woo replied. "I'll take care of it."

The commissioner crossed his arms. "Now, officially, we're going to keep quiet about Smithfield and investigate this incident as a suicide. I'll call Smithfield's family and see if they've heard anything, but if not, I'll make up an excuse about his sudden disappearance. Tell them he's undercover."

"That's not right," Leung protested. "They're his family. They deserve to know that he's in trouble."

Dayne shook his head resoundingly. "We don't know anything yet, Leung. And I don't want to stir up any panic until we do. For now, we'll gather information. We've had relative peace for a decade, so if something's changed out there, the situation is *troubling*, to say the least. We can't afford a war on our hands. Not now."

"Right-o," Woo said.

"The governor would be most displeased if the sovereignty negotiations were compromised. And Deng Xiaoping has threatened an invasion if there are any domestic *disturbances* during the course of these talks."

"Negotiations?" Leung asked.

The commissioner stared at him quizzically. "Don't you read the news?"

Inspector Leung had heard rumors that the British might give Hong Kong back to China, but this was the first time he'd heard anyone on the force say it aloud, let alone anyone important. Leung bore no love for the Chinese government—after all, their agitators had tried to kill him and his colleagues repeatedly at the height of the Cultural Revolution—and, for the most part, he'd been treated well by the colonial administration. But still, the thought was something to behold, even if it was unlikely to happen. A chance to show those smug *gweilos* once and for all who was really in charge.

"Don't worry," Woo said. "I'll be discreet."

The commissioner smiled. "Good boy."

***

Inspector Wong sat in his cubicle, twirling a pistol around his finger. His desk remained full of crumpled timesheets, but now he could no longer complain about them, staring wistfully at the Walled City far in the distance beneath the night sky. A plane came in low over Kowloon, making a sharp forty-seven-degree turn—the Hong Kong Heart Attack as it was known—through high-rise after high-rise before sticking a perfect landing at Kai Tak airport, itself hidden in the dense urban jungle. Wong's heart was like a church bell resonating down the tips of his fingers.

His first case wasn't going the way he had planned. He and his partners were supposed to solve mysteries, not become the mysteries themselves. He was supposed to fight crime for a few years, perhaps end a string of serial killings, before embarking on his inevitable acting career. The image was all so clear in his head, but now the whole plan was collapsing before his eyes.

In all of Raymond Lau's films, the plots were so simple. Sure, someone always died at the beginning the story. The hero was tested and had to fight hard to make his way back. But in the end, he always triumphed. The mystery was solved, and he *always* got the girl. In real life, though, there was no guarantee. And even if the image did become reality, it would be painted in blood. What Leung had said now finally rang true—a single glimpse of that viscous red fluid had changed everything. This was a killing. Someone *died*, and if he wasn't careful he might just die too.

A voice boomed out from behind him: "I hope the safety's on." Inspector Leung stood over Wong's shoulder. "If it's not, I think your probation's over."

"Of course it is," Wong replied, though he wasn't entirely sure. "How'd it go?" he asked nervously. "What'd the commissioner say?"

"He's taking us off the case."

Wong's jaw dropped. "What? *Why?*"

"He's assigning Inspector Woo instead. Like he always does."

"Who the hell is Inspector Woo?"

Leung looked back at his graduation photo—at his younger self and the short, hairy man lined up next to him. "A brown-nose runt from the Triad Bureau."

"Shit!" Wong exclaimed. "Well, I guess that's the end of that . . ."

Leung pulled out a Lucky Strike. "Welcome to the Royal Hong Kong Police Force," he said, flicking open his Yin-Yang lighter and holding the flame to the butt of his cigarette. "My advice is to take up smoking."

"You're a real depressing guy, you know that?"

"Reality is depressing," Leung said, puffing out smoke with each syllable. "If you want escapism, look somewhere else." His eyes were still fixated on the short inspector in the photograph. Back then, the little runt wore a mop cut, but the picture had deteriorated so much that Woo's young face was completely faded out. "We can't just sit back," he said. "Smithfield is *missing*."

"Commissioner's orders," Wong replied. "What are we supposed to do?"

"I can think of something," a gruff voice bellowed from behind. Inspector Woo stepped into Leung's cubicle, inflating his bubble gum to the size of a small balloon.

"Woo," Leung said as the gum popped like a firecracker. "What are you doing here? The commissioner wants you on the case, not us."

"Commissioner Dayne is being cautious, as he should be. But the truth is that your partner's life is in danger."

"How do you know that?" Leung asked.

"Look," Woo said. "When the Lucky Stone is involved, I just assume the worst."

"The Lucky Stone," Wong repeated. "That's one of the three big triads."

"The worst of them," Woo said. "More violent than the 14K and the Sun Yee On combined."

Leung leaned back in his chair, feeling the jagged scar on his lower back press into the faux leather. A pulse of pain rushed up his spine. "I thought they went quiet after the last triad war."

"They *won* the last triad war," Woo said. "Things tend to be quiet when business is going well. But I've been hearing strange rumblings from my informants lately. Their new leader, Marshal Hong, has staged a coup and has been consolidating his power."

"And you think this whole case has something to do with that?"

"Maybe," Woo replied. "I'd ask him myself, but he knows me too well. He used to be my most trusted snitch, but now he won't even whisper in my direction."

"So that's where we come in," Wong said.

"Right-o," Woo replied. "Marshal Hong doesn't know either of you, so you still have a chance to break in undetected."

"Break in where?" Leung asked.

"Their base of operations is a jazz bar in Wan Chai called Blue Girl. Hong spends half his nights there drinking himself into a stupor. If they have your partner, that's where they'll keep him. And if not . . ."

"A little violence goes a long way."

"Bingo. Bullets are the only language these people speak."

"I'll try my best to translate for them," Leung said, "but it could get messy. Are you sure about this? If the commissioner finds out, it could cost you your job."

"Maybe," Woo admitted. "But I'm not one to leave another inspector behind. You two came back for me, right?"

"That's true," Leung said. "And how well did that work out for us?"

Woo smirked. "Let's call it karma."

As Julian walked down from Central Plaza to the streets of Wan Chai, he encountered a motley crew of handsomely suited gentlemen that had assembled on Hennessy Road, one snorting a line of cocaine off the other's sleeve. Wiping their noses, they started walking casually across the street, lighting up cigarettes and conversing about the latest rugby match. They plodded forward at the pace of the stoplights' syncopated beeps—slower when the light was red, faster when the light was green—but always droning on, marching to the orders of an endless rhythm.

Julian descended the steps onto a gated sidewalk, then followed the pack of financiers back underneath the same bridge he'd just crossed. There he found himself on a long road filled with boisterous restaurants and bars, each with its own brightly lit sign hanging off the side of the building above it. QIBLAT, one read in green Arabic text as fruit-flavored smoke billowed up from the shishas below. CHIQUITA TITITA, another risqué sign flashed out, depicting a costumed banana hanging off a stripper's pole. Julian walked down the crowded road, observing the expatriate crowd in its natural habitat. In one bar he passed, he saw a group of Frenchmen salsa dancing as several older Chinese women shook maracas at their sides. In another, he saw a skinny Vietnamese man belting out Frank Sinatra's "My

Way" as his friends snapped their fingers and sung along, before one man stood up and started throwing punches.

As Julian continued down the road, moving from glow to glow, he overheard conversations in at least six different languages. And though he couldn't understand a word that anyone was saying, he realized that no one else could either, and it made him feel a strange sense of solidarity with these other dreamers he'd never met before. This was Hong Kong, he remembered. Everyone was an outsider here.

"Look at him," said a mascara-laden woman standing between the San Francisco Club and a bar called COCKEYE. "A handsome *gweilo.*"

"Like a stallion," her partner said.

It was nice of them to say, though he knew they were just fishing for a tip. Positive racism is still racism, but Julian wasn't complaining about it. By all rights, he should have been dead already. He came to this city with no plan, a guidebook-level knowledge of its culture, and three-thousand Hong Kong Dollars in his pocket, and here he was already succeeding beyond his wildest dreams. The position Dayne offered him was too good to be true—he was to be the Director of Analytic Consulting, whatever the hell that was supposed to mean, for a sum of forty thousand Hong Kong dollars a month and the down payment on a new flat in the Mid-Levels, right next to the escalators. It felt like taking hush money, but Julian couldn't tell what he was supposed to be quiet about.

Julian turned onto a side street and passed by a Pinoy Karaoke Bar and the Jockey Club, inside of which a mix of cab drivers and international businessmen were still placing bets. Even after work was over, the races never stopped in this city. At the end of the road, Julian arrived at a dilapidated old bar, just the kind of run-down dive he used to love back home. The shutters were broken, so the establishment looked more like a prison than a pub. The sign above the door depicted a crescent moon with a tear in its eye, but the letters themselves were broken, making it impossible to see the name.

Given his recent accomplishments, Julian figured he'd earned himself a tall glass of beer. And when nothing else made sense, he craved that familiar bitter taste, that buzz that breached borders and years.

The inside of the bar was as dilapidated as its exterior; the paint on the walls was chipping, and several of the chairs and tables were held together by duct tape, if not outright broken. While the old advertisements and propaganda posters littering the room lent the bar a certain retro charm, the smell was outright putrid—a musky scent masked only by wafting cigarette smoke and some kind of cherry plum perfume. It was like unearthing a time capsule, only to discover that the items inside were covered with mold.

In the corner of his eye, Julian spied a familiar face at the bar. The hostess of his guest house was sipping a martini while thumbing through the pages of her book. She was wearing a white buttoned-down shirt several sizes too big for her.

For all his good sense, he should have run. He should've known that this was just another trap, another chance to beat him and leave him for dead. But when he closed his eyes, he once again saw the woman from his dream—the dewdrop dripping on his shoulder as she smiled down at him—and instantly his legs started to push themselves, as if of their own accord, straight in her direction.

As he opened his eyes again, it seemed as though all of the bar's patrons were now staring at him directly. Unlike the more formal crowd outside, the customers here were mostly locals in tank tops and chains with long tattoos running up and down their arms and loose cigarettes dangling out of their mouths. Julian smiled lamely and inched forward to the nearest table, not far from where the hostess was sitting. An old Filipino waitress in a black vest and bowtie approached him with a notepad in hand. She had a faint scar on her throat that resembled a coiled dragon.

"Can I help you?" she asked.

"Yeah, I'll have a beer."

"Blue Girl or San Miguel?"

He hadn't heard of either. "The first one, I guess."

The waitress shook her head. "We're out of Blue Girl."

"Okay," Julian said. If there was no choice, he was unsure why she had even bothered to ask. But still she waited on his order. "San Miguel, then."

"Very good." The waitress wrote it down and walked back to the bar.

Julian twiddled his thumbs, trying not to look in the direction of the other patrons, who were now whispering amongst themselves. Within a few seconds, a pair of men stood up from their table and walked over to him. One was short, with two blood-shot eyes and the tips of his hair dyed blonde, wearing a pair of Jordan V's and a sweat-soaked tank top. The other was lanky, maybe three heads taller than his counterpart, and was wearing a Nike tracksuit and a flat rimmed NEW YORK hat.

"You," the shorter one said. "I know you."

"M-me?" Julian stammered, averting his gaze.

The man leaned in close. "Aren't you Mark Zuckerberg?"

The pressure dissipated. That was why they'd been staring, of course: a case of mistaken identity. This was real life, not a Raymond Lau film. There were no triad assassins out roaming the streets. Maybe they were real once, but now they were just a fantasy for the silver screen. A remnant of some lost era, superficially preserved.

"Yes," Julian replied in the best American accent he could muster, sounding like a Bostonian with a southern drawl. "That's right."

The shorter man smiled giddily and whispered in the ear of his counterpart: "*Ngo eegeng tung lei gong zhou hai koi lemah.*" The lanky one grinned, showing his blackened teeth. "Mr. Zuckerberg," the shorter man continued, "Could we get a picture together?"

"Sure," Julian said. "Why not?"

The man held up his iPhone and struggled to get all of them in the frame. The three men huddled close together.

"Say cheese," Julian said, holding up a peace sign.

"*Chee-tzee!*" the two men exclaimed as the shorter one snapped the picture.

"*Chee-tzee?*" Julian repeated, dumbfounded by the expression. He had heard it once before, out by the Golden Bauhinia statue. "What is that?"

"It means aubergine," the shorter man said. "I think you call it eggplant."

"Of course," Julian replied. "*Egg*plant."

The two men went back to their seats, gawking admiringly at their new treasure. As they sat back down, the Filipino waitress returned and plunked a tall glass of beer on the table, spilling foam off its sides.

"That'll be forty dollars," she said.

Julian nodded and handed her a fifty-dollar note. Even if he wasn't Mark Zuckerberg, he was feeling generous. "Keep the change," he said.

The waitress folded the note and put it in her pocket, the corner of her mouth rising upward by habit. Then she walked back to the bar, where the beautiful hostess was now staring straight in Julian's direction. She waved at him and winked.

Shit, Julian thought. There was no turning back now. He sipped his beer slowly, and, with each gulp, his legs gained strength and his mind grew more limber. He stood up, beer in hand, and approached her.

"That's a nice shirt," he said.

As the woman's mirrorlike eyes met his, his confidence sublimated from a solid straight to a gas. Just looking at the hostess made his tongue dry up like he'd swallowed talcum powder. Her eyes were almost perfectly round, but each eyelid drooped to a slightly different level. The effect of her gaze was disorienting, even intoxicating. She put down her book and ran her finger through the side of her smooth black hair. "Thanks," she said. "I picked it out myself."

"It looks familiar."

"Of course it does," she said. "It's yours."

Julian sat on the stool beside hers. "You admit it."

"Any items left unattended are not the hotel's responsibility. We cannot be held liable for wherever said items might end up."

"But you're wearing it," Julian said. "You're right in front of me."

"Yes, well . . . finders keepers." She winked.

"I want it back. Now."

"You want me to take it off? I should warn you: I'm a *mama*, not a whore."

"What does that mean?"

"It means I'm not for sale."

"Of course," Julian said. He froze in place, trying to think of something both intimidating and suave, but his internal monologue had reverted to an infant's level. When he opened his mouth again, all he could think of was a half-formed joke about a porcupine.

"Let's play a game," the hostess said. "You tell me a good story, and I'll give it back to you."

"Right here?"

"Wherever you want."

A story? Julian thought. *What the hell is she talking about?* "What kind of story?" he asked. "I like history. And action films."

"I don't want those types of stories. I want to know about you."

"Me?"

"Yes you."

"Why would you want to know about me?"

"Why not?" she asked. "I'm planning on writing a book one day, and I'm collecting interesting characters to write about."

"I wouldn't call myself interesting."

"Sure you are," she said. "What else would you being doing in this city? You stick out like a polar bear on the Yangtze River."

"Well," Julian said. "I guess I came here to find my dad."

"Your dad?"

"He was an inspector in the HKPF homicide department, but he went missing thirty years ago. Back when they used to call it the *Royal* Hong Kong Police Force. No one's heard from him since."

"And you came here to look for him?"

"Or to find out what happened, at least."

"A man on a mission," she said. "Alright, I like it."

Julian blushed. "It's not that big a deal."

"No, no. You're on a noble quest, like Xuanzang."

"Who's that?"

The hostess pointed to the large mural above the bar of a monk riding atop a gallant white horse. "Him," she said. "You've never read *Journey to the West*?"

"Can't say I have."

"Xuanzang was a monk who travelled all the way from Chang'an to India on a quest to find the original Buddhist scriptures."

"So he was a real guy," Julian said.

"He was," the hostess replied. "But the version we all know is from the stories."

"Like Mo Tai. Kwan Yu."

"Exactly," she said, tilting her head ever so slightly. "You know your history."

"Bits and pieces, really."

"When Bodhidharma first brought Buddhism from India to China, he didn't bring any books with him. He just taught his students what he knew, and then they passed the lessons on to their own students. But each one put in his own twist, and after years the religion got so corrupted that no one knew what it looked like in the first place."

"Like a spiritual game of telephone."

"Right. Everyone claimed to know the *one true way*, but no one knew what that way really was. You had some monks sacrificing animals to Buddha, some driving nails into their own skin, some having orgies and using sticks of incense to light their cigarettes. And Xuanzang just got sick of it. He decided to go back to the source."

"He was like me. He wanted to know the beginning of the story."

"Everyone thought he was crazy," she said. "To get to India meant crossing Sichuan, Tibet, and Afghanistan, vast tracts of desert filled with bandits, marauders, and worse. But once he made up his mind, there was no changing it. He had to follow that path until its very end."

"So, did he find them?"

"Spoiler alert."

"It's okay. This was a long time ago."

"He did," she said reluctantly. "He got all the texts he wanted and more."

"Good," Julian replied. "I like a happy ending."

"But he wasn't alone in his journey. If he was, he probably would have starved to death or been killed along the roads. Guanyin, the goddess of mercy, protected him from above. She gave him that horse, for instance."

"The dopey looking one?"

"That's Yulong."

"Yulong," Julian repeated. "A white horse."

"Actually, he was the son of the dragon king, but after he betrayed his father, Guanyin turned him into a horse and made him serve the monk."

"So that horse is really a dragon."

"You know what they say: When a white horse is not a horse . . ."

"I don't get it."

"It's a Chinese expression."

"That doesn't really help."

"It's a logical fallacy about the double nature of things, based on a dialectic discourse between two monks."

Julian stared at her blankly. "Who in the what now?"

"It's simple: If I ask you for a horse, you can bring me a white horse or a black horse, and either way I'll be satisfied, because you brought me a horse. Right?"

"Okay . . ."

"So the definition of a *horse* includes both white horses and black horses, yes?"

"Sure, why not?"

"But if I ask you for a *white horse*, you can't just bring me a horse. Because a horse can be white, black, brown, or anything else. And you have to bring me a *white horse* to satisfy my needs."

"You're awfully picky."

"Extremely."

"What if they only have black horses at the breeder?"

"Doesn't matter. It's not the same thing."

"Women," Julian said. "You just can't win with them."

"One thing is not the other. A grouping of objects is not the same as a subset of that group. Just like not every cop is a good cop and not every criminal is a bad person. But the flipside is true as well: not every good cop is even a cop and not every bad person is a criminal."

"Shouldn't you be teaching literature or something? Or philosophy?"

"I just like to read. And I have a lot of free time. One of the perks of my job."

"It just seems a bit odd. A girl like you working at a place like that . . ."

"What about your job?"

"My job," Julian laughed. "Don't even get me started."

"What do you do?"

"Well, back in London I was working in finance. Did some consulting, some business development. But my specialty was debt collection."

"You were hired muscle," she replied coldly. "Like a gangster."

"Not exactly. Mostly just issuing documents, maybe a phone call here or there. Never had to break anyone's legs, unfortunately."

"Sounds boring."

"That's why I quit."

"I envy you," she said. "If I could, I would."

"Don't feel too bad. I've got a new job now, here in Hong Kong. And it's shaping up to be as dumb as the old one, just better paid."

"Meet the new boss, same as the old boss . . ."

"I guess it's pretty much the same everywhere in the world."

As the two of them spoke, the lanky man in the flat-brimmed NEW YORK hat took a one-dollar coin out of his pocket and put it in a jukebox in the back corner of the bar. Golden rays shot out from behind the glass and reflected off the white smoke wafting through the air. The man flipped through the old Western hits until finally his hand rubbed against a notch in the wood, directing his finger toward the number ninety-seven. He pressed the button down, and the first piano notes rung out. As the saxophones blared, he stepped away, longing for something lost.

"This song is good," the hostess said. "But it's making me sad."

"It's not the song that's making you sad. It's life."

"That's a very negative attitude."

"I'm just being realistic. Look at me: I came to Hong Kong on a mission, but I just ended up doing the same damn things I was doing back in London. Working for a haughty arsehole, ending my nights at a smoky pub. Why even bother?"

"The same reason Xuanzang did: to gather the message."

"To learn the truth."

"And to share the company of those who help you."

"I guess I've been pretty lucky in that regard. There's been Flora, and even Shih-yin in his own way. Without them, I would have been lost."

The hostess closed her book. "Did you say *Shih-yin?*"

"Yeah," Julian replied. "He's an old monk who's been trying to help me."

"That's not even a Cantonese name. He's a character in this book."

"He is?"

"Sort of," she said. "He's part of the framing device." The hostess flipped open to the first few pages of the novel. "Look here. This is his speech." She read aloud from the text:

"*Sordid rooms and vacant courts,*

Replete in years gone by with beds where statesmen lay;

Parched grass and withered banyan tress,

Where once were halls for song and dance!

Spiders' webs the carved pillars intertwine,

The green gauze now is also pasted on the straw windows!

What about the cosmetic fresh concocted or the powder just scented;

Why has the hair too on each temple become white like hoarfrost!

Yesterday the tumulus of yellow earth buried the bleached bones,

Tonight under the red silk curtain reclines the couple!

Gold fills the coffers, silver fills the boxes,

But in a twinkle, the beggars will all abuse you!

While you deplore that the life of others is not long,

You forget that you yourself are approaching death!

You educate your sons with all propriety,

But they may someday, 'tis hard to say, become thieves;

Though you choose for your fare and home the fatted beam,

You may, who can say, fall into a place of easy virtue!

Yesterday, poor fellow, you felt cold in a tattered coat,

Today you despise the purple embroidered dress as too long!

Instead of yours, you recognize another as your native land;

What utter perversion!

In one word, it comes to this: we make wedding clothes for others.

We sow for others to reap."

Julian sat in stunned silence. "That's beautiful," he said. "But it sounds nothing like the Shih-yin I know."

"This was my father's favorite book. He gave it to me the last time I saw him."

"Sounds like an interesting guy."

"He was," the hostess said with a knowing smile. "A cop first, but then a triad. He was in the movie business briefly. Had some bit parts in a couple of films."

"Have I heard of him?"

"I doubt it. He wasn't a very good actor. But some people knew him back home."

As the piano solo began, she sipped her martini coldly. The smile on her face had melted—not into a frown, but something even more pained. She clutched the jade pendant strapped around her throat, rubbing her forefinger across its smooth surface.

"Where are you from?" Julian asked, trying to change the subject.

"Singapore, mostly. But I spent some time in Malaysia and Macau."

"Huh. I had you pegged for a local."

"What does that mean?"

"I don't know. You just seem like you're from Hong Kong."

"No one's really *from* Hong Kong. Everyone here's a visitor, a colonist . . . it's a very transient place."

"I was born here."

"But where was your father born?"

"Stratford-upon-Avon. England."

"Exactly," the hostess said. "Everyone's an expat. Even the locals . . . their families are from Guangdong, Fuzhou, Shanghai . . ."

"So how did you end up here?"

The hostess chuckled. "You know, everyone in Hong Kong asks that question."

"Well, why wouldn't you? You don't just pick up and move somewhere else without a good reason."

"In my line of work, the stories are all pretty similar, really: kidnapped by the triads, forced to pay their family's debts."

"Is that what happened to you?"

"More or less."

Julian sipped his beer, unsure what to even say. He'd heard stories about brothels and human trafficking on BBC, but it had all felt so distant then, almost like a cheap novel. It seemed too gross and cartoonishly evil to exist in real life, but here it was sitting right in front of him.

"It's wrong," he blurted out finally. "A girl like you shouldn't be stuck in a place like that. You should be free."

"Julian," she replied, "I'm just as free as you are. Look." She leaned in close and brushed her lips lightly against his. They felt like two little eggplants.

"Get it, Zuckerberg!" the lanky man screamed through cupped hands.

Julian sat frozen, his mouth agape. He felt like he was back in his dream, holding the carved stone in his hand, his lips now wet with succulent dewdrops.

"I never got your name," he said, staring down at her.

"Celeste," she replied. "Celeste Wong."

1984 / Chapter 4: 'Round Midnight

As Inspectors Leung and Wong entered the smoky bar, it was as if they'd stepped into a long-forgotten memory. The dark ambiance and the pink and blue-hued lights along the walls gave the room a distinctly nostalgic aura. Old campy ads for Coke, Pepsi, Campbell's Soup, and Spam littered the walls, bordering Maoist Cultural Revolution-era propaganda posters. "Scatter the old world, build a new one!" one sign declared, depicting a red guard holding a sledgehammer high above his head.

There was a dusty jukebox in the back corner of the room with a golden record spinning behind its front glass, but no music played. The only sound was the humdrum buzz of people's voices, conversations melding together into white noise.

Leung and Wong walked past the long walnut-stained bar to a booth in the back corner near the jukebox. A young Filipino waitress with long black hair approached the two inspectors with a notepad in hand. She wore a black vest and bowtie—the same attire as every other waiter in the bar—and had a jagged, snake-like scar on her throat.

"Can I get you something?" she asked.

"Whiskey neat," Leung replied. "The cheapest one you've got."

"Very good," she said, turning to the young inspector. "And you?"

"Oh, I don't drink," Wong said.

"He's joking," Leung quickly interjected. "He'll have a rum and Coke."

"Excellent," the waitress replied. She scribbled down the order and walked off.

"You're at a bar," Leung said coldly. "Who goes to a bar and doesn't drink?"

"I don't know," Wong replied. "A designated driver?"

Leung sighed. "If you want to be a good cop, you have to be inconspicuous. You have to blend into the crowd. If people think you're a cop, they won't act naturally around you."

Wong adjusted his Ray Bans. "Why would anyone think I'm a cop?"

"I don't know," Leung said, rolling his eyes. "The clothes? The sunglasses?"

Wong snickered. "What kind of cop wears Louis Vuitton?"

"A cop with rich parents."

"Hardly."

"So how the hell do you afford this stuff?"

"Simple," Wong said. "I don't eat."

Leung stared at his partner skeptically. "It's all fake, isn't it?"

"Nah," Wong sneered. "That's not my style."

"Then I don't get it. An inspector's salary barely covers my rent."

"That's because you don't know how to think outside the box. How do you think Smithfield could afford that fancy car of his? This is *Hong Kong*. Everyone has a little business on the side."

The waitress returned, carrying two glasses atop a square silver tray. One was short and rounded—almost pear-shaped—and was filled with a caramel brown liquid. The other was an antique Coca-Cola glass, filled to the brim with foam and crushed ice.

"Here you go," the waitress said, laying the drinks in front of them. "Do you want to pay now, or would you like me to open a tab?"

"A tab," Leung said. "It'll be a long night."

"You and me both," the waitress replied, winking at the old inspector. "Let me know if there's anything else you need." Leung nodded, and the waitress walked back to the bar, swaying her hips with each step.

"She's cute," Wong commented, "in a Connie Chan sort of way."

"She's a whore," Leung observed.

"Come on," Wong protested. "You barely know her."

"I know enough," Leung said. "And I know what a whore looks like."

"Hey man, that's racist."

"It's not that," Leung demurred. "It's that scar on her throat. It's the way she walks. It looks like she spent a long time in a shipping crate."

"A shipping crate?"

"That's how the triads transport them to Hong Kong. The Lucky Stone, Sun Yee On, 14K . . . they smuggle them onto cargo ships, then sell them when they arrive."

"Or maybe she has a shitty boyfriend and lives in an average Hong Kong apartment."

"Wong . . ."

"They're the same size, basically."

". . . I'm not joking."

"I know," Wong said, his nervous smile weighed down by gravity. "So what do we do now?"

"Now we wait," Leung said, taking a swig of whiskey that tasted like pure battery acid. He didn't flinch at all as he swallowed it. "We wait and observe." As he peered around the smoky bar, he spied a woman in a long beige trench coat and dark sunglasses sitting by herself at a table. "Who's she?" he wondered aloud.

Wong didn't respond; he was too busy staring at the mural behind the bar: an intricate, almost psychedelic painting of the monk Xuanzang sitting atop Yulong, his trusty white horse.

Leung snapped his fingers repeatedly. "Wong!"

"Huh?" Wong blurted out, turning back to his partner. "What's wrong?"

"Look at her," Leung said, pointing to the woman. She wore a beige trench coat and puffed incessantly on a cigarette, not even bothering to take it out of her mouth between breaths.

"Who's that?" Wong asked.

"That's what I'm trying to figure out." He scanned the woman up and down, but he couldn't get a good read on her. She kept turning her head towards the bar, obscuring any possible view of her face. "Why would someone dress like that in here? If she's on the run, it's too obvious. And if she's not . . ."

"She's hiding in plain sight," Wong said. "Same as me."

"Maybe."

Wong ran his forefinger around the rim of the glass, increasing in speed with each rotation. "Should we go talk to her or something?"

"Not yet," Leung said. "But you should drink that. If not, the tension will kill you."

"I'm warning you: me and alcohol don't go well together. I'm *very* sensitive."

"Good," Leung replied. "I'm going to need you loose. Tension means fear. And if you're scared, that means you look like a cop. So drink up." He raised his glass in the air, and his partner reluctantly followed suit.

"Cheers," Wong said as they clinked glasses. He took one sip, and instantly his face turned bright red.

***

An hour later, Inspector Wong was leaning over the jukebox, staring through its front glass at the glistening gold record spinning in circles. "I don't g-get it," he slurred. "Whyyy doesn't it stop?"

"Sit down!" Leung commanded. "You're making a fool of yourself."

"Hold on!" Wong said. The vein in his forehead was protruding so much that Leung was worried it would burst. "I want to put on a song."

The young inspector took a one-dollar coin from his pocket and pressed it into the side of the jukebox, making a notch in the grain as he struggled to locate the coin slot. Then, when he found the small slit, he missed by a half meter and dropped the coin onto the ground. He reached into his pocket for another, and, this time, by stabilizing his right hand with his left, he was able to get the coin inside. The jukebox lit up with flashes of gold so bright that Wong had to squint his eyes, even with the sunglasses.

"Woah," he said, still fixated on the spinning record. He pressed randomly on the keypad then stumbled back over to his seat as the first piano notes rang out from the machine. "This is good," Wong said. "What song is this?"

"You put it on."

"You sure?" Wong asked. "I've never heard this before."

"'Round Midnight," Leung said, sipping his whiskey. "By Thelonious Monk."

"Some kind of monk, huh? Never heard anything like this in the temple."

Leung looked at his young partner, who was now merrily snapping his fingers to the song. "You weren't kidding about the alcohol."

"I told you," Wong said, the corners of his lips curling menacingly upwards, as if held there by fishing hooks. "When I drink alcohol, I get either too happy or too sad to function. Sometimes both."

"Let's stick to happy for now."

"Yes," Wong agreed, still bouncing along with the music. "Let's."

As the young officer continued to dance, the front door of the bar swung open again, and a rail-thin Chinese man walked in wearing a fitted pinstriped suit and a fedora. He was holding a long cane with an ivory horse for a handle and had a thick black goatee with a pointed tip. From the moment he stepped into the bar, all the waiters trained their eyes on him. One walked over to grab his coat, and another led him over to a table at the center of the bar, where the woman in the trench coat was sitting.

"Wong," Leung whispered, trying to get his partner's attention.

Wong opened his eyes. "What's going on?"

"I think we found our man. Look."

The suited man sat down at the table and took off his fedora, revealing oily, shoulder-length black hair. He ran his hand through to straighten it out.

"You think that's him?" Leung asked.

"Only one way to find out," Wong replied. "*Mmgoi!*" he yelled without hesitation, raising his hand high in the air.

"Can I get you something?" the scarred waitress asked, appearing at the side of their table like an apparition. "Another rum and Coke?"

"He's fine for now," Leung said. "But I'll take another whiskey."

"Is that Marshal Hong?" Wong asked obliviously.

"Yes," the waitress whispered. "He's the owner of the bar."

"Is that right?" Wong mumbled, scratching his chin. He stood up and cupped his two hands around the sides of his mouth. "Hey, you!" he yelled across the room. "Marshal Hong! Get over here!"

"Wong!" Leung shouted in disbelief.

Marshal Hong turned in Wong's direction and pointed at himself calmly, mouthing the word "me?"

"That's right," Wong said. "I'm talking to you!"

Leung put his head in his palms. "You damn fool . . ."

The triad boss stood up from his seat and walked toward the two inspectors, slapping each table he passed with the tip of his cane. "You talking to me, *sei puk gai?*"

"I'm terribly sorry," Leung said. "My friend here just wanted to compliment you on your establishment. It's very stylish. Very chic."

"Ehhh, it's okay," Wong slurred. "Not *that* nice."

Hong glared menacingly at the young officer. "Who the fuck are you two?"

"Yeap," Leung said. "Xavier Yeap. CEO of Eight Immortals Shipping. And this is my associate David Fong."

"Eight Immortals," Marshal Hong repeated. "I know every shipping outfit in town, but I've never heard of you."

"We're new, but watch out. Soon, we'll make a big splash."

"Confidence," Hong said. "I like that." He extended his hand out toward Wong's, but Wong missed and shook Leung's hand instead.

"David," Leung said. "Are you alright?"

"Who's David?" Wong asked. "I've got to take a leak. Pop the cork, y'know?" He stood up and brushed past Marshal Hong, walking straight into an empty stool on his way to the bathroom. "Excuse me," he said as he continued on his way.

The triad boss sat down across from Leung. "He's a strange man."

"You don't know the half of it. Just last week, he tried to import eight tons of powdered milk. As if anyone would buy that."

Marshal Hong chuckled. "You can drop the act," he said. "I know who you are, Inspector Leung. Woo told me you were coming."

"Did he now?" Leung said, only half-surprised.

"The Lucky Stone and the Triad Bureau have always shared information."

"You're awfully cozy with your enemy."

"We're like yin and yang. They exist because of us, and we exist because of them. It's a symbiotic relationship."

"I'm not sure I follow."

"When you have laws against prostitution, against gambling and drugs . . . you create a demand in the market. One that can only be filled through illegal means. It's simple economics."

"Or simple exploitation," Leung said. "You prey on the weak."

The triad boss shook his head. "I'm not a bad man," he insisted. "I'm a businessman. And the chief business of Hong Kong is business, if you haven't noticed."

"I have."

"The *Royal* Hong Kong Police Force is a business too. You may act like white knights, but, in the end, you're all in it for a paycheck. And without the triads, there would be no Triad Bureau. Without us criminals, you wouldn't have a job."

"I'm not in the Triad Bureau," Leung scoffed. "I'm CID."

Marshal Hong shrugged. "It's the same thing. Only you rely on common criminals. And those are growing fewer and fewer these days."

"They're due for a comeback," Leung said.

"Maybe you're right, maybe you're wrong. Who knows what'll happen after the handover to China? Maybe Beijing will put us all out of business."

"It doesn't matter who's in charge," Leung said. "There will always be good and bad. Right and wrong."

"Right and wrong," Marshal Hong repeated wistfully. "It all depends on who you ask."

The last piano roll of 'Round Midnight echoed from the jukebox and the song came to a deafening halt. Now, the bar was utterly silent; there were no chattering voices or feet shuffling around the room. Leung turned over his shoulder and saw that all of the other patrons had seemingly disappeared. In their place, at least twenty waiters stood in their black vests and bowties, holding axes in their hands.

Leung stood up quickly. "Woo," he grunted. "That piece of shit . . ."

"Now," Marshal Hong said, raising his cane high in the air. "I have a few questions for you." He swung down, and the white horse snapped across Inspector Leung's face, breaking in two.

2014 / Chapter 5: Dream of the Red Chamber

Julian looked at the digital clock on the nightstand, which read two-forty-two in bright red numbers. He sighed and closed his eyes, but it was useless. No matter how tired he was or how much he had drunk over the course of the night—and it had been quite a lot—there was no way he could sleep right now. Celeste lay beside him under the maroon sheets, sprawled out and naked, with one of her breasts peeking out of the cover.

Her room was nearly as claustrophobic as his own, but its design was far more tasteful. The walls were painted red and adorned with ink paintings on parchment scrolls, each featuring a different animal of the Chinese zodiac. The horse, which was dressed in armor and carried a golden halberd, hung just beside the dragon, which had on a translucent purple gown and was blowing a fiery kiss in Julian's direction.

A loud noise rang out just outside the window, like the sound of a gunshot. Julian slipped his head under the velveteen curtain and stared out onto Nathan Road, which was still bustling even at this hour. To his disappointment, there were no cops and triads exchanging fire. Only tailors and fake watch salesmen and a lone red and white cab pulling up to the curb, its engine sputtering like a farting pig. A fat, bald man stepped out of the car, accompanied by the mascara-laden woman that Julian had seen the previous morning.

"King Chow," he muttered to himself.

"What was that?" Celeste asked, rising from her pillow.

"Nothing," Julian said, slipping the curtain back over his head. "Go back to sleep."

"Are you crying?"

"No," Julian said. "Who said I was crying?"

"It's okay," she replied. "It really wasn't that bad."

An awkward silence permeated the room. Julian looked down in shame, unable to even meet her eyes. "It's wasn't you," he said finally. "It's just that I get nervous sometimes. Especially when I've had too much to drink."

"Well, it was good while it lasted."

Julian sighed. "That makes me feel so much better."

"Hey, I've had worse."

"I can imagine."

She scrunched her face. "What do you mean by that?"

"Well, you know . . . with the types of guys who come to a place like this . . ."

"*You* came here, didn't you?"

"Well, *I'm* a perfectly respectable gentleman, of course. The only reason I came here is because that crazy monk sent me your business card." *And because I couldn't afford anything else*, he thought to himself, though he wasn't desperate to share that fact.

Celeste's eyebrow rose. "Monk?" she asked. "What monk?"

"You know, like Xuanzang."

"Never seen a monk around here."

"Well, he's not like other monks, really. You'd like him."

"I doubt it."

In the corner of his ear, Julian heard a loud buzzing sound coming from behind him. He looked down and saw that the belt of his crumpled trousers was jiggling on the floor. He retrieved the cellphone from his pants pocket and looked at the notification screen, which showed thirteen missed calls, all from the same number.

"Who's that?" Celeste asked.

"It's him," Julian replied as he held the phone to his ear. "Hello?"

"I'm sorry," Shih-yin said. "Did I wake you?"

"Of course not. I haven't even slept."

"It's past your curfew," the monk said. "Where are you now? Wan Chai?"

"No," Julian said. "Well, not anymore."

"You're with a whore, then."

"That's not true," Julian said, peering back at Celeste. "Okay, that's not *exactly* true."

"I'm not here to judge you," Shih-yin said.

"I did meet a girl, but it's not like that."

"Whatever you say. But now it's time to get to work."

"Now?"

"Yes, now. The early bird gets the worm."

"Well, the late bird gets some sleep. And I have work tomorrow."

"That's right," Shih-yin said. "You have to be at the office by 8am. But there's something you have to know about that place before you do."

"What, that it's a front?"

"Obviously. They don't even try to hide it."

"The only question is what they're hiding. Or whom."

"That's what I wanted to talk to you about. Get back to Man Mo Temple *now*."

"Alright, alright," Julian grumbled. He stood up and started putting on his disheveled underwear and trousers. "But it might take a while. I'm in Tsim Sha Tsui."

"What, on a park bench?"

"Chungking Mansions," Julian said. "I'm checking out of my room." He buttoned up his white dress shirt and threw on his suit jacket, still damp with sweat.

"It could be worse. At least you're not in Tsuen Wan."

"I thought I'm going to Sheung Wan."

"Forget it," Shih-yin said. "Just go across the street to the minibus stop in front of Kowloon

Mosque. Bus number ninety-seven. It will take you right to Man Mo Temple."

"What about the Star Ferry?"

"The MTR and the Star Ferry don't run this late. And most cabs won't take you across the tunnel. Not without a hefty tip. Besides, I don't want you ending up all the way in Tsuen Wan by mistake."

Julian examined what was left in his crumpled wallet, which had been cleaned out over the course of his night with Celeste in Wan Chai. He'd spent most of his money on oysters, apple shishas, and Long Island Iced Teas, then lost the rest of it playing snookers with one of Celeste's young friends, a real-life hustler who seemingly never missed a shot. All that was left was a single purple ten-dollar note and a double-ringed silver and bronze ten-dollar coin from before the handover. "Alright," he said. "I guess I don't have a choice."

"No," the old monk said tersely. "You don't. Hurry up."

"Yeah, yeah . . ." Julian ended the call and returned the phone to his pocket. Then, he sat down on the bed and laced up his white Converse sneakers, staring at Celeste all the while.

"You're leaving me?" she asked.

"I'll be back," Julian replied. "I promise."

Celeste sighed. "That's what men always say."

"Except it's actually true. I'll be back in a day or two."

"You don't mean that," she said, clutching the jade necklace still strapped around her neck. "You think you do, but you really don't."

Julian was silent, staring at the scroll ahead of him: a rat in an orange monk's robe, flying through the air. "I don't know what to say."

"Then don't say anything," she said, clutching his arm. "Just stay."

"I can't do that," Julian replied, feeling like he was choking a stray kitten. "I came to this city for a reason, and I have to see that mission through. I have to know what happened to my father or else I'll never forgive myself."

"What does it matter?" Celeste asked. "What did your father ever do for you?"

"I'm not saying he was a saint," Julian replied, "but that doesn't mean I can just abandon him. He might be in trouble."

She sighed. "Even if we learn from history we're still doomed to repeat it. We're like prisms caught between two mirrors. Only half the time, we don't even know what we're reflecting."

"That's beautiful," Julian said. "But I have no idea what that means."

She glared at him. "It means you know not why you act."

"Maybe not," Julian replied. "But it's not like I have any choice in the matter."

She sighed, staring at the dog on the far wall—a sleeping basset hound in a magisterial robe. "I guess everything has to end eventually."

"Not everything," Julian said, inching closer to her. "I'll be back. I promise."

He put his arms around her shoulders and kissed her lightly on the forehead. She let go of the jade pendant and reflexively squeezed back. Her jet-black hair bristled against Julian's nose, and the scent of figs and pomegranate filled his tarred lungs. "I wish I could believe you," she said, finally letting go of him. "Go," she said.

He stood up and stumbled over to the doorway, taking one last look at her as he turned the knob. His opened his mouth to say something, but just as the words came to him they were already gone. Celeste tilted her head sideways like an owl, her two eyes catching him in their hypnotic glare. Unblinking, he backed away, stepping into the hall and shutting the door behind him.

Well, he thought. *That went well.*

Tiptoeing quietly through the smoke-filled corridor, he made his way back out into the lobby and entered the lavatory to splash some water on his face. The aroma inside was putrid, like burnt rubber and dysentery blended in a food processor. The bathroom had one urinal and one stall, the front door of which bore a handicapped icon and a sign that read FOR WEAK ONLY. What passed for a shower was merely a hose attached to the far wall above a hair-filled drain. There was a cloudy mirror over the sinks, caked with black streaks of mold and dried pus. Julian could barely recognize the figure in its reflection; the bags beneath his eyes had blown up to moon-crater proportions, and his brown, curly hair was so oily now that large chunks of it were sticking together in a mohawk. He went to the sink to wet down his hair a little, but when he turned the handle a thick brown liquid came pouring out the spout. He inched backwards.

The bathroom door opened again, and King Chow waddled in wearing only his white briefs. His fat, hairy stomach distended out over the waistband of his yellow-stained underwear; every inch of his body was covered in wavy black fuzz, except for the top of his bald head. The stench was overpowering, like badly expired seafood doused in Drakkar Noir. He walked to the urinal next to Julian and dropped his briefs nearly to the floor, exposing his bare ass in the process.

Julian tried his best to ignore it, combing back his oily hair in the mirror. But then he felt a stream of liquid running down his calf. In the mirror, he saw that King Chow was peeing on his leg, soaking his canvas trousers past the point of saturation. The fat man shook his exposed penis vigorously, glaring at Julian with his lone bloodshot eye.

"That girl belongs to me," he said as he pulled his briefs back up. "Don't forget." He patted Julian on the cheek and exited without washing his hands.

***

As the minibus roared through the Cross-Harbor tunnel, Julian stared out the window, trying not to think about his encounter with King Chow. His leg had mostly dried already, but his heart was still racing madly, and his thoughts veered back and forth between anxiety and pure terror.

Outside, the fluorescent lamps on both sides of the tunnel were moving so fast that they looked like two long streams of light. Julian felt himself being carried along, hypnotized by their luminescence. The odometer hanging from the ceiling, which displayed the car's speed in red digital numbers, crept higher and higher. When it hit eighty kilometers per hour, the numbers stopped increasing, but instead started flashing ominously and dinging twice per second like a fire alarm. The bus shot out of the tunnel and made a wide turn onto the causeway, sending Julian careening into the window beside him. However, the couple in the next row, the only other passengers on the whole minibus, seemed unaffected by the winding G-forces. The man fed a pack of grape Hi-Chews to his girlfriend as she laughed and rubbed her hands up and down his tattooed arm.

For the next ten minutes, Julian sat utterly still, his hands fashioned into two claws clinging to his seat. He felt like if he let go, he would get sucked out the back window and get mowed over by a lorry. The syncopated dings continued like a demented breakbeat, until the boyfriend raised his arm and yelled "*Qin min yao lok!*"

The bus ground to a sudden halt on a curving, sloped road, its tires shrieking like four blind bats colliding midair. The laughing couple stood up and walked out the front door, pressing their Octopus Cards to the reader on their way out. Julian followed them, opening his wallet and taking out his last ten-dollar coin to hand to the driver. However, at the last moment, he stopped and reconsidered. The weight of the old coin had an almost gravitational force, like a magnet pulling his fist closed. Instead, he handed the driver the lone ten-dollar note left in his wallet and walked out onto the hilly street.

As he stepped outside, Julian tried to make sense of his surroundings. He didn't know where he was, but he couldn't take another second on that infernal minibus, which had already whizzed down the block past a red light. From the slopes alone, he could tell that he was somewhere in Sheung Wan, but the scenery was unfamiliar. There was a closed wet market across the street, with the remnants of pig carcasses still hanging from the bamboo scaffolding and fish guts strewn about on the sidewalk. Julian walked up the hill, stepping around the pools of bloody runoff. The smell of death was ubiquitous, but he was starting to get used to it. In fact, he was pretty hungry.

At the top of the hill, Julian reached a plateau of shuttered antique shops. He walked past them, staring through the windows at the ceramics, bronze idols, and opium pipes displayed behind the glass. There were jade stones and statues of every size and shape, but none as green and lustrous as the one hanging around Celeste's neck. It was impossible to tell what was real or fake.

Standing on the street corner in front of a 7/11 was a blonde-wigged woman with a powdered face and a pair of dark sunglasses resting on the bridge of her nose. She wore a long beige trench coat and was smoking a Lucky Strike cigarette, which was nearing its last embers. Julian recognized her from the immigration line at the airport.

"Hey handsome," she said, flashing him a lascivious glare.

"Good morning," Julian replied meekly.

The woman inhaled deeply until she was sucking on nothing but the filter. She exhaled it all in one blow, the smoke hanging above the sidewalk like a rain cloud. "What brings you here at this hour?" she asked. "Looking for a good time?"

"Actually," Julian said. "I'm on my way to the temple."

"Isn't it closed at this hour?"

"It is, but I'm friends with one of the monks."

"Wow. You must be really dedicated."

"I guess so," Julian replied. "I'm still learning."

"Well, say a prayer for me, too."

"Sure," Julian said. "You have anything particular in mind?"

"Prosperity," she replied. "I just started this job tonight, but I still haven't had my first customer. Tell the gods to send one my way."

"I'll, uh, see what I can do," Julian said, though he wasn't sure if he'd want the same thing in her position. He nodded and walked away, approaching the temple gate just as the sun was starting to rise. The traffic signals in the distance sounded like chirping crickets, and at least a dozen stray cats slept in front of the gate, most missing their tails. Julian took it as a bad omen. He pressed his hand against the handle and pushed it in, but the door wouldn't budge.

"Hello?" he yelled, trying to get someone's attention. But the only ones who seemed to notice were the stray cats, who awoke and scurried off. Julian stopped and stepped back, picturing the temple from afar. The dim streetlamps and the polluted haze gave the atmosphere a yellow-orange glow, like a van Gogh painting. The whole scene was very abstract.

Julian approached the temple again, this time noticing a small pathway between its side and the concrete gate surrounding it. He followed the narrow path into an orchid garden in the back, just in front of the hidden door to Shih-yin's study. There, the old monk stood before a stone screen wall—a relief of nine coiling, fire-breathing dragons.

"Took you long enough," he said.

Julian yawned vigorously. "Sorry. It's been a long night."

"Well, it's about to get longer. If what I believe is correct, you have only a day or two to acquire the necessary information. Maybe less."

"Information," Julian repeated. "About my father, you mean?"

"Yes," Shih-yin replied. "But first, it's time to finish your lessons."

"Another slap in the face, you mean?"

"Come," the monk said, opening the hidden door and leading Julian back into his study. He flipped on the lights and gathered the jar of Yulong from the book on the back shelf, just as he had the night before. The oil burner was still lit.

"Opium again?" Julian asked.

"I've been asking myself that same question for the last thirty years."

"Then why do you keep doing it? You know it's going to kill you."

"I can't help it," Shih-yin said. "Thirty years ago, those bastards fed it to me for two straight weeks, and I've been hooked ever since."

"Who fed it to you?"

"The Lucky Stone Triad," Shih-yin growled. "Your boss's boss."

"I've heard of them."

"I wouldn't be surprised. Along with the 14K and the Sun Yee On, they're one of the three big triads in Hong Kong. And for more than a hundred years, they've held a monopoly on the trade of opium and heroin, even as their competitors have moved on to other drugs. They used to funnel their money through the movie studios, but these days they've stepped up to high finance."

"And you want to expose them."

"It's not that simple," the monk said. "White Horse, Lucky Stone . . . they're two heads of the same dragon. But there are still seven others to worry about."

"What do you mean?" Julian asked. "What other heads?"

"Sit down, and I'll tell you the beginning of the story."

Julian did as instructed. "Can you not kiss me this time?"

"Then you'll have to handle it yourself," Shih-yin replied as he ripped a clump of the white goop from the jar and pressed it into the brass bowl as before. He handed the slender pipe to Julian, who held it hesitantly above the burner.

"Won't I get addicted to this stuff?"

"There's always that risk," Shih-yin said. "But that's the price you pay to go back. If you want to truly understand someone, you have to feel what they felt exactly as they felt it."

"But who am I trying to understand?"

"You'll see."

The pipe was heavier than Julian expected. He fumbled awkwardly with it, unsure where to place his hands between the snaking dragons. "I just hold this here?"

"Yes," the monk replied. "Then you close your eyes and let yourself float back. People used to call this a *yin cheung*—a dream stick. It will show you things you might not be happy with. The important part is not to fight what you see."

Julian placed his mouth against the pipe and held it upside down over the burner, imitating the old monk. He inhaled deeply, and the flame rose to meet the brass, igniting the white goop, which quickly shriveled into black ash.

The room started to swirl—the rush was so intense that for a moment Julian thought his heart had stopped. He placed two fingers on his jugular to make sure it was still beating, but his pulse was too rapid and jagged to be accurate. Julian closed his eyes, trying to make the feeling stop . . . trying to will himself back into bed with Celeste, to be somewhere he knew was real.

"Our tale," Shih-yin said, "begins in 1908, on Cochrane Street in old Victoria City . . ."

Julian opened his eyes again, but he was no longer in the study hall. He was lying on the floor of a small red chamber filled with white smoke. The clouds were so thick and the heat so sweltering that it felt like the devil's personal sauna. Several shirtless men lay on the ground laughing, puffing on their own pipes from a supine position. All of them had an identical haircut: a bald head with a long black braid hanging like a slender ponytail. Julian wondered if they could even see him, or, if they could, whether he was just a vision in the clouds to them as they were to him. At Julian's feet, the ornate pipe rested on the ground beside a lit burner. He looked around the room at the other men and their laughing faces, but he couldn't find the old monk. "Hello!" he called out. "Shih-yin! Where are you?" The other men didn't even flinch at the desperate cries, basking in their own personal heavens and hells. *That old monk is just like the rest of them*, Julian thought. He'd been abandoned yet again.

The front door burst open, and a ray of sunlight shone into the room. The addicts recoiled from the piercing light, shielding their eyes from the sun's intrusion. A tall British policeman with a pencil-thin mustache stood in the doorway, wearing a spiked helmet like that of a Prussian general. It seemed as though everyone inside was about to get rounded up and thrown in jail.

"Cheung-kee," the policeman said, looking in Julian's direction.

Julian pointed to himself incredulously. "Me?"

"*Aiyyya*," groaned a lanky man sitting right behind him. "Is it that time already?" The man stood up and put on his black *changshan*. He had a scar above his left eye and almost nonexistent cheekbones; it seemed like his face was held together by sheer will alone. The man dusted off his jacket and straightened out his braid. "How do I look?"

"Fabulous," the policeman replied. "Come on. We're running late."

The man and the officer exited the opium den together. Intrigued, Julian stood up and shuffled sideways through the prostrate addicts to follow them out the door. He exited onto a small hill filled with low-rise brick buildings, most with green sheets covering their windows and doorways. Bamboo poles hung above the road with wet laundry dangling off of them, swaying in the wind like tattered flags. Julian looked to the top of the hill, where Victoria's Peak loomed over the whole scene, only with no mansions or roads on the mountainside—just bare rock.

Julian recognized the road; it was the same hill where he had gotten off the minibus earlier that morning. The passersby wore *changshans* and their hair in braids, but the smell of death was just the same, only with slightly less pollution. Cheung-kee and the British officer continued up to the plateau at the end of the street where a rickshaw waited for them. Julian quickly flagged down one of his own.

"Follow them," he said to the wiry, shirtless driver, but the man just scratched the top of his head, unable to understand Julian's dialect. Julian pointed with frustration at the rickshaw ahead of them, which was now fading into the distance. The driver now seemed to get it; he picked up the two handles and carried the cart forward, keeping in hot pursuit at a fast walking speed.

Soon, the traditional Chinese characters, the braided men, and the dirty low-rise buildings morphed into regal Victorian structures made of white marble, with enormous columns and windows larger than the whole den he'd just come from. It felt like an oxymoron for two such neighborhoods to exist right next to each other. As the rickshaw turned a corner, Julian glimpsed the blue waves of Victoria Harbor in the distance, sparkling so cleanly that he could see traces of the rocks and coral reefs below. Dockworkers carried crates in and out of the anchored wooden ships, each flying the Union Jack.

The two rickshaws stopped in front of the largest building in the whole plaza, a Renaissance-style colonial palace with colonnades and arches. A fountain in front of the building depicted a cherub spitting a thin stream into the water below. Two Indian policemen stood guard at the sides of the entrance, each with a similar blue uniform as the British officer but with long beards and yellow turbans. Both were carrying long rifles on their shoulders and standing utterly still. Cheung-kee and the British officer walked into the building, and Julian jumped out of the rickshaw after them, not even bothering to pay. "*Mm man!*" the driver barked angrily, shoving his empty hand into the air.

"I'm with them," Julian said to the two stationed officers, who shrugged and said nothing; their eyes didn't even move in his direction. Whether in 1908 or 2014, it seemed, Julian would always blend into the background. It was his one useful skill.

The entryway was lined with gold-framed mirrors and classical art, and stone gargoyles were perched above in dockets on the walls. Light shone in from the windows and glinted off the marble floor, which was tiled black and white. The police officers standing guard at various checkpoints were as still as the gargoyles above.

Julian stopped in front of a mirror and looked at his own reflection. He didn't recognize himself anymore—his face was far rounder than he remembered, his nose was smaller and sharper, and his eyes and skin were both the wrong color. In place of his oily hair was a bald head with a single black braid, and his borrowed suit had transmogrified into a long purple dress. Julian staggered backward and looked away from the reflection, queasy at the unfamiliar sight.

In the mirror behind him, he caught a glimpse of the two men he'd been chasing. Cheung-kee and the policeman were speaking with a British captain, who smiled effusively and shepherded them through a wooden door. Julian followed them into a large chamber that resembled the House of Commons, hiding behind one of the columns near the entryway and peering out at the group gathered at the center of the room.

There were two merchants and a military officer seated at the table—a heavy-set admiral with bushy eyebrows and at least three chins. One merchant was young, with curly hair and a pair of gold-framed spectacles, while the other was much older, wearing a black petticoat and sporting a thick grey mustache. Beside them all, a stately-looking Chinese man in a white coat stood solemnly as Cheung-kee and the British captain approached the table.

"Dr. Sun Yat-sen," the captain said, sitting down beside the fat, tanned admiral. "This is the man I was telling you about."

The man in the white coat grimaced. His thin mustache was swallowed into cracks forming around his lips. "He doesn't seem like much."

"These men will vouch for me," Cheung-kee replied. "Sir Jackson and Mr. Matheson have used my services many times before."

The older merchant, Jackson, slammed his hand on the table. "I still don't agree with this," he protested in a thick Irish accent. "This is a dangerous game to play."

"And yet it serves our mutual benefit," the captain insisted. "After the Boxer Rebellion, we can't trust the Qing government to uphold our trading interests. They've given in to popular anger, shutting themselves out from the world."

"The market has dried up," the admiral said. "We have to do *something*, or else the whole colony will go broke."

"It's imperative that we ensure open access to the mainland," the captain said. "And Dr. Sun's group is the only one with any kind of legitimacy and local support."

"Ridiculous," Jackson said. "His Heaven and Earth Society has been eating into the local opium trade for years, and now you expect them to lead a revolution? They're common criminals!"

Dr. Sun crossed his arms. "The *Tiandihui* are loyal only to me and our cause. All that we do is in service to our revolution. To expel the Tatar barbarians and restore our homeland, we will do whatever it takes."

"I don't trust him!" Jackson exclaimed.

"You don't have to," the captain said. "This is a matter of mutual self-interest."

The younger merchant, Matheson, shook his head. "Enough with the bickering! What's the damned plan?"

"It's simple," the captain said. "Jardine Matheson, HSBC, and the crown will clandestinely fund Dr. Sun's revolution, officially funneling the money through the Tung Wah Hospital's Board of Directors. They hold regular humanitarian expeditions in the mainland, which will make for easy cover."

"And what's in it for us?" Jackson asked.

"Access," Dr. Sun replied. "Access and control."

The captain smiled. "Dr. Sun's administration will ensure our unfettered trade with the Chinese market."

"Interesting," Matheson said, scratching his chin.

Jackson gritted his teeth. "I don't like it," he growled. "His men run wild on the streets, and we reward him for it? Why not find someone more trustworthy?"

"Because we need those men. The Qing government has sealed off China, and the *Tiandihui* have seized control of our streets. My plan is to kill two birds with one stone."

"In return for your support," Dr. Sun said, crossing his arms, "I will install Cheung-kee as Marshal of one of the three *Tiandihui.* The branch in charge of opium distribution."

"Interesting," Matheson remarked. "A triad under our direct control."

"If the revolution succeeds," Dr. Sun said.

"That won't be trouble," the admiral insisted. "The Manchus fell quickly during the Opium Wars, and their grasp on power is weaker than it's ever been. They only survived the Taiping Rebellion because of us. They rule at our pleasure."

Dr. Sun nodded. "With your assistance and the support I've gathered from Hawaii, Malaya, and Japan, I'm sure it will be enough. These barbarians have caused us enough humiliation already. It's time to take our country back and make it great again."

"A splendid plan!" Matheson exclaimed.

"Hmph," Jackson grunted begrudgingly, "I suppose, with local distributors, we *could* penetrate into new communities. Sell opium beside their herbs and bitter soups."

"Should we put it to a vote?" the captain asked.

Julian clenched his fist tight, the veins in his forehead pulsing. Instinctually, he reached for an object hidden in the back of his waistband: a bone whittle with an ivory handle. Clutching the weapon, he stepped out of the shadows, his arms akimbo as he silently approached. He knew this wasn't really his city and it wasn't really his fight—he was just a colonizer who had set up camp on its beaches and chiseled a bit of gold for himself. But this was still his home, still his fatherland, and he had just as much a stake in it as anyone else. He couldn't just sit back and watch Hong Kong get carved up in front of him.

"I second the motion," the admiral replied, raising his hand in the air.

Holding his arms over his head like a great sledgehammer, Julian jumped out from behind the column, charging straight at the captain with the whittle.

"An assassin!" Forbes shouted out.

"*Toiiii!*" Julian shouted, doing his best Raymond Lau impression. He grabbed the captain by the collar of his uniform. But just before he sunk the killing blow, he looked into the man's eyes and let go of the knife.

"It can't be," Julian gasped.

Beneath his pointed hat, the young captain had the eyes and gaunt cheeks of Julian Kensington. The same face. *His* face. A look of sheer terror came over both of them, and the two men each backed away from the other.

Cheung-kee and the British officer ran over and quickly wrestled Julian to the ground. They kicked him repeatedly until his bones were crushed and

blood gushed from his mouth. The two businessmen cheered them on, but Dr. Sun covered his eyes
at the sight of blood.

"What should we do with him?" Cheung-kee
asked.

The captain had no reply. For the first time, he
was at a loss for words. He could only stare down at
his two hands in horror.

"The same thing we do with all filth," the admiral
said, breaking the silence. He drew a small revolver
from his holster. "We take out the trash."

The muzzle flashed silently.

As Inspector Leung woke from troubled dreams, he found himself strapped to a hospital bed. His hand was fastened to an electronic heart monitor, and there was an IV drip in his arm, connected to a butterfly needle under a sheet of gauze. On the opposite wall, Leung recognized the crest and shield of Tung Wah Hospital. Beside it, a grainy TV hung from the ceiling, playing the Bruce Lee classic *Fist of Fury*. The star actor was mowing through a crowd of Japanese martial artists like a hot knife through tofu.

An old nurse in scrubs checked Leung's vitals as a bespectacled doctor read through a chart at the foot of his bed. Leung could feel something sharp in his back and could see the bed sheets becoming saturated with blood, but there was no pain. In fact, each of his four limbs was numb, like he was floating on air. Even his teeth had lost all feeling.

"Inspector Leung," the doctor said. "Are you alright?"

"Why am I here?" Leung asked.

"You fell unconscious after the explosion."

"Explosion? The last thing I remember, I was with Marshal Hong at the bar."

The nurse turned to the doctor and whispered something in his ear. She had curly black hair and a pea-shaped mole in the center of her forehead, like a bindi. The doctor nodded at her, a sullen look painted on his face.

"Your memory may be a bit unstable," he said. "You took a sharp blow to the head. And unfortunately, we couldn't remove the shrapnel from your back without risking damage to your vital organs."

"Wait," Leung said. "I remember this."

"It's something you'll just have to live with."

With his left arm, Leung reached under the bed sheets and felt a sharp, jagged object lodged in his lower back. "Cock-Brand Fireworks," he said.

The doctor nodded solemnly. "I'm afraid Inspector Gibson didn't make it. But Inspector Smithfield escaped with only minor injuries."

"Smithfield," Leung said. "Where is he?"

The doctor tilted his head sideways. "Well, that's the question, now, isn't it?"

"It's time for his medicine," the nurse said. Her voice was raspy and about five octaves too low for her body type. "I'll get him set up."

"Very good."

The nurse rolled over a surgical cart, on which sat a brass oil burner, a jar of Yulong, and a long bamboo pipe. The nurse stuffed a pinch of opium into the brass bowl, then held the other end to Leung's mouth.

"What kind of hospital is this?"

"Take it," the doctor insisted. "It's good for you."

Leung resisted at first, holding his lips shut for as long as he could. But the nurse waited patiently, and inevitably he began to breathe in the seductive fumes.

Now, Leung remembered. The Lucky Stone had knocked him unconscious and dragged him to a prison cell in the dockyards. And for the last several days, he'd had only one visitor: a fat lumbering oaf named Little Chow, who came in every morning with a glop of food—some unspeakably disgusting gruel that he ladled directly into Inspector Leung's mouth—and came in every night to set up an oil lamp and a pipe beside his hospital bed.

It had been seven days. Seven days of lying here, his flesh wounds festering untreated, waiting for Little Chow to come and make the pain go away. It was getting harder to tell what was real and what was imagined—the exhaustion and hunger had clouded his brain to the point where dream and reality were blending together. His only clock was the door swinging open, Little Chow signaling a new day with his ladle or welcoming the night with the strangely crystal white opium.

"The problem with Yulong," the doctor continued, "is that you start to lose track of what's real. You'll talk whether you like it or not. But who knows if any of it will be true?"

Leung stared up at the young physician, who in the last five seconds had sprouted a goatee. "Are you Marshal Hong?" he asked.

The doctor grinned sickly. "Do you know where you are, Inspector Leung? Do you know when you are?"

"It's nighttime," Leung said simply. "'Round midnight, I suppose."

"Where is Smithfield?" the doctor growled.

"I thought you had him."

"No," the nurse replied in her deep baritone. "He stole something from us. And you know where he is."

"Think!" the doctor yelled. "What was that *gweilo* partner of yours up to?"

"I have no idea," Leung said. "Even if I did, I wouldn't tell you. But I don't."

The doctor grabbed Leung's chin and held a scalpel to his throat. In the glow of the dim red heart monitor, he looked like Satan incarnate. "Don't *fuck* with us, *sei puk gai.* You and Smithfield have always worked together. He must have told you something."

"Smithfield," Leung said blankly, but the name had lost all meaning.

"Your goddamn partner!"

Inspector Leung's eyes rolled backwards. His body began to tremble, and both his arms started shaking epileptically. Foam dripped out the sides of his mouth onto the ragged remnants of his coat. He closed his eyes and screamed.

"Jesus!" an Irish voice called back. "Leung, are you alright?"

When Inspector Leung opened his eyes again, he was seated in the passenger seat of a Morris Mini, a small British sedan that was speeding through the Aberdeen Tunnel at over a hundred kilometers an hour. Inspector Gibson, a fat man with bright red hair and freckles, was sitting in the driver's seat with a cigarette between his thick lips. In the back, a young Arthur Smithfield was splayed across the leather seats, drumming on his right leg to the beat of "Sympathy for the Devil" on the car's stereo.

"Smithfield," Leung said.

"Have you two met before?" Gibson asked. "Arthur here just started yesterday."

"I'm afraid we haven't had the pleasure," Smithfield said. "Pleased to meet you."

"Likewise," Leung replied.

"He's a rising star," Gibson boasted. "The commissioner assigned him to us personally. Says he wants young Smithfield to be our shadow."

"Shadow," Leung repeated blankly. The car sped out of the tunnel and out onto the main road, giving the three inspectors a clear view of Aberdeen Harbor. Leung pressed his face into the window, staring at the cargo ships and fishing trawlers anchored by the pier. "Déjà vu."

"What's the case?" Smithfield asked.

"A nasty one," Gibson replied. "Inspector Xiang was killed last week. Last we heard, he was posing as a member of the Lucky Stone Triad along with Inspector Woo. But this past Tuesday his body washed up on the shores of Aberdeen. Some dockworkers called it in."

"What about Inspector Woo?" Smithfield asked.

"Still missing," Gibson replied. He took a deep drag off his cigarette, scorching half its length in one puff. "Ricky Cheung says to check out the Cock-Brand Fireworks Factory in Repulse Bay."

"That triad rat," Leung said. "He's leading us into a trap."

"Maybe, maybe not. But it's the only lead we have. Our sources say this factory is the headquarters of the Sun Yee On."

"It's a front."

"That's what Ricky told me."

Smithfield peered up. "And he thinks Inspector Woo might be there?"

"That's right. Ricky says they're trading him to the Lucky Stone in exchange for an alliance against the 14K."

"A search and rescue mission," Smithfield said. "Sounds easy enough."

Gibson shook his head. "You picked a hell of a time to start. The three big triads are all at war with each other, killing inspectors left and right. Who knows when it'll end?"

"Maybe sooner than you think," Leung muttered under his breath.

"Maybe sooner than you think," Smithfield said aloud.

"If you're right," Gibson said. "I'm taking you both out to Wan Chai. My treat."

Leung scowled. "I'm not interested in *whores.*"

"You're not interested in *anyone*," Gibson laughed, slapping his partner on the back. "In all our years together, I've never even seen you with a girl."

"There's more to life than pleasure."

"God, you're dull. What about you, Smithfield? The girls in Wan Chai love a *gweilo* more than anything else. Especially a *gweilo* in uniform. I'm sure they'll give you a nice discount."

Smithfield flashed a golden ring on the fourth finger of his left hand. "I'm married," he said.

"So what?" Gibson said. "So am I."

"His wife's real lovely," Leung commented. "But maybe a little blind."

"I'm not that type of guy," Smithfield said. "I like peace and quiet."

Gibson laughed. "Then you're in the *wrong* city."

"That's not true," Smithfield demurred. "You just have to know where to look. Maybe it's noisy here on Hong Kong Island and up in Kowloon, but the New Territories are a whole other story. My father used to own a country house in Tai O Village. It's real sleepy there. No violence, no triads."

"No *people*," Gibson said.

"Sure there are. The local fishermen are very nice."

Leung scratched the side of his head, zoning in at a moment that he'd zoned out before. He didn't remember this part of the conversation.

"Where do you guys live?" Smithfield asked.

Gibson chuckled. "Central, of course. It's the only civilized part of town."

"How stereotypical of you," the young man said. "What about you, Leung?"

"I live with my parents," he grumbled.

Soon, the car arrived at the Cock-Brand Fireworks Factory on the south side of Hong Kong Island. They drove past the empty security booth and into the lot, which was filled with haphazardly parked sedans and SUVs.

Two guards standing outside the warehouse walked toward the Morris Mini, brandishing submachine guns. They were both dressed in tank tops and denim jackets and wore dark sunglasses. One had a thick goatee and bushy eyebrows while the other was bald and baby-faced, a cigarette dangling out of his mouth.

"Looks like we found it," Smithfield said, clandestinely removing the snub-nose pistol from his shoulder holster and holding it behind his back.

The bearded man approached the driver's seat, pointing his gun squarely at Inspector Gibson's head. "*Nei hai dou gaau mat ceon aa?*" he growled. "*Li dou hai xi yan de fong lei ga.*"

"We're looking for the Cock-Brand Fireworks Factory," Gibson said. "Are we in the right place?"

The bearded man grimaced. "Get the fuck out of here, *gweilo*, or I'll put an extra hole in your dick."

"Is violence really necessary?"

"If you don't fucking move, it will be. You have until the count of three."

His counterpart raised his gun. "Fuck that. The boss will kill us if anyone comes out of here alive."

Gibson turned over his shoulder. "Smithfield, now!"

Inspector Smithfield drew the Colt Cobra .38 from behind his back and shot the bearded man once in the head, splattering red over the car's white upholstery. In shock, his counterpart slipped backwards, falling hard onto the concrete.

"Drive!" Leung screamed.

Inspector Gibson pushed his foot down and the Morris Mini darted forward toward the warehouse entrance. From his back, the bald guard raised his submachine gun and shot aimlessly at the fleeing sedan. Smithfield clutched his pistol and rolled down the window above his door.

"Hard left," he commanded. "*Now!*"

Gibson jerked the wheel counterclockwise and Smithfield fired a single shot out the window, hitting the guard square in the back. The bald man crumpled to the ground; the cigarette fell out of his mouth and rolled down the pavement, smoking the whole way.

"Bullseye," Gibson said. "I told you, Leung. The kid's a star."

Leung got out of the car and knelt over the bearded man's corpse. The guard's denim jacket had a jagged red stone sewn into the left breast, and there was an identical tattoo inked on the inside of his right arm. Leung holstered his pistol and took the submachine gun from the pavement.

"What the hell are you doing?" Gibson asked.

"This time, at least I'll be ready," Leung said.

"Come on," Smithfield called out, already pressing his ear against the factory's front door. "The meeting's started already."

"What do you hear?" Gibson asked.

"It's hard to tell. All the machinery is still on."

Gibson pushed open the front door. "Then let's take a closer look."

"We shouldn't go in there," Leung insisted. "You'll die."

"We can't leave another inspector behind," Gibson said. "You know that Woo would do the same thing for you."

"I seriously doubt that," Leung replied, but before he could lodge another word of protest, his two partners had already ducked inside the factory. "There's no changing history," he muttered to himself.

The factory was lined with snaking conveyor belts, carrying colorful rockets to and fro in various states of assembly. All along the walls, shelves of fireworks were bundled together like joss sticks stacked up to the ceiling. As they ducked under and around the whirring machines, they spied a group of men at the far end of the factory, standing between a ring of massive fireworks patterned after the twelve animals of the Chinese zodiac. The three inspectors hid behind the snake, ox, and dog respectively, just close enough to hear the conversation. Marshal Cheung of the Lucky Stone stood beside nine of his men, holding Inspector Woo at knifepoint. Opposite him, Chairman Ping of the Sun Yee On sat in a simple folding chair, wearing a grey suit with a golden tie. Nine soot-covered factory workers stood at his side clutching steel pipes and wrenches.

"Marshal Cheung," the Chairman said. "*Wa jor zeng hai lei ya gou yan lei.*"

"*Lei dou mmhai zi ge ya gou yan lei!*" Cheung replied.

"*Lei dong ngo sor ga? Ngo seon lei xin zi kei.*"

"*Hhm,*" Cheung chortled. "*Gam lei yi ga yau seon ngo dey.*"

Ping spit on the ground in disgust. "*Lei yi wai ngo seon ga. Ngo mou dat gan. Ngo de sam min dou yau dik yan.*"

"*Hai sei fong,*" Marshal Cheung said. He snapped his finger, and twenty shirtless men stepped in from the shadows holding tommy guns. Each one had the same intricate tattoo on his back: a dragon, tiger, bird, and turtle all crossing swords. One man, the tallest and most muscular of the whole bunch, had the character 怒 penned in red ink on his chest.

"D-Dragonhead Wei?" the Chairman stammered. "Cheung! *Lei ceot mai ngo!*"

Cheung smirked. "*Dui mmzi.*" He untied Inspector Woo and escorted him out of the factory along with all of his men. The twenty shirtless triads surrounded what was left of the Sun Yee On leadership and raised their weapons to deliver the killing blows.

"Chairman Ping," Wei said. "*Ngo deng jor li gou gei wui deng jor hou loi.*"

"Wait!" Ping pleaded. "If we—"

But before he could finish his sentence, the twenty men opened fire, gunning down the factory workers and the Chairman in cold blood.

"Shit," Gibson whispered to his partners. "Stay down…"

"It's not over," Leung said. "Not even close."

The storm of bullets came to a halt, but, before anyone could even catch their breath, several bright sparks flew in from the windows at the top of the walls. Firecrackers arced into the room, shrieking madly as they burst into trails of colorful flames.

Wei scratched his head nervously. "*Fa saang mei xi?*"

"That's not good," Gibson commented.

"No," Leung said. "Not again." He dove on top of Smithfield just before the flames ignited the bundled fireworks along the walls, setting off a chain reaction. Blue, red, and yellow bursts shot out, tearing Gibson and most of the triads to shreds. A variegated inferno exploded out of the half-assembled rockets on the conveyor belt, and the twelve animals of the zodiac shot into the air. The dragon twisted at its apex and flew out sideways directly into the Dragonhead's chest, detonating in the center of his red tattoo. The conveyor belts themselves even burst into pieces, raining jagged metal onto the helpless triads below. A piece of shrapnel pierced one in the stomach, and another flung into the air and implanted itself directly into the small of Leung's back.

"*Gahh!*" Leung shrieked, collapsing onto Smithfield. The pain throbbed so violently that he couldn't even keep his eyes open. *There's no changing history*, he thought to himself again, his consciousness fading amidst the symphony of blood and colorful flames. *But maybe there's something to learn from it.*

The only problem was that he didn't know what.

"*Ng*," Julian groaned.

He felt a dull pain in his lower abdomen, like a bulge distending above his pelvis. He felt at it with his hand, even tried to push it back in, but the more he rubbed, the larger it grew. A din of panicked Cantonese voices rumbled all around.

Julian opened his eyes, nearly blinded by the sunshine glinting through the windowsill beside his bed. A nurse with the eyes of a bodhisattva stuck a needle in his left arm as she felt his pulse through the other wrist. The room was overcrowded; patients were stuffed so close together that their beds were practically adjoined. To Julian's left, a man's broken leg was held in the air by a makeshift pulley, using a bag of sand as a counterweight. Across from him, a young boy sat holding a dishtowel over his horrifically burned face. On the wall above hung a rectangular wooden sign with the words TUNG WAH GROUP OF HOSPITALS written in English under the seal.

"Julian!" a gruff voice barked from outside the window.

He looked out onto a familiar sidewalk: Hollywood Road. There was a crowd gathered outside, circled around two men in colorful armor who were dueling each other with halberds. Each man wore a ceramic mask with gaudy painted features: one had a thick black beard and resembled the angry god Mo Tai, while the other had two thick tassels coming out of his forehead like antennae. The latter charged at his opponent and swung his halberd, but the bearded man ducked and somersaulted out of the way. The audience cheered, and the two costumed warriors stopped and took a bow. With his head hung low, the bearded man turned his angry glare in Julian's direction.

"Haven't you slept enough already?" he asked. He took off his mask, revealing a plain white face with no features. His tasseled counterpart then removed his own mask, underneath which was the old monk himself.

"It's time for justice," he said.

The ground beneath the dueling warriors shook. The sidewalk cracked and split in two, and the gathered crowd screamed as the world twisted around them. Most were swallowed into the abyss, and others hung onto the fissuring concrete for dear life. One woman pushed her shrieking son to safety just as she was crushed by the shifting plates below. The featureless warrior fell to his death silently, but Shih-yin stood on solid ground, staring Julian dead in the eye even as the world fell apart around them.

"Get up!" Shih-yin yelled again.

Julian clutched at the walls, holding on for dear life, lest he too be sucked into the void. But after a few seconds he blinked and the earth was still. The room had not fractured like the world outside, though all the other beds and patients were gone. In one hand he held the obsidian pipe, in the other a thick black tome with the words *ROMANCE OF THE THREE KINGDOMS* etched in gold along its spine. He dropped the pipe and investigated the novel further. There was a flagged page seemingly three quarters of the way through, but when he turned to it all he found were scribbled notes, like a journal of some kind. It looked like his handwriting, though he couldn't be sure. *Did I read this?* he thought to himself. *Or did I write it?*

He laid the book down beside the pink mattress, and his surroundings came into focus. He was in Shih-yin's study, he realized, right where he'd been when he first breathed smoke from the pipe. The monk himself sat at one of the desks, reading casually from a Jin Yong novel. The oil lamp had long since fizzled out.

"You're awake," Shih-yin said casually. "Finally."

"What time is it?" Julian groaned in a groggy stupor.

"Seven o'clock," the monk said. "I couldn't wake you."

"Shit, I'm going to be late for work."

"You should have set an alarm."

"You shouldn't have drugged me!"

"Eh," Shih-yin said, "we're not here to review ancient history . . ."

"I thought that's exactly what we're here for. What the hell were you trying to show me? Who *were* those people? The captain . . . he looked just like me."

"That makes sense. He was your great-grandfather, after all."

"My great-grandfather?"

"John Smithfield," the monk said. "A titan in the history of Hong Kong. He lived here for ten years on assignment from the crown, and, in that time, he left an indelible mark on its future. He used his position to gain power and influence, and in a masterstroke, he linked the unlikeliest of partners: Jardine Matheson, HSBC, the Admiralty, and the *Tiandihui*—what we now call the triads."

"They didn't look like any triads I've ever seen."

"You've been watching too many films," the monk said. "Most of the triads these days are hiding in plain sight. They put on suits and ties, and everyone stops noticing them. But this goes much deeper than gambling rings and protection rackets; this was a formal partnership between the colonial administration and the criminal underworld. A state-sanctioned triad to protect the government's interests."

"The White Horse."

"They've gone by many names over the years. White Horse, Lucky Stone . . . Originally, they were called the *Suk Xing*. The Stars of Destiny."

"How do you know all this?"

"Your great-grandfather's journal," the monk said, pointing to the thick tome at his bedside. "Your father gave it to me. He was working with them too, for a time."

Julian picked the book up again, running his fingers along its etched spine. Feeling its grooves. "When?" he asked. "What happened to him?"

"It was his last gift to me," the monk said. "Just before he died."

***

On the train from Sheung Wan to Wan Chai, Julian and Shih-yin stood in serried ranks like soldiers in the terra cotta army. Some of those massed around them wore suits and ties on their way to work, but most were dressed casually and held umbrellas and large placards. Julian's body was nearly crushed by their weight, his hands caught between a meathead's sweaty gym bag and the ass of a fat American tourist, who kept remarking to her husband how clean the trains were.

"*Yen san yen hoi,*" Shih-yin said. "People mountain people sea."

Julian's mind, however, was somewhere else.

What did you expect? he asked himself silently. Realistically, he had always known that it was unlikely for the old man to be alive. Even if he had survived his "disappearance," he would now be almost eighty years old, around the life expectancy for any man, let alone a police inspector. There had been no contact for all these years and seemingly no record even of his existence. His father was like those men who failed the Imperial Exam: he'd simply been forgotten. Erased. Yet, now Julian knew that there might be a reason for all this madness. There might be someone to blame.

He had come to Hong Kong to follow this crazy dream—this nightmare—all to escape the endless drudgery of another day inside a cubicle. But now that he'd woken up, the ghosts were still there. They were scarier than he ever could have imagined, and it was his job to put them to rest once and for all—his job to make amends for all that his family had ever done. All these years, he'd looked back on them with pride. Even when his mother ranted and raved at him in her final years, her mind shattered by abandonment and alcohol, Julian still admired her. She was struggling to survive, all alone raising a boy who'd been broken by the world. Both of them fractured by the very same forces he was chasing now. But they were survivors—both of them. Even if he was the only one left standing. And his old man was a cop, still leading the charge against the forces of evil. A good guy. A white knight defending his kingdom from bandits and murderers.

Only he wasn't really. Sometimes a white horse is not a horse.

"Did my mom know about this?" Julian asked.

"About his death, yes. About the rest, no. I thought it best to keep her in the dark."

"She told me he disappeared."

"He did disappear. But then I found him. And then they found us."

"How could she lie to me?" Julian wondered aloud, his voice cracking. If his body weren't held up by the sheer mass of his fellow passengers, he would have sagged to the floor like a ragdoll leaking its stuffing. "All these years, she let me hope."

"I'm sure she had her reasons. And if she hadn't, we wouldn't have this chance we do now."

"This chance for what?"

"Vengeance."

The train came to a halt at Wan Chai, and half of the crowd diffused out of the car into the neon-green tunnels of the station. Julian and Shih-yin were carried along with them, waddling up an escalator and scanning their Octopus Cards to exit the paid area of the station. Escaping the crowd, they ascended the steps up onto the street, and a trickle of light poured in from above, illuminating the innumerable advertisements lining both sides of the stairs. EARTH-WORM PROTEIN PILLS, one read, showing a bespectacled doctor giving a thumbs-up with one hand and holding an earthworm in the other. Another depicted a disembodied white hand with what looked like a dried stool pinched between its first two fingers: YOUR PREMIER CATERPILLAR FUNGUS SOLUTION.

They exited onto the street, finding themselves on a sidewalk beneath the raised concrete bridge which connected the MTR entrance to Central Plaza and the Immigration Tower. The wide walkway hung over Hennessy and Lockhart Road—the Red-

Light District—all the way to the reclaimed land on which the city's latest skyscrapers stood. Both sides of the street were fenced off and lined with policemen and call girls. Instantly, a rush of vomit shot up Julian's esophagus and out onto the concrete.

"*Lei hai lid zhou mat tza?*" a passing businessman snapped, having evaded the flecks of vomit by mere inches.

"Subways," Julian groaned. "This always happens to me. It's like a reflex."

"It's all in your head, Julian."

"Really?" Julian said as a slender woman stepped directly into the pool of undigested oysters. "Because it seems like it's out on the sidewalk." The woman, who wore a pixie cut and was tall and thin enough to be a model, glared at the two men, biting her lip in anger. She took off her puke-covered stiletto and charged at them in rage.

"He's sick," Shih-yin tried to explain.

But it was no use. The woman beat the old monk repeatedly with her shoe until Julian pulled him away onto an escalator leading up to the bridge. She continued to curse at them from the base of the moving steps, even as she faded out of view.

"Crazy *sei ba po*," the monk said, wiping the vomit out of his eyebrows.

"Call it karma," Julian said. As they reached the top of the bridge, on which an army of businessmen was marching back and forth like stormtroopers, he spotted dozens more police officers lining both sides of the walkway, peering repeatedly into the horde. Shih-yin ducked behind a column, staying out of sight.

"Why are there so many cops here?" Julian asked.

"Because you're walking into the belly of the beast."

"What the hell am I even supposed to do, then? You think they're going to put drug sales on their financial records?"

"Of course not," Shih-yin replied. "They move that money through two holding companies in the mainland. This is where they invest the profits."

"And how do you know this?"

"Because I used to work here," Shih-yin said. "I was the boss's right-hand man."

"Huh," Julian grunted, grinning slightly. "So the monk was once a triad."

"As much as you are now," Shih-yin replied. "But my former relationship with them yields certain advantages. How do you think you got that job in the first place?"

"It wasn't my charming personality?"

"My position left me privy to some highly incriminating information. If I told the right people, I'm sure it would cause quite a stir."

"I'm surprised they left you alive."

"That's *why* they left me alive," Shih-yin said. "If I die, who's to say where it might end up? I have a dead man's switch in place should anything happen to me. Hidden records that will automatically come to light upon my death.”

“Smart.”

“However, there is one thing that they always managed to keep from me.”

“What?”

“Who’s actually in charge of the whole operation. In theory, their leadership left when the UK gave up the colony in ’97, but it’s possible the British government retains a vested interest. They could have left the organization in the hands of a caretaker while raking in the profits. Or maybe they have nothing to do with it at all. Maybe they sold it all to someone else.”

“How are we supposed to find out?”

“Simple. I need you to find the names of the men and women on their board of directors. And their addresses too.”

“Planning to pay them a visit?”

“I’m planning to send them a message.”

Julian gulped. “W-what kind of message?”

“You let me worry about that,” Shih-yin said. “Meet me at the MTR entrance during your lunch break, the same exit we just came out of. See if you can access the information now that you’re hooked up to the company’s server. If not, we’ll regroup.”

“Alright,” Julian said. “I’ll try. But if I end up in jail, I’m going to tell them this was all your idea.”

"Be careful," Shih-yin said, putting his hand on Julian's shoulder. "If it's too risky, you don't take the risk. Understand?"

"Yeah," Julian said, steeling himself for the task ahead. "I got it."

"No heroics," Shih-yin said. "This is Hong Kong, not Hollywood."

This is Hong Kong, Julian thought, squeezing his fists tight. *I'm an undercover cop. A spy sent to take down the triads*. He was just like Tony Leung in *Infernal Affairs*, only this was real life. Saluting the old monk with two fingers, he shuffled off in one direction with the mob of businessmen. Even if he wanted to turn back now, the force of the crowd was such that there was no way for him to change direction. Soon, he approached the green and gold skyscraper and was deposited by the masses into the lobby through the glass double doors. The scene was at once familiar and strange: the palm trees and imposing columns still stood over the marble floors; the vapid industrial art still hung on the walls, giving the gaudy space an aura of tastefulness. But now, in addition to the businessmen rushing in and out, there was a conspicuous presence of security personnel brandishing riot gear and assault weapons. By the elevators, a group of men in black suits and sunglasses waited patiently with their hands behind their backs, silently watching as the office crowd walked past them and went upstairs.

I'm a spy, Julian told himself again, only this time the comment took on a different tone. Maybe the White Horse had caught onto him. Maybe they knew all along who he really was, and Mr. Dayne was just luring him into a trap and using him to strike back at Shih-yin. He was an ant caught beneath the shadow of these greater men, and a foot could come crashing down on him at any second. His resolve fading, he slunk back outside to the building's food court to regroup. *Deep breaths*, he told himself as he walked toward the Starbucks for a coffee. *If you can't get inside, you'll have to make them come out to you.*

As he opened the door, the smell of arabica beans tickled his nostrils. He approached the counter, but a snaking line had formed like a twisting anaconda. He went all the way to the back, gazing back out the window to ensure that the suited men hadn't followed him. There, he saw a familiar face beside the glass: the same girl Mr. Dayne had screamed at just the day before on his way to the interview. She was staring intently at her tablet with a pair of thick headphones over her ears. *That'll work*, Julian thought, exiting the line abruptly.

He approached the girl from behind, catching a glimpse of the TVB program playing on her tablet—some soapy melodrama about the power of love and the pain of betrayal. "Hello," Julian said, lifting the headphones off his coworker's ears.

"Hey!" she yelped, startled by Julian's presence. Reflexively, she exited her app and opened up a blank Excel sheet.

"Relax," Julian said. "Don't you remember me?"

"Oh," the girl replied. "You're the one who interviewed yesterday."

"What are you doing down here?"

"This is Station six zero seven," she said. "Sometimes, when the office is overcrowded, they have us work out here on our mobile workstations. Spatial efficiency, Mr. Dayne calls it. I'm sure he can explain it better."

"Can that tablet access the company's server?"

"Of course," she replied. "It wouldn't be much good otherwise."

Julian smirked. "Listen," he said. "I wasn't at your office for an interview yesterday. I'm an auditor from Ernst & Young. Mr. Dayne hired me to look over the company's finances for any irregularities. It seems that the board of directors have made some risky, perhaps even criminal investments. So, I will need access to the minutes of all of their official board meetings."

"Is that right?" the girl said. "Well, I can give you their names, but you're going to have to ask their permission for access to the minutes."

"Why is that?"

"Because the only ones who can see those are the board members themselves. And, of course, Mr. Lau, the CEO."

"Mr. Lau?" Julian said. "*Raymond* Lau?"

"Of course," the girl replied. "Who else?"

***

Emptyhanded, Julian walked back across the crowded bridge from Central Plaza to Wan Chai. He had failed in his mission, he knew, and the fact that he never even set foot in the office meant that he'd likely never get the chance again. Knowing Mr. Dayne, the second the clock ticked past 8:01, his pink slip would be postmarked immediately, his visa ripped up, and perhaps a warrant for his arrest issued.

Deflated, Julian knelt down and hung over the railing, looking to the east and to Hennessy Road below. For now, at least, the streets were empty, but there was a rumbling far in the distance—a cloud of dust, or perhaps an optical illusion. The longer he stared at it, the thicker the cloud grew. Unblinking, Julian's eyes fell out of focus. His only reference points were the advertisements crowding the second stories of the buildings along the four-lane road: Standard Chartered, Public Finance, and, far past the weathered rainbow residential towers—which in their pattern resembled the old flag of China after the Xinhai Revolution—a massive billboard for the Bank of China, featuring a grizzled face that Julian recognized right away: *Raymond Lau.* His mullet was salt-and-pepper grey now and his eyebags seemingly bore one ring for each year past his heyday, but his coy smile was just the same. Julian's hands trembled, and his head began to spin, so much so that he would have fallen over the edge of the walkway if not for the handrail that he leaned against.

Ever since he was young, Julian could watch one of Raymond Lau's films and be swept up in that alternate reality—that vision of Hong Kong as a land of warriors, honor, and pride. The films were campy, the dialogue was terrible, and the plots were absurd, but no matter what happened in the world, he could turn on *A Symphony of Fists* or *Horse in the Dragon's Claw* and watch Raymond Lau save the day.

There had to be some mistake. It couldn't be the same Raymond Lau he knew. Or even if he was involved, there had to be some other explanation. Maybe he was just the public face of the organization—a famous smile that they could hide behind—and he had no idea of the nefarious activities that his company was engaged in. Or, better yet, maybe he'd infiltrated the White Horse just to tear them apart from within. But he couldn't be the villain.

The whole reason Julian had come to Hong Kong was to follow the dreams that Raymond Lau and Charlie Yip had cooked up for him. It was just like Flora said: the whole quest felt like an action movie, and this was Julian's one chance to live out that fantasy for real. Art imitates life and life imitates art, and the only thing Julian had wanted his whole life was to move beyond the monotony of work to a world of heroes and villains. Cops and triads. And so far, the journey had brought him closer to that world than he ever could have expected. It was a real Hong Kong Drama—an homage to the New Wave of Hong Kong Cinema, brimming with classical allusions. But now that his dreams were becoming reality, he missed those simpler days.

He missed his mom more than anything else. As lost as she'd been at the end, when alcohol and Alzheimer's had stripped her of her memories and good sense, she was the one pillar that had kept the whole foundation from collapsing. She was the only one who was always there for Julian, protecting him when he needed it and giving him space when he grew so anxious and paranoid that every gesture felt like a slight against him. If it hadn't been for her, he would have come here long ago, but she forbade him to come back to Hong Kong, knowing instinctually the danger that he was now in. She always warned him not to idealize his father—always warned him that cops were no better than anyone else—but she'd never warned him about Raymond Lau. In fact, she was all too happy to put on one of Julian's favorite VHS tapes and spend some quality time with a glass bottle. Alone. She even laughed at some of those films from her perch in the kitchen. That innocent escapism was one of the few happy moments left in their lives, one of the few delights that they shared. But every great film had a great twist and, as much as it hurt, perhaps this was it.

Now, the rumbling in the distance came into focus. A crowd of protestors marched down the four-lane road, holding up signs and wearing yellow t-shirts, buttons, and bandanas that read PEOPLE POWER. Organizers on both sides held up flags and yelled through their megaphones, spurring their supporters on. There were young kids in the crowd passing out merchandise and old men handing newsletters to passersby. Although it wasn't raining, most of the women were holding up a colorful assortment of umbrellas to block out the midday sun. Between their parasols, the placards, and the rainbow signs and buildings looming over the sidewalk, it almost looked like a parade.

"*Zeng fu hai fuk mo sou yau yan man!*" one marcher yelled. "*But lun pan fu!*"

"*Zan zing dik man zyu!*" an organizer screamed through a megaphone. "*Mui yat gou yan dou ying goi dak dou yat piu!*"

Several marchers raised their fists and umbrellas high in the air in solidarity and, for some reason, Julian felt his own arm creeping towards the sky. Their anger infected him—the cacophony of the crowd and the pulsating, almost rhythmic chants from the megaphones physically shook his bones. He could feel the hairs on his arms rising as if by static electricity. *If Raymond Lau really did have something to do with my father's death*, Julian thought, *it's my job to hold him responsible*. He had to bring the villain to justice, even if it had been his hero all along.

"You're early," a voice said dimly through the crowd behind him. Julian turned around and saw Shih-yin standing at his side, holding a long, slender object behind his back that stretched from his waist down to the ground.

"What's going on here?" Julian asked. Several camera shutters went off from the bridge above. Julian winced and turned away, blinded by the flash.

"It's July first," Shih-yin said. "The anniversary of the handover to China."

Julian rubbed his eyes, but his vision was still bleary. "What are they protesting?"

Shih-yin laughed. "What do you think?"

As Julian's eyesight again came into focus, he saw a group of protestors holding a red Chinese flag in tatters. Beside them, another group of teenagers were dragging a stuffed wolf with a meat cleaver lodged in its head.

"It's a day of outrage," Shih-yin explained. "We yell and scream until we get our way. And if we don't, we yell even louder."

"That sounds like a temper tantrum."

"That's exactly what it is," Shih-yin admitted. "But it's the only power we have."

"I got the names of their board of directors. Four men: Wu Song, Song Jian, Jia Baoyu, and Kwan Yu."

"All characters from the Chinese classics."

"And there were no addresses listed either."

"I'm not surprised," Shih-yin said. "Say what you want about Raymond Lau, but he's not stupid."

Julian stared down, his anger momentarily abating. "Why didn't you tell me he was the one behind this?"

"If I told you," Shih-yin said, "you probably wouldn't have believed me."

Julian looked up at the monk with pleading eyes. "But he was my hero."

Shih-yin grimaced. "Mine too, if you can believe it. But it's thanks to him that this whole operation is possible. He's been their point man for years, using his network of contacts in both Hong Kong and the Mainland to shield their illicit activities from any kind of prosecution or official oversight. I've been chasing him for thirty years, but he's never let down his guard. He's like a tortoise hidden in its shell."

Swept up in the outrage below him, Julian clenched his fist so tight that his knuckles cracked. "Then we drag that bloody bastard out."

"Wrong," Shih-yin said. "If you threaten a turtle, it'll just burrow even deeper into its shell. But if you leave a carrot at its doorstep . . ."

"What did you have in mind?"

Shih-yin reached behind his back and revealed the large object—an old metal shovel covered in dust and soot.

"What's that for?" Julian asked.

"A family reunion."

Inspector Leung was jolted awake by a sudden upward movement, like the room was lifting off the ground and listing slightly to one side. At first, he'd thought it was just vertigo—a side of effect of Yulong—but as the room continued to rise, a crack of light shone through a slit in the metal wall. It was then that Leung realized that he was getting higher for real this time. He wanted to rub his eyes, but his wrists were tied together behind his back. He was lying flat, his neck atop a ceramic pillow, as white balloons were stacked over him like packing peanuts. Like a jade burial suit draped across his corpse.

What the hell is happening? Leung thought to himself. The last thing he could remember was the explosion at Cock-Brand Fireworks. As his head continued to spin, the smell of salt and sulphur singed his nostrils. *The ocean*, he thought, slightly nauseated by the acrid aroma. *Victoria Harbor.* He craned his neck to escape the pungent odor, noticing only then that he wasn't alone. Another man was lying supine at his left, balding, bearded, and blindfolded with his hands tied behind his back. He was wearing a white tank top and a pair of baggy grey trousers.

"Wong?" Leung exclaimed. "Wong, is that you?"

After a long second, the man replied simply: "No."

"Smithfield?"

"No," the man said again. "I'm Delin."

"What's going on?" Leung asked. "Where are they taking us?"

"Burma," he said.

"Burma?"

"Yes. That's where they cook the product. I don't know about you, but I've been sentenced to five years of hard labor. Or at least harder labor than I had before. You know, it's not so easy lifting boxes."

"You're a dockworker?"

"That's right."

"What did you do?"

"I spoke out," Delin said. "Marshal Hong was going to get us all arrested. It's one thing to transport illegal cargo. That's been the business model of Hong Kong for the past hundred years. But it's another thing to kidnap cops and piss off the authorities."

"I'm a cop," Leung said. "I'm one of them."

"*Aiyyya*," he said. "Just my luck. Locked in a shipping crate with a *gweilo* cop."

"*Ngo mmhai gweilo. Ngo hai zung gwok jan.*"

"Hm," Delin grunted. "*Gam ngo dei ho neng wui ya gei wui.*"

"Is there any way to escape?" Leung asked.

"Not unless you know how to get these ropes untied."

Leung struggled to free his hands, trying to pull the coarse ropes apart with brute strength, but the knot wouldn't give. The more he pulled, the deeper it cut into his skin, peeling off bits of the epidermis. It was no use.

Then, Leung remembered his dream—remembered the first gift that the Lucky Stone ever gave him. It was risky, perhaps, but it was the only chance he had. He pressed his back as hard as he could into the ground and pushed with his two bound hands against the sides of his back. The shrapnel dug through the underlayers of his skin, inching toward the surface. Each second yielded another pulse of pain, like a sadistic bassline droning on. Leung grit his teeth so hard that they could have shattered from the sheer pressure, and fists were curled so tight that his fingernails drew blood from his palms. The agony alone would have killed almost any man, but with the Yulong still left in his system it was just bearable enough to survive. Slowly, the sharp piece of shrapnel popped out through a thin gash. Leung rubbed his back up and down against the rope, each swipe sending another shockwave up his spine. Tears welled up in his eyes, but Leung pushed through, rubbing harder the worse the pain got. Finally, the rope snapped, and Leung slumped over, breathing heavily. "I," he said, struggling to catch his breath. "I did it."

"Nice job!" Delin exclaimed. "Now come help me."

Leung crawled over to the man, using his arm like a machete to knock away the thicket of stuffed balloons between them. "Why should I?"

"Because you're a cop," Delin said. "It's your job to save people."

"It's not my job to save a triad."

"I can help you," he pleaded. "Don't just leave me here!"

Leung got up on one knee, starting to regain his strength. He looked down at Delin's bearded face, tilting his head. Considering him. "Who killed Eddie Yang?"

"Eddie Yang? What do you know about that?"

"He used to work here, didn't he? Did you know him?"

"Of course I knew him. He's the son of a Red Pole."

"And how did the son of a Red Pole end up on the set of major motion picture?"

"I think you just answered your own question."

My own question? Leung thought. "Are you saying there's some connection between Jianghu Studios and the triads?"

"What have you been living under a rock?" Delin asked. "Not just Jianghu Studios. Orange Sky, TVB . . . all the major channels."

"And Raymond Lau," Leung said, "he was a dock-worker too, wasn't he?"

"What, do you need me to spell it out?"

My god, Leung thought. The idea was so patently ridiculous that he hadn't even considered it. "Raymond Lau's a triad."

"That's right," Delin said. "He's the son of a Red Pole himself. And the nephew of our old boss,

Marshal Cheung. How else do you think a little runt like him could become an action star."

It made sense, Leung had to admit. The bound man didn't seem to be lying. "Alright," Leung said. "I'll help you." He helped Delin sit up, then got to work untying the knotted rope around his wrists.

"Thanks," Delin said. "I guess not all cops are bad people."

"Just most of them," Leung said. The rope was no Gordian Knot—it came undone easily. Delin stood up, his body limber, raising his arms as high as he could before hitting the container's ceiling.

"Freedom!" he exclaimed.

"Not yet," Leung replied. "Now what do we do?"

"What else? We have to get out of here before they get us loaded on that ship. Let's charge the door together and try to force it open."

"But we're moving. We're rising into the air."

"Exactly. The longer we wait, the harder we'll fall."

Leung stood up and tried to regain his balance. He'd lost a great deal of blood and had been drugged for more than a week, so it felt strange just to stand, let alone balance himself inside the listing container. "Wait a second. There must be a better idea."

"There's no time for hesitation! Charge!"

Delin barreled straight through the opium-stuffed balloons like a raging bull aiming at the crack of light. The door burst open upon impact and Delin fell straight down over the edge. The container tilted downward at a 45-degree angle as the balloons slid forward toward the open end. Leung pressed his hands against the metal grooves on the ceiling to keep himself steady, until friction gave out and he plunged out the bottom along with all the merchandise. *This is it,* Leung thought. For all he knew, he was fifteen stories high and plummeting to his death. But, sooner than he thought, he hit the water with a loud splash, like a bellyflopping whale. He was bruised all over, but he remained conscious. He kicked his legs and jumped up above the surface, gasping for breath.

Not far from the edge of the dockyard, the container hung suspended just two or three stories in the air, pointing straight downwards. A frightened crane operator stuck his foot into the water and prepared to jump in to salvage the lost product. But then, from below the surface, Leung reached up with one arm and grabbed the knife from the man's ankle holster.

"*Diu lei!*" the crane operator screamed. He clutched his pistol, but before he could pull the trigger, Leung buried the knife into his submerged foot. The crane operator shrieked in pain, and Leung pulled himself up onto solid ground and landed a right hook across his face, knocking him to the ground. Leung grabbed the man by the collar of his orange vest and held him over the edge of the water.

"*Where's Marshal Hong?*" Leung snarled.

"I d-don't know," the crane operator stammered.

"I have a message for him," Leung said. He pressed the knife up against the man's chin. "And I'd like to deliver it in person."

The crane operator pointed toward a group of brick structures near the entrance of the dockyard, his hand shaking violently the whole while. "The warehouses," he said meekly. "That's where they keep the product . . ."

"Which one is he in?"

"I don't know!" the man cried. "Don't kill me! Please!"

Leung slit the crane operator's throat. Blood gurgling out of his mouth, the man clutched in vain at his severed arteries, trying somehow to keep them closed, but his fingers loosened and his eyes glazed over.

Leung stuffed the knife and the dead man's pistol into the back of his waistband, then donned the crane operator's vest and hardhat before kicking the corpse into the harbor. The water bubbled red as the corpse sank below the surface. However, just as soon as it fell under, another body came back out.

Leung raised his pistol. *A ghost?* he thought. *He couldn't be alive after that.* "Put your hands where I can see them!" he exclaimed. The body came alive, gasping for breath and choking out polluted water. *Delin,* Leung realized. He put the pistol back in his waistband and approached the edge of the shipyard, helping the dockworker ascend onto the surface. "Are you alright?" he asked.

"Never better," Delin said. "I told you it would work."

"We got lucky."

"It's better to be lucky than skilled. That's what I always say."

"I'm going to find Marshal Hong," Leung said. "And then I'm going to kill him."

"Understandable. You have to do your job."

"And what about you?"

"What about me?"

"You have to do your job too."

"Don't worry, I'll stay out of your way. I don't think I'm well suited for the triads anymore. Maybe I'll head off for Guangzhou or something. Start fresh."

"That's a fine idea. If I could, I would."

"So why don't you? Why get involved in this whole mess?"

"Because I have something to finish," Leung said as he walked away from Delin toward the warehouses, passing stacks upon stacks of shipping containers. Amidst the crates, more men in orange vests and hardhats carried wooden boxes between them. As he walked by, Leung lowered the hardhat over his bloodshot eyes to avoid detection. He ducked under a forklift, passing through the shadow of a massive green container overhead, and arrived at a group of brick warehouses near the dockyard entrance. There were more than ten buildings, each one identically built with rows of yellow forklifts parked in front of them. There, amidst the aromas of salt, algae, and oil, Leung caught a whiff of a distinctive odor. After the last week he'd spent tied to the hospital bed, forced to inhale those noxious fumes, he would recognize it anywhere. He removed the pistol from his waistband and followed the smell to a warehouse at the far end of the lot. The number four was emblazoned in a red circle on the front door. His heart quivering, lured in by the redolent scent, Leung turned the knob with his free hand and stepped inside.

The warehouse was smaller than it looked, with four grey walls and a high arched ceiling. What little light there was seeped in from the small windows along the top of each wall; rays of sunshine slanted down onto three workers wearing surgical masks as they unloaded crates of Yulong, stacking the product in a pyramid of white balloons. All the workers were dressed in jeans and tank tops and had small axes hanging from their belts. Leung clutched the pistol and approached the three men directly.

"Where the hell is Wong?" he demanded.

The men stopped what they were doing and broke into a fighting pose. One held two claws in front of him like a tiger, another stood with his legs spread wide like he was riding a horse, and the last held his arms and left leg up in a crane stance.

Without hesitation, Leung shot the first two men square in the forehead, sending a torrent of blood gushing onto the snow-white bags. The third man panicked and broke out of his stance, but then steeled himself and charged at the inspector. Leung shot the man once in the stomach and then again in the kneecap.

"*Argh!*" the man screamed, clutching his leg atop a mountain of red and white.

"Gun beats crane. Once again," he seethed, "where is Wong?"

"In the back," the man replied, wincing in pain. "But—" Leung pressed the trigger again and the man went limp.

Leung checked the clip of his gun. He had just four bullets left, so he would have to conserve them carefully. There was no telling how many guards might be hiding in the back. As he made his way through the labyrinthine corridors, he could hear the sound of moans, but it was hard to tell whether they were from pain or pleasure. Leung traced the sound to a metal door in the deepest corner of the warehouse with a blinking red light hanging over the entryway. Leung took a deep breath and kicked the door open, revealing a tiny room with pipes along the walls and a lone hospital bed at its center, which Inspector Wong was strapped to. Wong's designer clothes had been torn apart, and his sunglasses lay shattered on the ground. Little Chow stood at the center of the room holding open Wong's mouth and ladling gruel inside.

"Wong," Leung exhaled. He pointed his gun at Little Chow, but before he could get off a shot, the fat man turned around and swung the ladle, smacking the pistol out of Leung's hand. Hot gruel splashed onto the floor, and Little Chow charged again with the utensil, battering Leung repeatedly over the head. In desperation, the inspector shielded his face with his left arm and took the knife out with his right, depositing the blade in the side of Little Chow's blubbery stomach. The fat man howled in pain and wobbled backwards, but it was just a surface wound, the fat having absorbed most of the damage. He charged at Leung again and the two men grappled together, each trying to force the other to the ground. Slowly but surely, Little Chow's immense weight overpowered the old inspector and buckled his knees. Grinning, the fat man took a syringe from the surgical cart and held it high in the air.

"Leung!" Wong cried out.

At the last moment, Leung punched the handle of the knife, which was still buried in Little Chow's stomach, knocking it deeper into his gut. Little Chow staggered backwards and slipped on the hot gruel, falling on his back with a loud thud. Leung took the syringe from the ground and tried to force it into Little Chow's eye, but the fat man grabbed Leung's arm just before the needle went in. They both pushed mightily, the pinpoint raising and lowering millimeters at a time, until the fat man's strength eventually gave out. Little Chow screamed horrifically as the syringe pierced his cornea. Then, as Leung pressed the plunger down, the fat triad went quiet, gazing vacantly at the ceiling with his lone remaining eye.

Leung stood up, huffing in exhaustion and trying to collect his breath. He removed the knife from the side of Little Chow's belly and walked over to Wong, who was strapped to the hospital bed with three leather belts.

"Wong," Leung said, smiling for the first time in days. "Thank god you're alive."

"Not god," Wong choked out. "Thank *you*."

Leung cut the belts and helped his young partner to his feet, but Wong's legs were too weary to even stand. Leung walked a few steps with him until he could maintain his balance alone.

"Take this," Leung said, handing Wong the bloodied knife. "We have to get out of here before they find us. After all this commotion, they'll be coming after us hard."

"Who?" Wong asked. "Who the hell are these people?"

"Everyone," Leung replied. "The Lucky Stone, Woo, Raymond Lau . . ." He picked the pistol up from the ground and cocked it.

"Raymond Lau?"

"It's a long story," Leung said. "I'll tell you once we're safe."

Weapons in hand, the two inspectors exited the room and followed the corridors back to the front of the warehouse, where the three workers lay dead atop the balloons of Yulong. Wong stared in awe at the mountain of opium, his jaw hanging slack. "Is that what I think it is?"

"It sure is," Leung said. "We stepped onto the main nerve."

"You think we should take some for evidence?"

Leung slapped his partner across the face. "Will-power," he said. "Come on, we have to get out of here *now.*" He grabbed Wong by the arm and pulled him toward the entrance, the young inspector looking back the whole way.

As the two stepped outside, a black sedan veered in through the dockyard entrance and skidded to a halt beside the warehouse.

"Oh shit," Leung groaned. He and Wong ducked behind the nearby forklift, staying out of sight. The car doors opened, and three men in denim jackets stepped out brandishing pistols, followed shortly thereafter by Marshal Hong himself.

"That's him," Wong whispered.

"I know," Leung replied, aiming his pistol carefully around the corner of the truck.

"Go in there and flush him out!" Marshal Hong ordered as he pulled a golden Beretta out of his waistband. His three men entered the warehouse in a military formation. "Damn *puk gai,*" Hong said. "Should have killed him when I had the chance."

Leung lined the triad boss up in his sights and took a deep breath to steady his hands. Then, he stood up and stepped out from behind the forklift, keeping the pistol trained on Marshal Hong's head. "Drop the gun," he commanded.

Hong shuddered. "My, my, my," he said, caught off-guard. "You *are* resourceful. I'll give you that."

"I mean it!" Leung shouted. "Put your hands where I can see them!"

"You're a lucky man, Leung. But I can make you luckier."

Leung pressed the muzzle of the gun against Marshal Hong's chin. "You're not going to talk your way out of this one," he said. "I figured out your whole game."

"Is that right?"

"It wasn't pride that killed Eddie Yang. It was you."

"Do you have any proof?"

"Raymond's the son of a Red Pole, nephew of Marshal Cheung."

"Wait," Wong gasped. "Raymond Lau's a *triad?*"

"There's no way that Eddie would risk taking him on over some petty dispute," Leung continued. "Unless, of course, he had some kind of official protection. Your word of honor."

Marshal Hong smirked. "A promise that unfortunately could not be kept."

"You just wanted blackmail. Something you could hold over Raymond's head to keep him in line. You had just killed his uncle, after all."

"He who controls the Emperor controls the Empire."

"You filmed the whole thing, didn't you? And when Smithfield found the footage, you made him disappear."

"I didn't make Smithfield do anything. It's thanks to him we're in this mess."

Leung's eyebrow shot up. "What are you talking about?"

"One head bites the other," Marshal Hong said. "You wouldn't understand. Besides . . . it's your own head you should worry about."

"Freeze!" a voice commanded. One of Marshal Hong's guards stood beside the entrance to the warehouse, pointing his pistol directly at Inspector Leung.

Shit, Leung thought. He glanced back at Inspector Wong, but he was nowhere to be found. "A life for a life," he said. "An even trade."

"Make it then," Hong insisted. "Well?"

The forklift's engines blared on and the vehicle revved up. Wong sat behind the wheel, pressing the pedal down to the floor. The forklift charged at the three men, its ferocious roar freezing them in their tracks.

"Boss!" the guard shouted as he was crushed under its massive weight. Blood shot out onto Hong and Leung like the body had been passed through a woodchipper. At the last second, they dove out of the vehicle's path, the wheel of the forklift missing them by mere inches. Hurriedly, Leung jumped onto the back as Wong sped into a row of shipping containers.

"*Diu lei lomo!*" Marshal Hong shouted from the ground, firing aimlessly at the vehicle. "Come on!" he yelled to his two remaining men inside the warehouse. "Get in the car!"

Wong turned the forklift into another row of containers. The vehicle was slow and shaky, and it took all of Wong's energy just to keep it moving straight. Most of the dockworkers were able to get of the way, but one wasn't so lucky. The forklift bounced into the air as it hit him, jolting both inspectors.

"*Nghh!*" Leung groaned. "Can't you keep this thing steady?"

"Cut me some slack, I've never driven one of these before."

Marshal Hong's black sedan was gaining on them quickly. The triad boss and his two men stuck their heads out the windows, firing their guns repeatedly. One of the bullets grazed Leung's shoulder, and the inspector struggled to maintain his grip. "I'm hit!" he yelled. "We're sitting ducks out here!"

"You got any ideas?"

"This was your plan, not mine!" Another bullet brushed Leung's cheek, nearly taking his head off. The inspector swung around to the side of the forklift, trying to shield himself from the incoming gunfire. As he did, he saw another vehicle ahead of them, carrying a massive green container the size of sperm whale. "Up ahead!" Leung screamed. "Aim for the back-left wheel!"

"You want me to hit him?"

"That's right," Leung said, waiting for the sedan to pull up directly behind them. Marshal Hong stuck his head out of the passenger seat and aimed his pistol at the inspector, grinning madly. "Now!" Leung yelled.

Wong veered his forklift into the other, knocking it off-balance. The green shipping container listed heavily and slipped off the arms of the forklift, barreling down.

"*Sei puk gai,*" Marshal Hong groaned as the container fell toward his car. It crashed into the top of the sedan, flattening the top of the vehicle and sending glass and blood shooting out in all directions, like the guts of a crushed cockroach. Wong stopped the vehicle and Leung jumped down, still ready for a fight.

"We got him!" Wong exclaimed.

"Looks like it," Leung said as he approached the crushed vehicle. Amidst the wreckage, Marshal Hong's bloody arm hung out the window of the car, still clutching the golden Beretta. Leung handed his pistol to Wong and took the triad's weapon for himself, along with two stray clips that had fallen out of the car.

"A memento?" Wong asked.

"Something like that," Leung said. He put the safety back on and tucked the pistol in his waistband. "Come on," he said. "We still have work to do."

The two inspectors hurried back into the forklift and retraced their steps down the rows of containers. Near the entrance, a crowd of dockworkers had gathered around one mangled corpse—a bearded man in a white tank top with a fresh tire track across his chest. Leung stopped and gazed at the scene vacantly, holding his hand over his mouth.

"Don't worry about it," Wong said. "It's just a dead triad."

2014 / Chapter 7: The Uncanny Valley

Julian and Shih-yin sat onboard the MTR travelling west to Lantau Island. The old monk dozed in and out of consciousness, resting the shovel on his shoulder as he slept with his arms crossed. The sleek, modern train darted down the tracks at such a rapid pace that a strong wind blew through all the cars, ruffling the hair of everyone seated inside. None of the passengers seemed taken aback; all stared into their electronic devices seemingly without blinking.

The train exited the tunnel and continued along a raised track by the harbor. Light shone in through the windows, and Shih-yin turned to shield his eyes from the light, burying his head into Julian's shoulder. Julian blinked rapidly as light seeped into the car, and when his vision came back into focus, he could see Lantau Island far in the distance—a sea of green mountains that looked out of place in this venal metropolis. The island was an oasis: endless trees sprouted upward defiantly, as if challenging the skyscrapers to match their beauty. The pinnacle of nature beside the pinnacle of man, competing like all other things in the city.

Then, as soon as the island had come into view, the train turned into another tunnel, and the window went black. Where there had been a sea of life just moments earlier, darkness whizzed by. Julian looked down the train car and caught sight of a familiar face—a pudgy woman lying across one of the benches, taking up at least three or four spaces on her own. She wore what looked like a Dutch maid's outfit and rested her head on a Pikachu backpack, holding a tablet computer just a few inches from her face.

"Flora?" Julian said aloud. He stood up and approached her, plucking one of her earbuds out. "Hey you."

"*Nei hai dou tso mat ye?*" she roared before emitting a laugh. "Oh," she said. "You again. Are you following me?"

"What are you doing here?"

"I should ask the same of you. You know this train is headed to Tung Chung, right?"

"I know," Julian said. "I think I found my dad."

"You did?"

"Yeah. The monk told me that he's in a place called Tai O."

Flora cocked her head. "Tai O," she said. "Now, that's strange."

"What's strange about that?"

"I'm heading up there too, actually. Off to visit my grandfather's grave."

"Is that right?"

"Your dad is living with the Tanka, then?"

"The Tanka," Julian repeated. "I think I had one of those."

"The Boat People," Flora said. "Sea Gypsies. Maybe your dad shacked up with one of the *ham sui mui*—the 'salt water girls.'"

"What's going on here?" a voice groaned from behind. The old monk was standing over them with the shovel in hand, gripping it so tightly that his hands turned tomato red.

Flora sized him up. "So, you're the monk, huh? You don't look like much."

"Who is this?" Shih-yin asked. "What have you told her?"

"Relax," Julian said. "She's just a friend. Friends are important, right?"

Shih-yin grimaced. "I wouldn't know anything about that."

***

Over an hour later, Julian, Flora, and Shih-yin were seated onboard Bus number eleven traveling from Tung Chung station to Tai O. The path to the remote village was tortuous and torturous, up and down mountains covered end to end with lush foliage. Julian was amazed that such a large vehicle could navigate those twists and turns; the stereotypes he'd heard about Asian drivers were clearly unfounded. The branches dangled so low that their leaves brushed the side of the coach, emitting loud screeches like the warning cries of a chimpanzee. Julian stared out the window, trying to distract himself from the winding G-forces and the incessant squawks that rattled his innards. The sun glinted off the water in the distance, giving the lemon and tangerine trees that lined both sides of the road an almost neon glow.

"It's beautiful," Julian said.

Flora smirked. "That's the thing about Hong Kong. Just when you're ready to give up on it, it finds a way to draw you back in. It's intoxicating, addictive . . ."

"Infectious, even. It changes you."

"Infectious," Flora repeated. "Maybe that's the right word."

"Have you ever been infected by a place?" Julian asked.

"Sure," Flora replied. "When I first moved to London, I couldn't get enough of it. My flat was smaller than this bus, but we had this killer rooftop that overlooked the Thames. We spent half our days up there drinking, smoking, getting high as a kite. My boyfriend and I used to munch on Xanax and Valium like they were M&M's."

"Your boyfriend?"

"Ex-boyfriend, I should say. At least until he gets out of jail."

"Sounds like a real character."

"We used to sit over the side of that rooftop, our legs dangling twenty stories high, shouting insults at everyone who passed below. Half the time, we didn't even know what we were saying. But it didn't matter. It was the feeling we were after."

"I don't remember London like that," Julian said.

"Well, it's not just places that change you," she said. "Have you ever been infected by a person?"

"What, you mean like chlamydia?"

"No," Flora replied. "I mean have you ever been in love?"

Instinctively, Julian thought of Celeste—not of the real woman who lay beside him in that bed, but of the one from his dreams, sitting above him in the fig tree with the etched stone in hand. "I'm not sure," Julian replied. "Maybe."

"I think you'd be sure."

The bus came to halt at the foot of the village, stopping in front of a large wooden arch. Almost in unison, the passengers stood up from their seats and broke for the entrance, clogging up the aisles. As Julian stumbled out of the bus, he was unnerved by the sudden stillness. His legs were wobbly, and his insides still twisted and turned, bellowing like a groaning bear. He struggled to retain his balance as Shih-yin and Flora calmly exited the bus, the former clutching his shovel and the latter draping her Pikachu backpack across one shoulder.

The village ahead of them looked frozen in time. It was dilapidated but serene, with shanty houses built on stilts above the mud. Tanned men in rags sat on the edge of the dirt beside empty buckets. They were holding fishing rods and staring at the procession of tourists now passing through the village gate. Wooden bridges broached the canals that lined the rural oasis like the waters of Venice. Small, rusty speedboats buzzed through the narrow corridors and out into the vast sea. On both sides of the road, shopkeepers clapped their hands to attract customers to their restaurants and stands, most of which were selling some form of dried fish that looked like shriveled yellow mucus. A thin old man skillfully bowed his two-stringed erhu beside the gate, producing a melancholy wail.

As Julian stepped into the village, the smell of shrimp paste and rancid seafood overcame him. He rushed to the side of a wooden bridge and vomited over its edge, causing all of the tourists and shop owners to freeze and back away. Even the old man playing the erhu stopped his song mid-note.

"You sure know how to make an entrance," Flora said.

"It's alright," Shih-yin said, patting Julian on the back. The music began again and the shopkeepers and passersby fell back into their routines. "It's better if you get it all out of your system now."

"I'm fine," Julian insisted, wiping the flecks of vomit dripping from the corner of his mouth. "Must be something I ate."

He stood up and, helped by Flora and the old monk, continued past the arch into the village, approaching a rickety bridge on which tourists were snapping selfies with unenthused fisherman crowding both sides of the frame. Two salesmen stood at the shore, holding signs that read PINK DOLPHIN TOURS: $10.

"Pink Dolphins?" Julian wondered aloud.

"It's a tourist trap," Flora said. "You're not even guaranteed to see one."

Julian stopped and looked into the still, greenish water, which was so cloudy that he couldn't see an inch below the surface. "They sound pretty cute."

"They're dolphins," Shih-yin said. "Who cares what color they are?" The old monk continued plodding forward, using the shovel as a cane.

Flora whispered to Julian, "He's not really well put together, is he?"

"He does have his quirks."

"I've never seen a monk like him before. He looks the part, but there's no compassion. He has the stern demeanor, but that's it."

"Well, he used to be a triad."

"A *triad?*"

Shih-yin turned around and called out, "*Will you two hurry up?*"

They continued past the bustling shops over another dirt road into the mountains. A long red fence lined the pathway up the hills, on which tombstones were clustered in rows stacked one behind the other, like seats in a movie theater. Some of the graves bore crosses and others bore fading photographs of the deceased, but most were largely unadorned, with just a single black panel and golden characters etched into the marble. As they moved up the hill into the nosebleed seats, the noise from the shops and restaurants faded into the background. Crickets and frogs croaked as heartily as the shopkeepers, but none of them got in Julian's face. Passing through the tombstones, Julian thought back to the last time he'd set foot in a graveyard: at the Brompton Cemetery three years ago when they'd buried his mother. He had been asked to deliver the eulogy, but when he stood at the lectern with his prepared speech in front of him he froze, and his uncle had to step in. The words on the page lost all meaning when he realized that the woman who'd raised him was not the one they were lowering into the ground. That woman had died long ago, and all that was left was an empty shell. An echo. Inanimate flesh putrefying rapidly. Yet, now, Julian didn't mind the stench of death around him. Next to the fermented fish and salted egg yolks, it was like breathing in fresh air.

Soon, they arrived at another mountain of graves along a set of stone steps ascending to the peak. At the base of these was a metal rack in which three long bamboo sticks stood with wide red tassels on their ends like oversized brooms.

Julian scratched his chin. "I recognize these from somewhere."

"For putting out hill-fires," Shih-yin explained.

"No," Julian said. "That's not it. Wasn't this place in a movie or something?"

"That's right. Raymond Lau's *Water Margin*."

"Oh, yeah!" Julian exclaimed. "The one about the pirates! He fought off two soldiers with these fire-stoppers, remember?"

"Of course I remember," Shih-yin said. "I was there."

"You were?"

"And you were here too. You really don't remember, do you?"

"I'm sorry," Julian said, searching his mind but finding nothing. "I don't."

"You lived here with me for a few months. You and your mother. I thought it was the safest place to keep you, but I was wrong."

"Wait a second," Flora said. "You lived in Tai O Village?"

Julian looked around at the lush foliage. A water buffalo stood at the edge of the forest, gazing and grazing at the same time. Julian tilted his head as he stared back at the animal. "An ox," he muttered to himself, hoping it would spark his long-forgotten memories. But all he could think of was that movie—was Raymond Lau riding in on horseback to defeat the emperor's corrupt lieutenants. "Maybe," he said.

"The only *gweilos* I ever heard of in Tai O were the Smithfields. But you said your name is Kensington, right?"

Julian looked ahead at Shih-yin, still plodding forward with the shovel in hand. Even now, the old monk's story felt more like a fairy tale than reality. A gust blew furiously at Julian's back; reflexively, he gripped the handle of a bamboo stick from the bin and twisted his neck around. But there was no team of trained assassins behind him, no triad hitmen with axes in hand. Only wind.

"Come on," Shih-yin said. "We've lingered long enough."

The old monk started up the mountain, and Julian put the firestopper back and followed behind him, laboring up the steep steps paved into the mountainside. The sun shone brightly overhead, baking the three of them alive. Julian's skin turned the same shade of red as a perfectly cooked Dungeness crab. When they reached the top of the hill, he doubled over in exhaustion. Even Flora fell onto one knee, and Julian was sweating so profusely that he unbuttoned his whole dress shirt to cool off. But Shih-yin kept on walking at the same pace as before.

"Wait a second," Flora called out. "Hey! Monk!"

Shih-yin stopped and craned his neck. "What?"

Flora pointed her thumb over her back shoulder. "My grandpa's grave is right over here. I came to say a prayer for him."

"So go," Shih-yin said. "I'm not stopping you."

"Do you want to say something for him?"

"Not especially."

"*Sei puk gai*," Flora seethed. "Come on, Julian." She stepped off the path toward a large headstone, which was in a cluster of three on the side of the hill, set apart from the other graves. Like their own private box.

"Julian," Shih-yin grumbled, his arms folded. "We don't have time for detours. The dead aren't going anywhere, but we're living on borrowed time."

"She just wants to pay her respects," Julian said. "It'll only take a minute."

Shih-yin sighed and leaned atop the shovel for support. "Make it quick."

Julian nodded and approached the graves, which were just off the side of the pathway. Two looked like black ornamental mirrors and the other, in the middle, like a golden Washington Monument spearing the sky. All three bore black and white photographs of men and women with jet-black hair. At the middle grave, Flora was hunched over with her backpack open. She took out a small bucket and a wad of green paper bills, each with the picture of a demonic Chinese king on its front. The notes read BANK OF HELL GOVERNMENT and had outrageous sums printed on them, ranging from a million on some bills to five hundred million on special bills with gold leaf around the edges.

"Is that money?" Julian asked.

"Ghost money," Flora replied. She dropped the whole stack of notes into the bucket, then took one special $500,000,000 note from her bag and lit it on fire with a match. She threw the burning note into the bucket, setting all the other bills aflame.

Julian stepped back, reeling from the heat. "Talk about throwing your money away."

"Everyone needs an allowance in hell," Flora explained. "My grandpa might need some spending money. Not to mention the rent . . ."

"You have to pay rent in hell?"

"Of course you do. It's hell."

Another strong gust blew in from the ocean, sending embers flying in Julian's direction. He ducked his head, but a flaming strip of paper singed his damp suit. "Isn't there any easier way to send it to him?" he asked, beating his arm to put the fire out.

"It's a little dangerous," Flora admitted. "But he's my family. It's my job to take care of him."

Julian dusted the soot off his jacket. The wind was blowing so furiously now that the bucket itself began to shake. "I guess," he said uneasily, the image of his mother's coffin once again flashing in his mind. He looked back down the hill at the bucket of bamboo firestoppers, but they were so far away that they might as well have been back in Kowloon.

Shih-yin approached the pair from behind. "Are we done here?"

"Yeah," Flora said. "Mission complete."

"Good," Shih-yin said. "Julian, your father's grave is just up this hill."

"Wait," Flora gasped. "Your father's *grave?*"

Julian shrugged. "So he says."

Flora blushed. "You never told me he was dead."

"You didn't ask."

He walked back onto the main path, following Shih-yin up yet another set of stairs to the top of the mountain. Flora bowed once toward the still flaming bucket, then ran ahead to catch up to them. At the apex of the hill, they arrived at three small, unassuming crosses etched with the name SMITH-FIELD. They were all identical except for the dates: the leftmost one read 1880-1952, the middle read 1906-1971, and the rightmost one read 1949-1984. The grass in front of the latter was younger and far shorter than that in front of the others, perhaps only a few weeks old.

Julian knelt down and ran his fingers along the white cross, feeling the grooves of the letters carved into the stone. It was definitely real.

"Why's he all the way out here?" Flora asked. "Most cops get buried in Wo Hop Shek at the police cemetery."

"He was killed for betraying the police force," Shih-yin said. "Or at least that's the official story. And his family has owned this plot of land for more than a century."

"What do we do now?" Julian asked. "Burn ghost money?"

"No," the monk replied. He thrust the shovel into the dirt and let go of the handle. "You came all this way. It would be rude if you didn't say hello."

"You want me to dig him up?"

"That's right," Shih-yin said. "Your father has a present for us."

"You know," Flora interjected, "it's bad luck to dig up the dead."

"Then that's a risk we'll have to take."

Julian picked up the heavy shovel, sagging in his already tired arms. He struggled just to dig its head into the dirt, and after only four heaves he was already out of breath. Eventually, however, he was able to remove a fair amount, and when he got tired, both Shih-yin and Flora took turns as well. The more Julian dug, the more surreal the moment became. His whole life his father had been a phantom hanging over his shoulders. The mystery had always unnerved him but, in a way, it also kept his existence bearable. It was all he had, really. It was all that separated him from the other boys at school or the other drones at his office. Even when his life was at its most monotonous, Julian could stop and remind himself that there was some greater truth out there—a call to adventure just waiting to be heeded—and that he, just like Raymond Lau and his father, could step out of the shadows to right the wrongs of the world. To eliminate its rot. That was what a hero did, after all, and Julian never doubted that he had the blood of a protagonist.

But with each heave he came a little closer to the truth. He stripped away the dirt, and sooner much rather than later he'd come face-to-face with what his father really was. The mystery—the *dream*—would only last until he realized he was sleeping. Until his suspension of disbelief could no longer be maintained. And then it would lose all of its meaning, like the words on the page the day he stood at his mother's grave. Only now he wasn't putting the past to rest. He was drenched in sweat, struggling to his last breath to unearth it.

After a few hours, Julian hit pay dirt: a cherry wood coffin, which was damaged and partly decomposed. He brushed off the soil and pulled the casket open. The nails holding the lid shut had already been removed. Instinctively, Flora and Shih-yin pinched their noses at the fetid stench, but Julian breathed it all in. Even savored it.

Finally, he stood opposite his father: a corpse in a silken robe, with spirals of incense on all sides of his body. His flesh had mostly burned away, but his eyes were still discernable: two peaceful slits blackened by the passage of time. "Old man," Julian muttered. "I came back for you."

There was only silence. He reached out to touch his father's bony knuckles, which felt like those of the dummy skeleton from his A-Level Biology class. As he put his hand upon the corpse's cold fingers, he realized that they were clutching something: a VHS tape with the word INSURANCE written on its side. "After all this time," Julian said, "is that all you have to say to me?" He picked up the VHS and looked at it quizzically.

"Did you find it?" Shih-yin called down.

Julian looked back up at the monk. "We did all this for a videotape?"

"Believe me," Shih-yin said. "People have done worse."

After escaping from the shipyard, Inspectors Leung and Wong flagged down a cab and plotted a course to Tai O Village, on the western side of Lantau Island. It was a long journey, and the driver, an older man with cropped grey hair as sharp as a porcupine's razors, was busy puffing on a cigarette as the cab twisted and turned through the winding roads. The smell of nicotine tickled Leung's nostrils.

"Can I get one of those?" he asked.

The driver produced a carton of Lucky Strikes, from which Leung removed a slender cigarette. Then, in the middle of a winding turn, the driver dropped the box and lit a gleaming Zippo seemingly without taking his eyes off the road. Leung leaned forward, igniting the tobacco, which quickly turned from brown to red to black.

"What are we doing out here?" Wong asked.

"We're going to find Smithfield."

"You really think he's hiding in Tai O?"

"I'm not sure," Leung said, taking another long drag and blowing the exhaust out of the half-open window. "Call it a hunch."

The sun was finally setting; rays of orange light shone across the tree-lined mountains. Inspector Wong pressed his face against the window, staring out at the lush foliage below. "It's beautiful," he said. "Isn't it?"

"I have to admit," Leung replied, "it is quite a view."

Wong spotted a herd of water buffalo marching down the side of the road. They had black fur and curved white horns on both sides of their heads. The driver honked and swerved around them.

"It doesn't even feel like Hong Kong anymore," Wong said. "Without all the skyscrapers and office buildings, it's like another world."

"And yet, without this island and all of the New Territories, this city couldn't exist in the first place. They provide ninety percent of our water and electricity and pretty much all of our arable land. That's why the British are negotiating. They own Hong Kong Island and Kowloon forever, but the lease on the New Territories comes due in 1997."

"What, China's trying to increase the rent or something?"

"No, they want the whole city back."

"Really?" Wong said. "I don't pay much attention to politics."

"I don't trust them," the driver brusquely interjected. "I remember the riots back in '67. The whole city almost fell apart."

"The height of the Cultural Revolution," Leung said.

Wong shrugged. "I was eight years old."

The driver removed the dangling cigarette from his mouth, staring into the distance rather than the road ahead. "Who's to say it won't all happen again?"

He jammed on the brakes and the cab screeched to a halt in the middle of a dirt road, in front of a fraying wooden gate into the village. There were no other cars for miles. The driver looked at the fare ticker, which read five hundred and two dollars.

"Just call it five hundred," he said. "If it wasn't you boys in blue, we'd all be speaking Mandarin."

"Call it zero," Leung replied as he and Wong stepped out of the car.

"*Zero?*" the driver gasped.

Even if they'd wanted to pay, the inspectors hadn't a dime in their pockets. "I'm sorry," Leung said. "Police business."

The driver put the cigarette back into his mouth. "*Diu lei lomo,*" he muttered as he shifted the car into gear.

"I feel bad for the guy," Wong said. "He drove us all the way out here."

"If I'm right, it was for a worthy cause."

"*If* you're right."

They passed under the gate into the sleepy village, which looked the same as it had for the past hundred years. It was dilapidated but serene, with shanty houses built on stilts above the mud. Tanned men in rags sat on the edge of the dirt, reeling in their daily catch at a rapid pace. Their buckets were filled with flopping carp and gobies, splashing water onto the inspectors as they passed. The sea was bubbling with activity; two pink dolphins breached the surface of the water, squeaking shrilly before they flopped back headfirst into the sea.

"What the hell was that?" Wong asked.

"Pink dolphins," Leung replied matter-of-factly. "They're native to Lantau."

"And these stilt houses. I've never seen anything like this before."

"It's a village for outcasts," Leung said. "The first stop out of the mainland. It used to be a haven for smugglers and pirates, but these days it's mostly refugees. Tanka fishermen, Hakka and Hokkien outlaws, Cantonese who escaped from the Civil War."

"And you think Smithfield is here?"

"I can't be sure," Leung said. "But he said his father owned one of these houses."

As they walked further into the village, the two inspectors soon approached a long row of stilt houses at the end of the pier. A boy played dice with his younger sister on the boardwalk in front of them. Both were dressed in rags with withered and unkempt hair and were laughing wildly.

"Only one way to find out," Wong said. He tapped the sitting boy on his shoulder. "*Gweilo?*" he asked simply. "*Gou gweilo hai bindou?*"

The boy considered them carefully. "*Lei hai kui gek peng you?*" he asked.

"*Zhou hai,*" Wong said. "*Koi hor leng neng ye wo seong san.*"

The boy tilted his head back and forth, as if inspecting their faces. "Ok," he said finally. "*Lei tai lou mmtsi wai yan.*" He stood up and led the two inspectors down to the house at the very end of the row, which was painted red and had a curved thatched roof. The front door was hidden behind a large metal gate with a lion's head for a doorknocker. Next to the rest of the shanty houses, the place looked like a veritable mansion. Wong shook the gate to see if it was already open.

"*Hau,*" the boy said.

Inspector Leung banged the door twice with the metal lion, each time making a loud clang like a gong. As the last reverberations faded, the front door creaked open, and a gaunt-faced man with a bushy mustache peered out from behind the gate, wearing a white bathrobe. His green eyes were bloodshot, with stark red blood vessels that snaked like rivers on a map.

"W-what the hell are you two doing here?" Smithfield slurred, his breath smelling like pure turpentine.

"Smithfield," Leung said. "May we come in?"

***

Inspector Smithfield led his two partners into the dimly lit house, whose grim interior belied its intricate construction. Dirty clothes were strewn about alongside empty ramen containers and a mess of unmarked VHS tapes. The living room was just a red couch facing a large-screen Toshiba television, on which played a *wuxia* film masquerading as an old historical epic. Three bearded figures stood in the midst of a sorghum field, fighting off a host of Japanese invaders using only their hands and fists.

Smithfield plopped back down on the couch and lifted a bottle of *baijiu* off of the coffee table. He spread his legs wide, revealing the yellow-stained briefs hidden beneath his bathrobe. "How rude of me," he said. "I haven't offered you a drink." He retrieved two dirty shot glasses from the edge of the table and filled each one to the brim, emptying the rest of the bottle. "Come on," he said. "Take a seat."

Wong sat down but pushed the shot glass away. "I'll pass," he said. "If I drink that stuff, I'll puke."

Leung looked out the window, eyeing the boy playing with his sister. Clouds began to gather behind them like a gray fog, obscuring the skyline in the distance.

Smithfield hiccupped. "What about you, Leung? Don't make me drink alone."

Leung shut the drapes and sat down on the couch beside him. "*Gambei*," he said, lifting the shot glass and immediately draining it in one gulp.

"How's that?" Smithfield asked. "That strong enough for you?"

As he opened his mouth again, Inspector Leung felt like a dragon. The *baijiu* burned so fiercely that he wondered if Smithfield had perhaps fed him pure magma. He coughed violently as the room around him began to fade at the edges like a Gaussian blur. "You actually like this stuff?" he gasped, wiping his mouth with his sleeve.

"I don't like it," Smithfield said. "But right now, I need it."

"What's going on?" Wong asked. "What the hell are you doing out here? We've been looking for you for more than a week, and we're not the only ones."

"That makes sense," Smithfield replied. "When you cross the people I have, they tend to go after you. And they usually don't leave you alive."

"Who are you talking about?" Leung asked.

Smithfield looked down at the remaining shot glass on the table. "*Gambei*," he said with remarkable clarity. He lifted the glass into the air and downed it all at once, savoring the burn of fermented sorghum. "It's easier to list the people I *haven't* crossed at this point. Where do I even start?"

"At the beginning," Leung said. "Where else?"

Smithfield leaned down on the table, resting his chin in his hands. "When I first joined the Criminal Investigations Department," he said, "it wasn't really my choice. It was my only option. I used to work in the Financial Crimes Unit, but I was nearly fired for . . . let's just say *mishandling* evidence. My wife likes her gifts, and on an inspector's salary, hawking that stuff was the only way I could afford them. God knows my father didn't leave me anything. Besides this house, at least."

"You worked with the FCU?" Leung asked.

"As an undercover," Smithfield said. "But after I got caught, Commissioner Dayne offered me a deal. My grandfather and his were old friends, you see.

The two of them served together in the Navy and later went into business together. A very profitable endeavor, as I'm sure you can tell. But everything comes with a cost."

"What cost?" Wong asked.

"Loyalty. Commissioner Dayne demands my absolute obedience."

"You're a mole," Leung said. "Dayne's spy in CID."

"That's right," Smithfield admitted. "I have been for the last twelve years."

"You were selling us out the whole time."

Smithfield nodded. "Usually, that just meant passing him information. Most of the dirty work he saved for the Triad Bureau. But after Eddie Yang's death, I stumbled upon something at the studio. A key piece of evidence."

"What evidence?" Wong asked.

"It's easier for me to show you," Smithfield said, reaching underneath the couch and pulling out a blue Adidas shoebox. He lifted the lid, revealing an VHS tape with a single word written on its side: IN-SURANCE.

"Colm O'Callaghan gave me this for safekeeping," he said. "He told me to deliver it straight to the commissioner."

Leung took the tape from the box. "What is it?" he asked.

"Evidence," Smithfield replied. "I told you."

"Yes," Leung said as a shadow passed behind the red drapes, "but evidence of *what?*"

"You'll see," Smithfield said, taking the tape from his partner and inserting it into the VHS player built into the television set. The screen turned blue for a moment as the Jianghu Studios logo flashed upon the screen: two masked warriors crossing halberds.

"Is this a movie?" Wong asked.

"In a sense," Smithfield replied. "It's the raw footage from Jianghu Studios." Raymond Lau appeared onscreen dressed in an orange monk's robe as a makeup artist applied the final touches to his face. The crew cleared out, and two men in demonic masks stood across from the star actor. Charlie Yip called action, and the second assistant snapped the clapperboard. All three men dropped into their battle stances.

"*Wong Fei-Hung!*" one of the demons shouted, charging at Raymond Lau with his fists drawn.

"Ooh!" Wong exclaimed, clapping his hands together. "This is gonna be good."

There was no editing, no music . . . no effects of any sort. The punches were so quiet that they didn't seem real—because they weren't. Smithfield dug the remote from beneath the cushions and pressed fast-forward, causing the action to zip by at a rapid speed.

"Hey, I was watching that!" Wong protested.

"Wait," Smithfield said. "The good stuff starts about five minutes in."

The action was going so fast it looked like a battle between three gnats. After an intense burst of artful dodging and wire-fu, Raymond Lau defeated the demons with two powerful kicks. "Now," Smithfield said, pressing a button which caused the action to slow back to real time. Grinning with self-satisfaction, the star actor stood over one of the demons and removed its mask, revealing the face of Eddie Yang. Lau stepped back in sheer horror, as if recognizing his own reflection, while a wealthy family dressed in cheongsams and magisterial robes entered the frame behind him. The women emitted a din of shrieks as Eddie Yang rose from the dead and started throwing punches for real.

It wasn't much of a fight. Raymond Lau was unable to block even a single blow, and his counterpunches looked like a baby swatting at the mobile above his crib. Eventually, Lau simply curled into a ball and accepted the abuse. But Eddie wouldn't let him lie there and take it; he lifted Lau's body like a baggage handler at the airport and threw him headfirst through the triptych screen in the center of the room, punching a large hole in the fabric. Then, saying nothing, he sat at the foot of the spiral staircase and calmly pulled a cigarette from his pocket.

The other actors and crewmembers rushed over to help their star and carry him off set, but Eddie Yang just sat there smoking with a grin on his face.

"That was brutal," Leung said.

Wong crossed his arms. "Pathetic."

"Hold on," Smithfield said. "It's just starting to get interesting."

A group of suited men entered the frame. At their lead stood a bald man with a birthmark in the shape of South America just beneath what used to be his hairline, and arriving just behind him was a short man with vertically spiked hair, wearing a Hawaiian shirt with printed pineapples.

"That's Colm O'Callaghan," Wong said. "The chief of security."

"And do you know who that is right there?" Smithfield asked.

"Woo," Leung growled. "That fucking rat."

At once, the suited men and Woo trained their guns on Eddie, who looked up at them in disbelief. The cigarette fell from his mouth, but before he could say anything Woo opened fire, sending a bullet straight through his head. Blood sprayed out onto the spiral staircase, and Eddie Yang's body slumped dead upon the steps, his body contorted just the way it was when the two inspectors found him. The tape faded to noise and Smithfield turned it off, returning to the *wuxia* film on TVB. The two heroes stood over a mountain of corpses, huffing in and out in exhaustion.

"I don't understand," Leung said. "Why wouldn't they destroy this? It incriminates everyone. Woo, O'Callaghan . . ."

"It's not a good look for Raymond either," Smithfield said. "Which means that whoever got their hands on it would have the Triad Bureau, the studio, and Raymond Lau all under their thumb."

"It's the ultimate insurance policy," Leung said.

Smithfield nodded. "And right now, it's more valuable than ever—especially to the commissioner. But I couldn't just take it back to him. I know what he's planning to do, and I can't go along with it. It would be the end of us all."

Another shadow passed behind the drapes and several loud footsteps could be heard creaking on the boardwalk. Leung lifted his head to see what the source of the commotion was, but, as he did so, several loud bangs flashed upon the screen: the three bearded heroes were felled by machine gun fire as the villagers looked on, screaming. An army of Japanese invaders entered the frame, razing the sorghum fields to ashes and killing anyone they could get their hands on.

"I get it," Leung said finally. "He's planning a hostile takeover of the triads. He's trying to line his own pocketbook, just like every other criminal in this city."

"You're getting closer to the truth," Smithfield said, "but that's still not it."

"There is no *closer* to the truth," Leung insisted. "Either it's wrong or it's right: there is no in-between."

"Tell us," Wong said. "What is he planning to do?"

Smithfield sighed. "For starters, he doesn't need to take over the triads. The Lucky Stone is already his. It has been for almost eighty years."

Leung's eyebrow rose. "What are you talking about?"

"My grandfather and his. What business do you think they were involved in? You know what they say: when a white horse is not a horse . . ."

"It's opium," Leung said as the smell of gasoline tickled his nostrils. "I knew something didn't smell right." This time, unmistakably, he saw a dark silhouette just behind the drapes. "What is that?"

Wong too picked up on the odorous scent. "Smithfield, did you leave the oven on?"

"I don't cook," Smithfield replied as he stood up and opened the drapes. Standing just outside the window were three suited men holding submachine guns. Colm O'Callaghan stood at the vanguard with a Lucky Strike dangling from his lips.

"Shit!" Leung yelled. "They followed us!"

O'Callaghan smiled, then flicked the cigarette toward the stilt house. As the flames ignited, the suited men opened fire, riddling the burning building with bullets. Feathers sprang up from the dusty couch, which Leung and Wong ducked behind for cover. A bullet flew straight past their heads, depositing itself in the center of the TV and shattering its glass, even as the massacre continued on screen. Inspector Leung removed the golden Beretta from his waistband and returned fire, hitting two of the guards square in the chest. He stood up and approached the window, firing two more bullets to keep

O'Callaghan pinned down, but there was no sign of the burly chief of security.

"The tape!" Leung squawked, peering through the flames.

"Right," Wong replied, darting out from behind the couch and pressing the eject button on the VCR. "I got it!"

The stilt house began to sway as the blaze compromised its already fragile structure. Chunks of burning wood fell from the ceiling and Leung dove to the ground, dodging them by mere inches. "We have to get out of here," he said flatly. "Now."

"I'm afraid I'm not going anywhere," Smithfield replied, lying beside the windowsill, his legs crushed by the debris. He raised his hand from his chest, revealing a bullet hole in the center of his stomach. Blood was soaking through the fabric of his bathrobe: a red dot growing in the center of a white expanse, like a setting sun.

"Smithfield!" Wong cried out. "You're hit!"

"I'm afraid so," he said. "But it's not too late for you two. Go out through the back window. There's a boat down there tied to docks. You can still make it in time if you hurry."

"We're not going to leave you behind," Leung said.

The fire was drawing closer; plumes of black smoke filled the room, shrouding the inspectors in a toxic haze.

"You don't have a choice," Smithfield said. "You can't save me this time, Leung."

Gritting his teeth, Leung stood up and fired the rest of his clip out the window at random. "*Diu lei ham ga caan!*" he exclaimed like a demon amidst the flames. "I swear to god, I'll kill you all!"

"W-wong," Smithfield choked out, his skin growing ever paler. Wong leaned in close to his fallen partner, who whispered something in his ear. As the last syllable exited his mouth, Smithfield slumped over, and his eyes rolled back. Dead.

Inspector Wong stood back up and reached under the bullet-riddled couch, removing a thick black tome with the words ROMANCE OF THE THREE KINGDOMS etched in gold on its spine.

"He's gone," Leung said, stepping away from the windowsill as the fire closed in. His face was drenched with sweat and tears and he was quickly losing consciousness from the smoke. "I can't find O'Callaghan."

"Let's get out of here!" Wong exclaimed, shrouding both the tape and book under his tattered clothes. "Otherwise, it'll be all three of us!"

"What is that?" Leung asked. "What are you carrying?"

"I'm not sure," Wong replied. "He told me to give it to his son."

Leung looked back at Smithfield's corpse. "His son . . ."

Wong grabbed his partner by the wrist. "There's no time!"

"You're right," Leung said. His engines ignited by his partner's words, he took Wong's hand and sprinted for the window at the other end of the room. Leading with their shoulders, the two inspectors jumped through a wall of flames and broke through the cracked glass, descending two stories onto the dock below as the stilt house was swallowed by the raging inferno.

They couldn't look back.

2014 / Chapter 8: Black Rain Signal

The sun was setting as Julian stepped back into the village, cradling the VHS in his arms. Orange light shimmered through the gathering clouds, stretching across the lush mountains in the distance. There were still plenty of tourists on the dirt roads, but most of the shops were beginning to close. Shirtless workers scooped up bottles of XO-Sauce and wrapped up the dried fish with newspaper to put into storage. Flies buzzed endlessly around the salt-cured egg yolks, which looked like a hundred little suns.

"It's going to rain," Flora said, approaching Julian from behind.

"There's no rain in the forecast," Shih-yin said tersely. "I checked the weather." The old monk's head darted back and forth like a squirrel's, reacting to even the slightest movement in his periphery.

"Just look at the sky," Flora said. "And the wind is blowing already."

Shih-yin crossed his arms. "It's not that storm I'm worried about."

As they stepped across the bridge, Julian stared into the greenish water. The calm river belied the cacophonous village it passed through; not even a bubble rippled out. He looked across at the stilt houses, which, in the crepuscular glow, looked like a photograph in sepia. One stood out from the rest, colored red with a curved thatched roof.

Julian stopped and gazed at it in silence. "That house," he said. "That's where I used to live, isn't it?"

"That's impossible," Flora replied.

"Why is that impossible?"

"Because all those houses burned down thirty years ago. Those are just 'restorations' for tourists to gape at. Convincing fakes."

Another gush of acid shot up Julian's throat. He clutched his stomach and keeled over, putting his head between his knees and his hand in front of his mouth, but the vomit squirted through the cracks in his fingers.

Flora inched away from him. "Are you okay?"

"*Nghhh . . .*"

"Hey monk!" Flora called out. "Monk!"

Shih-yin said nothing, staring at the fleet of black Mercedes Benzes that had amassed at the village entrance, next to where bus number eleven was parked. A group of men in black suits and sunglasses stepped out of the cars, drawing the attention of the villagers and tourists by the gate. At the vanguard was a bald, aging man with a birthmark on his forehead in the shape of South America. He removed a golden Beretta from his shoulder holster and directed his men to spread out and search.

"It's him," Shih-yin muttered to himself.

"Hey asshole!" Flora exclaimed, grabbing the old monk by his robe. "Julian needs a doctor ASAP! Let's get him back to Tung Wah."

"We're not going to Hong Kong Island," Shih-yin said.

"You're right, Kwong Wah is way closer. Good thinking!"

"You don't understand," Shih-yin replied. The old monk rushed over to Julian, who by now was vomiting profusely into the still water off the pier, and seized him by the collar. "They're here!" he snapped, pulling Julian by the hand. Chunks of undigested food trailed off Julian's chin as he stumbled along.

"Hey!" Flora shrieked. "What the hell are you doing?"

Julian and Shih-yin sprinted at full speed toward the village entrance, staying off the main road and jumping through branches and thicket to remain unseen. The thorns and needles cut at Julian's damp suit, and mosquitos and worse feasted off his exposed ankles, but he was too dazed to even respond. It took all of his focus just to keep from bursting again.

They reached a clearing of trees just beside the parking lot, ducking behind a large Banyan tree and peering out. Alongside the black sedans, Julian spotted five or six white coach buses ferrying tourists away from the village. A single blue and white cab sat alone beside them, almost turquoise in the twilight glow.

"I think we lost them," Shih-yin said.

A shadow burst through the thicket behind them. With a tenacious scowl on her face, Flora doubled over, dropping her Pikachu backpack to the ground. "W-why," she huffed, nursing a stitch in the side of her stomach. "Why are we running?"

"We need to get out of here," Shih-yin replied. "Hong Kong isn't safe for us anymore. That tape is practically a target on our backs."

"So shove it back in the ground!" Flora gasped. "The man is sick!"

Julian took two deep breaths to center himself, still clutching his hand tight as if the etched stone was nestled in his palm. He opened his eyes.

"I'm fine," he insisted. "I think it's the pills. I haven't had one in three days, so my body's in withdrawal."

The suited men emerged through the village gate, brandishing their weapons. They walked across the parking lot straight in the direction of the forest clearing. As they rapidly approached the Banyan tree, Julian reached out and squeezed Flora's hand.

She squeezed back. "It's alright," she said. "You're going to be fine."

This is it, Julian thought. *This is the end.* He closed his eyes and thought of Celeste, picturing himself under the fig tree, the dewdrops falling onto his shoulder as she looked down at him from above. The pangs of terror and withdrawal continued, but as long as his eyes stayed focused on her, the dizziness and twisting pain were bearable, even if they didn't go away. He opened his eyes again and saw that the guards were only ten paces from the tree. His chest vibrated with tension, and he nestled closer against the mop-like trunk. *I'm the hero*, he told himself as if struck by some divine providence. A crack of light burst in through the clouds and orange rays shattered across the rugged countryside. As the light hit Julian's eyes, the vibrations stopped, and the tension disintegrated like crumbs in the dish drain. In fact, he felt the urge to laugh, but checked himself at the last moment. "They won't find us," he said.

Shih-yin glared in his direction. "They will if you keep talking."

"No," Julian replied. "That's not how this story ends."

Sure enough, the guards turned off and ascended the steps of the coach bus nearest to the tree. "Now's our chance," the monk said. He grabbed Julian by the hand and sprinted into the parking lot, making a beeline for the lone taxi.

"Hey!" Flora yelled. Still out of breath, she stumbled out from behind the tree and went after them. "Not fair!"

Shih-yin opened the back door of the cab and shoved Julian inside. Then, with Flora only a few steps away, he ducked into the car and slammed the door shut.

"*Chek Lap Kok!*" Shih-yin barked to the driver. "Airport!"

As the driver shifted the car into gear, Flora reached for the door handle and pulled with all her might. What she lacked in speed she made up for in power. Shih-yin struggled to restrain her, barely holding the door closed with all his strength.

"Hey!" Flora yelled, pulling as hard as she could. "Julian! Wait!"

"Drive!" Shih-yin commanded, unable to constrain her any longer. The driver stepped on the pedal, and the blue-and-white cab sped off down the road, sending Flora tumbling to the ground. Soon, she looked like a black speck in the distance.

"You didn't have to do that," Julian said, staring out the back window. "She was trying to help . . ."

"I know she was," the monk replied. "That's the problem."

***

Within the hour, Shih-yin and Julian had reached the end of line at the Cathay Pacific ticket counter inside Chep Lap Kok Airport, on the north side of Lantau Island. The terminal was especially crowded for a Tuesday night. Moonlight crept in through the triangular windows that lined the high ceiling. A dense fog was gathering outside.

"It looks like a typhoon out there," Julian said.

"It's Hong Kong," Shih-yin replied. "The skies are moody. But it'll pass soon enough. The clouds are never sad for long."

235

Julian was unconvinced. He looked at the departures board and saw that nearly every flight had been delayed, most for several hours. Even the morning flights still hadn't gotten out.

"We can't go back now," he said. "It can't just end like this."

"We have to," Shih-yin replied. "If he finds out we have this tape, Raymond Lau will kill us to get it back."

"What's on this thing?"

"Proof."

"But proof of what?"

"That Raymond Lau is as fake as ghost money."

"All actors are fakes," Julian said. "That's the point of acting."

"But most aren't involved with the triads."

"What about Bruce Lee? I heard stories about him."

"Bruce Lee didn't kill your father. Raymond Lau and his organization did. And if they killed him over that tape, what do you think they'll do to you?"

Again, acid ran up his esophagus. Whatever divine inspiration he'd felt behind the Banyan tree had been sapped already. *I'm th-the hero*, he told himself again; even his internal monologue was quaking with tension. *Unless I'm not.* He gulped, swallowing the vomit, which felt like an effusion of lava trailing down his digestive tract. "I think I'm gonna be sick," he said.

"Well, don't throw up here," the monk said. "If you do, you'll never get past the medical inspectors. And that will be the end of us right there."

Julian looked around for any sign of a restroom, eventually spotting one at the other side of the terminal. "There," he said. "I'll be back soon."

"Hurry," Shih-yin replied. "The next flight to London leaves in an hour, and we need to get through security!"

As he stumbled away, Julian looked again at the departures board, which now listed several canceled flights in addition to those delayed. "As if that will happen . . ."

In front of the restroom, a tall woman in a bright pink shirt and fake glasses was holding a clipboard, collecting signatures. "Dolphins!" she hollered. "Save the pink dolphins!"

Julian averted his gaze and made his way straight into the first open stall in the bathroom. He vomited out the remaining contents of his stomach, which didn't amount to much. But there was no relief—if anything, the knot in his stomach seemed to wind up tighter. Even if his stomach was empty, there was still more he needed to expel.

Julian looked down again at the VHS, which he had dropped onto the piss-stained floor beside the pubic hairs and half-burned cigarette butts that formed concentric rings around the toilet. *Maybe I should just throw the tape into the bowl and be done with it,* he thought. He picked it up and held it over the bowl, intoxicated by the proposition. Like the monks of old, he could drop a sacrifice into the fire, and his problems would burn away. The smell of piss was his incense, and the man in the next stall was groaning "*Ommm!*"

But Julian couldn't let go. When he tried to unclasp his fingers, he thought back to the graveyard—not to his father's body, but to the bucket of bills that Flora burned for her grandfather. He had failed to save both of his parents—was unable to even muster up the courage to say a few words at his mother's funeral—but he couldn't just give in to fear and abandon them the way that they'd abandoned him. *I'm his son*, Julian thought to himself. *It's my job to take care of him.*

He stood up, clutching the tape even tighter than before. His death grip wouldn't let go even if they riddled him with bullets. This was one debt that he could never forgive.

He exited the stall and bathroom, passing by the tall woman with her clipboard in hand. "Excuse me," she said, "do you have a moment for the pink dolphins?"

"I'm sorry," Julian replied. "I need to catch a flight."

"Oh, don't worry," she said. "No one's leaving here tonight. They put up the Black Rain Signal already." She smiled, disarming Julian with her warm gaze. Her shoulder-length black hair smelled vaguely of figs and pomegranate, like Celeste's.

"I'm sorry," Julian said. "How can I help?"

The woman went into her rehearsed spiel: "We're fighting the construction of a third runway at this airport. The pink dolphin is already an endangered species and creating a new landfill will only threaten it more. Reclaiming land means stealing it from the sea, and we've taken so much of the dolphins' habitat already."

"That makes sense," Julian said. "I never thought of it that way."

"Most people don't. That's how it always is in this city. It's always about money above all else. No one thinks about the dolphins . . ."

The dolphins, Julian thought. He wondered if there was something he was forgetting. Something more important than Raymond Lau, the triads, or even his father's death. He looked back at the old monk, who by now had reached the Cathay Pacific counter and was purchasing the tickets back to London. Shih-yin looked toward the bathroom and caught Julian's eyes, which shot wide open.

Of course, Julian realized. *Celeste.* He couldn't just let her toil away in that brothel forever. His parents were long gone, but she was still alive and still in trouble. His own debts could wait until hers were settled.

Shih-yin's eyebrow rose slightly. He gathered the tickets from the counter and rushed out of line toward the escalators. Without a word, Julian sprinted away from the dolphin lady to get a head start on the old monk.

"Hey!" she called out. "I need your signature!"

But Julian was already gone. He stutter stepped down the escalator, juking past the tourists hanging lazily onto the railing. Then, at the bottom, he jumped over a turnstile and ran through the glass doors of the Airport Express train just before they closed. Shih-yin slid down the railing after him, but when he reached the bottom, his orange robe got caught in the escalator and he fell face-first into the ground. "Julian!" he screamed from afar, trying in vain to escape the machine's clutches.

By the time he freed himself, ripping a chunk out of the thin fabric, it was too late. The train had started moving already. For better or worse, Julian was going back.

***

As the Airport Express train rumbled past Tsing Yi and Kowloon Station on the way to Central, Julian rubbed his temples, making little circles with his forefingers. His head throbbed violently, and he was so tired he felt like he was melting into the plush seat. He wanted nothing more than a warm bed and a Xanax, but there was no drifting off now. The businessman sitting in the next row peered up from the real estate section of his newspaper and glared at Julian, who was huffing the sterile air in and out like a cow chewing cud. The man typed a quick message into his phone as the train pulled into Central

Station, then made his way to the other end of the car to retrieve his luggage. Eyeing the man, Julian sprung up and sprinted through the glass double doors on the other side of the car. Shrouded by a crowd of travelers rolling their luggage into the station, he again jumped the turnstile and made his way up the escalator.

He didn't have a plan. He didn't know how to get back to the guest house or how he would deal with King Chow if and when it came to that. The fat pimp had sent a clear message: Celeste belonged to him. But Julian couldn't just abandon her. As strong as she was, she needed his help.

When he reached the next floor, he spied a large subway map on the red ceramic walls. He looked for the words "Tsim Sha Tsui," and, sure enough, found them along the Red Line to Kowloon, only two stops away. With the tape in hand, Julian sidestepped through the crowd, but the platform was cordoned off by several men in black suits and sunglasses: the same men that had come after him in Tai O.

Julian covered his face and made his way toward the exit; if the trains were a lost cause, he could take the tram to Wan Chai and catch the Star Ferry back across the harbor. And if the police or the triads were stationed at the boat, then he would jump in Victoria Harbor and swim across instead. After all, he desperately needed a bath.

Julian ascended the long escalator rising out of the station to Statue Square. As he ran up the moving steps, stiff-arming his way past a group of statuesque protestors, he heard a cacophony of voices that rumbled deeper and deeper the higher he went, like a fault line had cracked.

At the top of the steps, in shadow of the triangular-paned Bank of China Tower and the HSBC Headquarters, thousands of protesters were jam-packed together, chanting slogans for democracy. They looked like the same marchers from before, but in the darkness their colorful signs and outfits were obscured by an oppressive gloom. There were dozens of riot policemen stationed in front of the bank buildings, holding up plastic shields and nightsticks to keep the marchers at bay. Young students stood atop the statue of Sir Thomas Jackson, the older merchant from Julian's dream, shouting, "*Wan ngo zi yau wan xi pun ngo sei yang!*" They waved a British flag high above their heads.

Julian couldn't help but find the whole scene ironic. As much as he sympathized with those around him, he couldn't stand to see the Union Jack waved high again in this part of the world. It was the flag of *colonists*. The flag of Julian's ancestors—the same people who had locked this city into a cage of oppression. Just because they'd handed over the key to the prison didn't absolve them of enslaving these people in the first place. Hong Kong was a part of China now. There was no disputing that. It was *Chinese*. One only needed to look around to see the obvious. But it was also something more. Battered by forces from without for the past two centuries, its denizens had coalesced into a self-conscious community. A people. A white horse is still a horse, except when it's not. And it wasn't Julian's place to tell them what they did or didn't want.

He tried to work his way through the crowd, but there were so many people that the only way through was to push others aside. When even the tiniest space opened up, another flood of protestors instantly rushed in to fill it like a runny egg in an omelet pan, pushing their way closer toward the government buildings and banks. Most of the marchers held up their smartphones, snapping pictures and taking videos of raucous crowds. Meanwhile, Julian had only a VHS in his hands.

The crowd began to sway forward, and Julian felt a rush of marchers pushing at his back in the direction of the riot policemen. Whether they were trying to storm the building or just get a better photograph, all of the protestors pressed forward and several cylindrical cannisters rained in from above. "*Ceoi loi dan!*" one marcher screamed as the grenades went off, leaking tear gas into the crowd. Protestors opened up their umbrellas to shield themselves from the noxious fumes. Julian's own eyes began to water heavily, and as he tried to run away, another canister landed at his feet. Luckily, a young student in glasses saw the tear gas steaming from the grenade and held his Doraemon umbrella in front of Julian's face, shielding him from the haze.

"*Mmgoi,*" Julian choked out, barely able to breathe. The young man simply nodded and continued shouting his slogans at the police, who entered the crowd and started throwing people to the ground. The marchers began to scatter, and Julian sprinted alongside them down Hennessy Road.

The scene was like a war zone. Policemen chased after protestors, who threw stones and bottles in response. Catching up to the marchers, the cops beat them furiously with their nightsticks and slapped on pairs of plastic handcuffs to keep them docile. Then the cops continued their pursuit, beating and clubbing whoever else they could catch up to, even those already on the ground.

A hole opened in the foggy sky, and rain started dripping out like the first tears of a nervous breakdown. Julian ducked under one of the fleeing protestors' umbrellas and hid the tape inside his suit jacket, protecting it from the coming storm. Cracks of thunder echoed in the distance and the sky flashed several times in a row as if a circuit had just shorted out. Gusts of wind blew at the marchers' backs, pushing them east towards Wan Chai.

By the time Julian reached the bridge to Central Plaza, the downpour had grown so heavy that he had to hide beneath the underpass to keep himself dry. The rain was coming down in diagonal sheets at such a volume that the individual rain drops blended together into a massive wave. It almost looked like the whole city had fallen underwater, and everyone—good or bad—would be swept away in a hell storm of Biblical proportions. He was maybe a hundred meters from the White Horse office, but there was no way around it if he wanted to reach Kowloon. If he was going to the Star Ferry, he would have to pass directly by the tower, whatever the risk.

Two other protestors ducked beside Julian under the bridge—a student and his mother—both soaked to the brim and doubled over. Julian recognized the boy by the Doraemon umbrella in his hand. A riot policeman was hot on his trail, so the boy rushed down the steps into the Blue Line MTR entrance. The mother stayed behind and pleaded with the approaching officer: "*Koi tseng hai yik gou sai lou le tse ma!*"

"*Heng hoi!*" the cop yelled. He brushed past her and approached the top of the stairs. The woman jumped on his arm, and the policeman beat her savagely with his nightclub, knocking her onto her back. While she was down, he hit her twice more for good measure, then strapped a pair of plastic handcuffs on her wrists.

Julian felt the veins in his forehead pop, and his free hand instinctively clenched shut. Raising his fist, he approached the cop and reared his arm back to deliver a haymaker, but not before another hand caught it from behind. Julian turned around and stood face-to-face with Colm O'Callaghan.

"Mr. Kensington," O'Callaghan said. "Or should I say, Mr. Smithfield?"

"What's it to you?" Julian asked.

"You're a hard man to track down," he said. "The boss has been looking for you all day."

"Well, sorry to disappoint him. I've been busy."

"We know, Mr. Smithfield. Trust me, we know."

The policeman put his knee on the woman's back and pressed her face against the sidewalk. Tears and raindrops were streaming down both of her cheeks.

"A pity," O'Callaghan said. "All this violence . . . and for what? It'd be a shame if the same thing happened to you."

"Don't worry. I'll go peacefully."

"Good choice," O'Callaghan said. He took Julian by the elbow and led him up the stairs to the bridge. As they walked down the elevated pathway toward Central Plaza, they passed more riot cops and suited guards carrying assault rifles and wearing bulletproof vests. They looked like two columns of a military parade. But the grand lobby of Central Plaza was empty; it seemed that Julian and his escort had the whole building to themselves.

O'Callaghan pressed the up button, and one of the golden elevators rang open. "When you get upstairs," he said, pushing Julian into the lift, "you'll find him in the back office. He's expecting you."

"You're not coming with me?" Julian asked.

"No," O'Callaghan replied as the door closed behind him. "The boss wanted to speak with you alone."

1984 / Chapter 8: Burying the Lede

Inspector Leung sat alone in a booth at the Dou Jiang Diner, a small restaurant just inside the Kowloon Walled City. The place didn't look like much, but the austere furnishings and generally spartan ambiance were one of the few sources of comfort left for him in these ever-changing times. It was the type of place that couldn't be found on Hong Kong Island anymore; the city's increasingly gentrified neighborhoods and taste for Western brands had pushed restaurants like this into obscurity. But Kowloon was another story altogether. For years, the triads had used the fortified settlement as a base of operations, and it had been only five years since most of the gangs were forced out. The name Kowloon still sent shivers down most officers' spines; the younger constables were trained to simply avoid the neighborhood altogether, and memories of the last triad war were still fresh in many of the senior inspectors' minds.

Leung sipped on an overly sweet *si wa nai cha*—"silk stocking" milk tea, a local favorite. The taste was the same as always: scalding hot, smooth, but with a distinct bitterness that hung in your mouth long after taking a sip. As a young inspector, Leung would meet Ricky Cheung—then a triad informant—at this same restaurant for information on triad and Communist plots. Back in those days, the danger from both was real. Wars between the triads left hundreds dead and countless lives destroyed. Leftist riots incited by subversive agents from the mainland were myriad, and policemen were targeted regularly in assassinations and bombings. Now, though, with the triads and the police both after him, Leung longed for those simpler times. Back then, right and wrong were clear as day. The good guys had their uniforms and the bad guys had their tattoos and red armbands. But the year was 1984, not 1950 or 1967; things were far more complicated now. Men with tattoos were as likely to be artists as triads, and policemen were as likely to be corrupt as not.

Inspector Leung regretted coming alone, but there was no other option. Smithfield's family wasn't safe in Hong Kong, so he sent Inspector Wong to shepherd Victoria and young Julian to safety while he waited patiently for Ricky Cheung to arrive, just as he used to. Only now Ricky wasn't an informant but a respected journalist, having used his time in the underworld to develop a crack network of sources. In many ways, the two professions required the same skills—the best informants and journalists were great communicators, with gregarious personalities and a total inability to filter their thoughts. In other words: real blabbermouths. And Ricky Cheung was certainly that.

The front door swung open and a short, stocky man stepped inside the diner. He was balding, with a thin black comb-over and a scraggly, untamed beard. His eyes were so dark and weathered that it looked like he hadn't slept in thirty years, and between them was a thick, crooked nose—the result of multiple beatings, one or two from Inspector Leung himself. His face never won him much love from the girls, and yet it suited his needs perfectly—just the right balance of ugly to be at once goofy and threatening. If he said he was in the triads, anyone would believe him, but if he said he was a clown no one would even bat an eye.

"Ricky," Leung said. "You got fat."

"That's a nice way to say hello," Ricky replied as he sat down across from the inspector. "How long has it been?"

"Five years. Maybe six."

"There's not much crime these days."

"You'd be surprised."

Ricky raised a hand to the only waitress in the whole restaurant. "*Mmgoiii!*" he shouted. "*Yit yuenyeung!*"

"I have no idea how you drink that stuff," Leung said. "Half-coffee, half-tea . . . It's disgusting. Just pick one or the other."

"It's good for you. It promotes balance."

"Sounds like bullshit."

Ricky shrugged. "It works for me. How else could I have lived this long?"

"You do make some pretty questionable decisions with your health," Leung said. "Crossing the 14K, working with the police . . ."

"... associating with *you*," Ricky said, pulling out a carton of Lucky Strikes. "How's Gibson doing these days?"

"He died twelve years ago."

"That's a damn shame," Ricky said, putting a cigarette between his two plump lips. "What happened to him?"

"You led us into a trap, remember?"

"Huh," Ricky grunted. He took a rusty Zippo from his pocket and flicked it open. "Should've had more *yuenyeung*." He smirked and lit the cigarette, blowing a cloud of smoke in Leung's direction. The smell tickled the inspector's nostrils, filling them with an intoxicating mix of tar and nicotine. "So what do you have for me this time?" Ricky asked, breaking the silence. "The last story you gave me was a dud."

"What was wrong with it? Everything I said was true."

"No one cares about lead in milk powder. It didn't sell papers!"

"Well, I can assure you that this one will. It's the crime of the century."

Ricky crossed his arms. "I don't do crime stories anymore. I got moved to the entertainment beat three years ago. It's a steadier business."

"Even better," Leung said. "It's about Raymond Lau."

Ricky's left eyebrow shot upward. "I'm listening . . ."

***

After an hour-long conversation, Leung finished his deep-fried Hong Kong-style French Toast while Ricky Leung picked at the remains of his baked rice. The table was covered with dirty napkins, cigarette butts, and tomato sauce.

"If what you're telling me is true," Ricky said, "you're in way over your head. To think . . . all this over a videotape."

"It's the one thing that can damage their operation. Without Raymond Lau's films to launder their money with, where are they going to hide all that cash?"

"At HSBC, just like they used to."

"The banks aren't willing to take that risk anymore, not with this handover looming over everyone. They don't want to get shut down by the new government."

"This is Hong Kong," Ricky said. "The banks can do whatever the hell they want."

"Not for long."

"You're a real optimist," Ricky said. "But some things never change."

"Just look around: *Everything's* changed."

The stocky reporter leaned in, pointing his fork at Leung. "Listen, even if you could take Raymond Lau out of the picture, what difference would it make? If this whole operation is as big as you say it is, they'll just find another actor's films to hide their money behind. There's a new action star every day. Jackie

Chan, Sammo Hung, Yuen Biao . . . one of them will play ball."

"This isn't about the money," Leung said. "It's about *justice.*"

"So take it back to your commissioner. We don't hold trials in the press."

"I can't do that," Leung insisted. "I told you."

"I'm sorry," Ricky said. "But there's nothing I can do."

"Of course there is! You take this story to someone at your newspaper. I don't care if it's the entertainment section or the front page, but you get someone to write about it. If you're smart, it'll be you."

"Smart?" Ricky scoffed. He stabbed the lone grain of rice left on his plate, splitting it in half. "Do you know how dangerous it was just for me to come back to Kowloon? There are people on these streets that want to have me killed. And now you're trying to get me involved in a *triad conspiracy?*"

"This will sell a million papers."

"Maybe it will," Ricky said. "But I'm not going to take that risk."

"You little coward," Leung snarled. "You haven't changed a bit."

"Hey, I have a wife now!" Ricky protested. "I have a daughter!"

Leung reached across the table and grabbed the fat reporter by the collar, pulling him forward and staining his white shirt red. "Once a rat, always a rat," the inspector growled.

"Watch it," Ricky said, reaching for his waistband. "I'm warning you."

Leung drew Marshal Hong's golden Beretta and stuck it into the reporter's fat gut. "You're warning *me?*" he seethed, pulling the hammer back. One patron seemed perturbed by the sight of the gun, but most of the crowd didn't even look up from their newspapers. These types of outbursts were commonplace here.

"You don't know what you're dealing with, Leung! The Lucky Stone is only one leg of the operation. They just move the product."

"Then who else is there? The studio? The commissioner? I'm not scared of them."

"Not just the commissioner," Ricky said. "The Marshals of the Lucky Stone have always reported to the police superintendents. And who do you think they answer to?"

"The governor."

"That's right. The same man you work for. Every single one of you pigs: Gibson, Smithfield, Woo . . . you're all on the same team. Just tools of a faded empire."

"You think you're any better?"

"No, but at least I get paid for what I do. And I'm not about to give that up so you can take on the whole British Empire. These people will *kill* you, Leung. They don't care about you. Thirty years on the force and they'll still slit your throat if it helps them earn a buck. Hell, look what they did to Bruce Lee!"

"What are you talking about?"

Before Ricky could answer, the front door burst open, and a young uniformed police officer stormed inside, aiming his pistol at Inspector Leung. "Freeze!" the officer screamed. "Put down the weapon!"

Ricky smirked. "You'd better do what he says."

Thinking quickly, Leung put the fat reporter in a chokehold and pressed the golden Beretta to the side of his head. "Take one step closer and he dies!" Leung yelled, inching backwards towards the kitchen.

"What the hell do you think you're doing?" Ricky exclaimed, trying in vain to wrestle his way free.

"Release him!" the officer commanded.

"Step back outside if you want him to live!" The officer didn't move; Leung knew that the young man was trained to hold back when there was a hostage at risk. No field officer would want to be found responsible for a civilian casualty—the paperwork alone would inspire fear in any man.

"You don't have to do this!" the officer yelled. "Surrender peacefully!"

"I'm afraid it's too late for that," Leung said.

As he reached the kitchen door, a gruff voice boomed out from beyond the restaurant's entrance: "He's right, you know." The front door swung open, and Inspector Woo stood in the doorway with a cigarette in his mouth, puffing smoke from his nose like a bull. "At this point, I'm afraid we can't let you live."

"How'd you find me?" Leung growled.

Woo smirked. "Some of your friends have big mouths."

Leung clutched the reporter's collar tightly. "Ricky . . ."

The reporter's eyes bulged like a fly. "I swear to god, it wasn't me!"

Woo laughed, and the other policeman tepidly chuckled alongside him. The young officer didn't really understand the joke, but he was trained not to break rank.

"Officer," Woo said. "These two men are triad assassins, both armed and extremely dangerous. Kill them both *immediately*. I'll take full responsibility."

"*What?*" Ricky howled. "Wait!"

"Yes sir!" the officer replied. He fired his pistol repeatedly, hitting the stocky reporter's torso, legs, arms, and face. Using the dying man as a shield, Leung kicked the door behind him open and fell through it. He fired two shots at the young cop, hitting him once in the arm and once in the head.

Now all of the patrons scattered like bugs. Some hid under their tables, but most stood straight up and sprinted out the door. Inspector Woo ducked behind one of the booths and fired in Leung's direction, but the bullet missed and flew through Ricky's cheek. Leung fired his last three bullets back; two of them hit the ceiling fan, sending the fixture crashing down onto the ground and crushing what was left of the young officer dying on the floor.

"You son of a bitch," Woo growled. He made his way around the wreckage toward the kitchen door, then kicked it open, sending a quarter-inch of sea-food-scented water flooding out into the restaurant. There were dirty pans and pig carcasses on the counters alongside several oversized meat cleavers. Woo peered around the room, scanning for any sign of movement, stopping only when he saw a tooth-less chef cowering behind a hunk of roasted pig.

"Do you really think you can run forever?" Woo snarled.

"I don't need to run," Leung said. From across the room, he charged at Woo with a pot of hot soup. In-spector Woo raised his gun, but not before Leung threw the boiling liquid at him.

"*Yeaarggghhh!*" Woo howled in a high-pitched voice. Broth and elbow macaroni seared his chest like a tuna steak. His hairs were singed off and his epidermis melted, turning bright red from the heat, blood, and tomato soup sticking to what was left of his torso. It smelled a bit like borscht.

Inspector Leung charged at his counterpart and pinned him to the counter. He thrashed Woo merci-lessly, then reached for the meat cleaver on the cut-ting board beside him. Woo thrusted his pistol into Leung's stomach, but, before he could pull the trigger, Leung swung the cleaver as hard as he could, making a loud thud as it hit the counter.

Inspector Woo's right hand came off in one swing. He shrieked horrifically, stumbling to the ground. Torrents of blood gushed out of his wrist onto the floor, mixing with the cloudy seafood-scented water, which was quickly turning pink.

"You're right," Leung said, standing over him with the cleaver in hand. "I can't run forever. But I can get revenge."

"P-please!" Woo howled, clutching his severed wrist. "I was just following orders!"

"Of course you were," Leung seethed. "Gibson gave his life for you. *I* almost gave my life for you. What did we ever do to you?"

"It was the commissioner!" Woo exclaimed. "He's the one who's behind it all! I didn't want to kill any of you, Leung. But you know it's not you and me who gives orders around here. *Fuk mo wai bun jing yit cao jing.* We *serve*, Leung. I thought you'd understand that."

Leung gripped the cleaver tightly and held it over his head. "It's not me who doesn't understand. It's you."

Woo held his remaining hand forward. "W-wait!"

"Bad dog."

He swung down with all his might.

2014 / Chapter 9: The Handover

As Julian entered the White Horse office, he noticed the smell of asparagus and lavender oil coming from the back. There was no trace of any other employees; even Mr. Dayne's desk was empty. Julian approached the metal door to Raymond Lau's office, nestled in the vertex of the triangular floor plan, the camera above following his every move. *No more running*, Julian thought. *If he wants a fight, then goddammit, he'll have one.*

Staring directly into the lens, he squeezed his fist tight and pulled the door open.

"I'm here," Julian declared. "What do you want from me?"

But there was no response. The leather chair at the far end of the desk was turned to face the window, which offered a glimpse of Victoria Harbor far below. On the left, at least a hundred television sets were stacked across the whole wall, each one tuned to a different security feed. The light from the screens shone so brightly that all the posters and photographs across from them looked overexposed. It was almost eerie to look at those images: Raymond Lau sparring with Jet Li. Raymond Lau locking arms with Jackie Chan, Tony Leung, and Stephen Chow at a Communist Party gala. Raymond

Lau playing Mahjong with the former Chief Executive Donald Tsang.

Julian's chest was so tight it felt as if his lungs were caught in a metal crane lifting higher and higher into the air. But he steeled himself. He took a deep breath and shifted forward slowly, neither fighting the tightness nor dismissing it, but embracing it and making it his own. This was his fight. His moment. Holding his two fists in front of him, he marched toward the oak desk.

"Raymond Lau!" he barked. A crack of lighting flashed out across the harbor. "Do you know who I am? Do you know why I'm here?"

Julian clutched the top of the chair and swung it around to face him, ready to deliver a final blow straight across the star actor's face. But someone had beaten him to the punch. Slumped over in the leather chair, with a pistol in one hand and a bullet hole in the side of his head, Raymond Lau was already dead. His slim brown suit was stained red, dripping blood onto the Persian rug below.

Julian heard a toilet flushing from behind the walls. An oversized *Mahjong Royale* poster swung open, and Mr. Dayne walked out of the hidden bathroom wearing a blue shirt and red tie with a pair of nylon suspenders holding up his trousers. The stocky man rumbled toward Julian, wearing the same wide smile as always, hidden beneath his bushy brown mustache.

"Mr. Kensington!" he beamed. "Or, should I say, Mr. Smithfield? I didn't hear you come in." His piercingly blue eyes so disarmed Julian that for a second he forgot there was even a corpse in the room. "Are you feeling better?"

"No," Julian replied. "I'm feeling a bit dizzy."

"I'm sorry to hear that. Please, please, have a seat."

Julian sat down at the oak desk across from Raymond Lau's lifeless body. Dayne reached for a clay teapot. "Tea?" he asked.

"Yes, please."

Dayne poured from the teapot into two small earthenware mugs, then reached under the desk and removed a can of evaporated milk from a hidden mini-fridge. "Would you like it Hong Kong or British-style?"

"When in Rome, I guess . . ."

"A man after my own heart." He opened the can of evaporated milk and poured it into the two mugs until the liquid hung a millimeter above the edge. It seemed to defy gravity for it to not spill over. "I see you've met Raymond Lau already."

"Yes," Julian said. He stared over at the motionless corpse, gaping at the sight of blood dripping from the star actor's head. Lau's two eyes were rolled backwards and half his forehead was missing, but it was the same face that Julian had seen a thousand times before. Wrinkles formed around both sides of the actor's mouth, the result of his beaming personally and unflinching extroversion, though he wasn't smiling anymore. "What happened to him?"

"A suicide, it seems. I suppose he couldn't take the stress at work any longer."

"You killed him."

"Murder, suicide . . . these are just semantics. Sugar?"

"Yes, please."

On the desk, there were three figurines of wooden dogs—one covering its eyes, another its ears, and the third its mouth. Dayne took the latter and un-screwed its head, revealing a canister of white pow-der in its base. He carefully scooped two teaspoons and deposited one into each cup. "I always forget if this one is the sugar or the cocaine," he said. "I know that 'See No Evil' is the Splenda." He handed Julian one of the mugs, which trembled in his hand as he grasped it, causing the liquid to drip over the edge. "Well, either way, it should lift our spirits. Cheers."

Hesitantly, Julian took a sip, and thankfully it tasted sweet. An awkward silence permeated the room; the only sound was the slurping of tea, which Dayne devoured all in one gulp, staring up from his glass ambiguously at the scene before him. Finally, he put the glass down and wiped his mouth. It felt as though Dayne was waiting for Julian to speak—to point out the obvious question: *Why?* But Julian couldn't open his mouth, frozen at the sight of a man who was at least two steps ahead of him. "Won't you

say something?" Dayne asked. "This should be a celebration!"

"A celebration?"

"Of course! The villain is dead, and you didn't
have to lift a finger to stop him. This is what you
wanted, isn't it?"

"What *I* wanted?"

"Yes, of course. That's all I care about, Julian. I
just want to make you happy."

Julian scratched his head. "I'm confused. You're
not going to kill me?"

"*Kill you?*" Dayne gasped, offended by the supposition. "Of course not, Julian! I would never kill you.
Is that what Wong told you?"

"Wong?"

"Yes, Jack Wong. Or whatever that drug-addled
loon is calling himself these days. Do you really trust
a single word that comes out of his mouth? The man
killed his *own partner*, for Christ's sake! And in exchange for what? A mountain of opium to drown
himself in. And, of course, a part in that hideous TV
series."

"He told me you killed my father."

"Not *me*," Dayne said.

"But it was your organization. Your father."

Mr. Dayne sighed. "It was an unfortunate mistake, yes. And if I could take it back, I would. Your
family and mine go back generations. It was our
great-grandfathers that started this whole venture
in the first place."

"But it was your father who killed mine."

"We can't change the past, Julian. All we can do is look forward. That's what this company is about. And I want you to have a part in it. A real stake."

"Don't lie to me," Julian seethed. "You're just a drug dealer. That's all you are, and that's all you've ever been. Selling opiates to the masses."

"Opium," Dayne scoffed. "A shameful relic of a simpler time. And one that shall be eliminated from our inventory soon enough. Bespoke Tranche Opportunities, NINJA-Mortgages, Credit-Backed Securities . . . these are the products of the future. And the best part is: They're all perfectly legal."

"Empty numbers," Julian said.

"Better that than a cloud of white dust," Dayne said as he poured himself another glass of tea. "Tell me, Julian. Would you rather be poor and dead or rich and alive?"

"Is that a real question?"

"Yes," Dayne said, putting down the kettle and filling his cup again with evaporated milk. He tipped the can upside down and shook it to exhume the final drops. "But that's the choice you're facing now."

"You want to pay me off."

"Precisely, Julian. *Precisely.*" He stirred two teaspoons of sugar into the glass. "I want to pay you off. You see, my father used violence to achieve his goals, but I prefer the carrot to the stick. If you look at history, commerce brings peace wherever it goes. Think about it: no two countries with a McDonald's or a Starbucks have ever gone to war. That's a matter of historical record. So, let's trade."

"I don't want your money."

Dayne sipped his tea pensively. "Of course you do. Why else would you even be here with that tape? You've either come to blackmail me or kill me, and frankly you don't strike me as a murderer."

Julian's fists loosened. "I'm not."

"Tell me, what will satisfy you, Julian? An extra ten thousand dollars a month? A second flat on Lamma Island?"

"I want my father back."

"Well, I can't bring back the dead, Julian. This is a flourishing enterprise, but we don't have magic powers."

"I don't care. I want him back."

"How about a promotion then? I'll raise your title to Senior Executive Consultant and add another fifty thousand to your monthly salary. You can even work from home if you like. Or not work, if that's what you prefer."

Julian slammed the VHS on the table. "How about a hundred million dollars or I send this tape to the press."

Dayne raised an eyebrow. "That's . . . a bold offer. A little high to start."

"I'm negotiating."

"I think you're overestimating your leverage. Raymond Lau is already dead. Even if you exposed him as a fraud, what difference would it make?"

"He was the CEO of your company. If it comes out that he was involved with the triads, you think anyone will buy your stock anymore?"

"You have such faith in the Hong Kong people. But they will follow the money, as they always have. And they won't care where it came from."

"Not anymore," Julian said. "Just look outside. The people are through with scum like you."

Dayne snickered, setting the mug on the table. "You don't know this city like I do. This is my home, after all. And it's always the same thing here: delusional protestors, marching year after year for something that will never come. Democracy, reform, you name it. But things will never change, Mr. Smithfield. Hong Kong and greed go hand in hand. It's part of the local flavor. And *no one* is going to change that . . . not Beijing, not the Hong Kong people, not me, and not you. Never."

"Maybe you're right," Julian said. "So how about two hundred million then?"

Dayne smirked. "Now that's the Hong Kong spirit," he said. "Tit for tat. But I think we can come to an acceptable compromise. I know what you want, and I know what Jack Wong wants. And, conveniently, they're the same thing."

"What are you talking about?"

"Since the moment you set foot in Chungking Mansions, I've been watching you. *We've* been watching you. See?"

Dayne took a remote from the top drawer of the desk and pointed it at the wall of televisions. He pressed a button, and every set turned to the same grainy security footage. Julian recognized the location immediately: the lobby of Lucky Guest House, where Celeste sat behind the counter as usual, flipping through the pages of her book. Julian's eyes swelled wide.

"Raymond was very impressed by your taste in women," Dayne said.

"You bastard. I swear to god, if you hurt her . . ."

"Every man has the same weakness. The damsel in distress."

Julian stood up and clutched his fist tightly again. "I'll kill you!"

"But how would Jack Wong feel if he found out about you and his daughter?"

Julian froze and fell backwards into his chair. "His daughter?"

"Yes," Dayne said. "She's been paying his debt for seven years, while he smokes his pipe and chases myths. I wonder if this was part of his plan. A bit of complicated matchmaking. You *are* a good catch, after all."

"What are you talking about?"

"I'm talking about giving you both what you want. Her."

Celeste flipped her hair then turned the page yet again. "Her," Julian repeated, as if in a trance.

"If you give up that tape, I will call off her debt and let the two of you live in peace."

"That's a generous offer," Julian said.

"Very generous. Far more than you possibly deserve."

Julian slouched back, staring into the ceiling. *What choice do I have?* he thought to himself. To take the deal was to be no better than his great-grandfather—was to be in league with triads and the dark forces that had corrupted this city in the first place. But to reject it was suicide. He stared at the pistol dangling from the fingers of the Raymond Lau's corpse. Perhaps if he was fast enough, he could grab it and dispatch with Mr. Dayne, and then, his revenge complete, he could go out in a blaze of glory, exchanging fire with the guards and cops in the lobby until he met his inevitable end. *But what good would that do?* he thought. What was he even trying to accomplish? Even without Mr. Dayne, the organization would endure. Someone or something would take his place. There's a new star every year, and he wasn't about to give his life just to accelerate the process. To change the scenery. *There's no stopping the wheels of history*, he thought. All he could do was to be crushed by it or to stand behind the wheel, steering it ever so slightly in the right direction—away from those who would be flattened by its course. Away from the innocent. Or away from Celeste, at least. "I'll do it," he said, sliding the VHS across the table.

Dayne smirked as he picked the tape up and held it in hands, betraying no surprise at Julian's choice. "You're too noble for your own good," he said, leaning back and placing his legs on the table just beside Raymond Lau's corpse. "You've been watching too many of his films."

***

A half hour later, Julian sat in the backseat of a black Mercedes Benz, moving at a snail's pace through the Cross-Harbor Tunnel back into Kowloon. Colm O'Callaghan was chauffeuring him back to Chungking Mansions on Dayne's orders and was growing increasingly frustrated with the slow-moving traffic. He honked repeatedly at the cars ahead of him.

"Come on!" he yelled. "Fucking protests always hold up traffic . . ."

But Julian was thankful for the delay. He didn't quite know how Celeste would react to the news. Would she think of him as a white knight saving her from danger or just another greasy man buying used goods? Maybe he would save the girl only for her to run away from him. Or perhaps he would get her back and she would resent him for it, as if the act of saving her entitled Julian to her body in some medieval sense.

Julian didn't want her to think that. He wanted her to know how he saw her the very first time, when he dreamed of the etched stone by the riverbank. The gods had used thirty-six thousand

268

five hundred stones to build the heavens, and she was the one left over, the only one who could fill in the cracks. So much of Julian's past was robbed from him, and it was Celeste alone who could fill that gap and make him feel whole.

But of course he couldn't say *that*.

When the car finally exited the tunnel, Julian gazed in awe at the lights of Nathan Road. Hong Kong at night was so lush with neon that it seemed almost sacrilegious to walk the city in daylight. This city fed on the darkness and embraced it like no other. Soon, the car sped toward the curb and screeched to a halt. Julian stepped onto the sidewalk and stared up at the entrance to Chungking Mansions. The unlit lettering above the doorway was shrouded in darkness, and even the entryway was barren for the first time he could remember. There were no watch salesmen, no tailors, no Arab men whispering in his ear about Numidian hashish. Just a uniformed policewoman leaning against a parking meter. O'Callaghan stepped out of the car and threw the keys to her.

"*Bo ci hei ce yan king wan jyun,*" he said. "*Hou fai ceot loi.*"

"Yessir," the officer replied, saluting back.

Julian and O'Callaghan walked through the gate unmolested by the usual assortment of hawkers, restaurateurs, and hostel owners who typically lined the building's front hallway. The salesmen were still there, but they were all huddled along the walls as if standing at attention. When the two men reached the elevator, Julian pressed the 3M button, and the doors rattled closed.

"Here we are," Colm said. "This girl must be important to you."

"She is," Julian replied. "She's a *bodhisattva*. A goddess in a fig tree."

"Like in that TV show," O'Callaghan said. "What was it called again?"

Julian cocked his head. "What TV show?"

The elevator doors ringed open, and the two men stepped out and walked through the dark gunmetal hallway toward the guest house. Julian tiptoed around the crushed cockroaches, but Colm simply walked through them.

"*Dream of the Red Chamber*," O'Callaghan said. "That mini-series with Raymond Lau."

"Raymond Lau was in *Dream of the Red Chamber?*"

"It was on TVB two days ago. I think they were running a marathon."

Julian thought back to his first night in Hong Kong—zoning in and out after King Chow punched him out in the very lobby in front of them. Celeste had dragged him into bed and turned on the TV to cover the noise coming from the next rooms—the pounding and moaning that continued long into the night. When she first switched the set on, a grainy image faded in and out: a towering banyan tree amidst a lush world of rivers and lakes. Karen Mok sat up on the top branch in a flowing purple dress with overlong sleeves, and a monk stood below her in an orange robe, clutching an unremarkable etched stone. Now, Julian remembered the actor's face clearly.

"Shih-yin," he said aloud.

"Right," Colm said. "He was the one who found the stone by the river."

Julian froze and looked down at his palms in sheer terror. Whose hands were these in front of him? Whose dreams was he chasing in the first place? As they arrived at the front door of the guest house, he saw himself as he really was: a cog in some greater machine, clinging to the patterns of the past. A tool of someone—of *something*—that was utterly out of his control. He had allowed himself to be led on by men like Wong, Dayne, and even Colm O'Callaghan for far too long. He had been entranced by a mythic image of this city, obsequious to an idea of something that never was—to a dream long since dead in this venal metropolis, or perhaps even the world. But this was the path he walked, and for better or worse he had to see this story to its end.

"It's coming back to me," Julian said. "Bits and pieces."

"You know," O'Callaghan replied as he pushed the front door open. "The director, Charlie Yip—he didn't even read the book."

The lobby was deserted. Where Celeste had been sitting just a half hour earlier, there was now just an empty stool gathering dust. The only sign of movement was the creaky, old security camera, which blinked red and stared directly at them, practically nodding up and down.

"She's not here," Julian said.

"She's here," O'Callaghan insisted. "We just saw her." The burly chief of security marched down the hallway and knocked twice on King Chow's door. When there was no answer, he simply raised one foot and kicked the door open, knocking it off its hinges. Instantly, a waft of smoke floated out, filling the entire guest house. The two men entered the room, batting the noxious fumes away with their hands.

The haze was so dense that Julian could scarcely see a foot in front of him. The ground was covered a mess of drugs, sex toys, and cigarette butts—it was as if every square inch of the floor could both get him stoned and get him off. Amidst the mess, he spied a familiar orange pill bottle, missing its cap. He reached down and picked it up, holding it close to his eyes to read its label: JULIAN KENSINGTON it displayed on its side. Only that wasn't his name anymore.

King Chow himself was splayed atop a king-sized bed, completely naked save for the black eyepatch on his right eye. A woman was tucked under the covers beside him, but her face was blanketed by the sheets.

"*Lei zhou mat ye?*" King Chow yelled, his gruff baritone shaking the whole room. His lone eye was horribly bloodshot.

"Celeste," Julian said. "Is that you?"

O'Callaghan stepped forward. "We're confiscating this property."

"*Koi hai ngo ge yan!*"

"The order comes from Mr. Dayne."

"*Fuck* Mr. Dayne."

O'Callaghan removed the golden Beretta from his shoulder holster. "You might want to pick your words more carefully, Mr. Chow. You may be a big fish around here, but men like you are easily replaceable."

King Chow turned his head and saw Julian standing in the doorway. He squinted through the haze until he recognized the face. "You," he fumed. "You did this." He stood up and curled his right hand into a fist.

"I wouldn't do that," O'Callaghan said.

But King Chow was delirious. "I told you," he snarled. "That girl belongs to me!" He kicked his feet like a bull and charged at Julian with clenched teeth.

Seemingly without aiming, O'Callaghan fired a single shot, and King Chow fell to the floor with a bullet hole in his calf. "*Gyahhh!*" he shrieked.

Startled by the noise, the woman in bed woke up and threw off the sheets. It wasn't Celeste, but rather a blonde-wigged woman with powdered cheeks, whom Julian recognized. "*Lei se koi!*" she shouted at the top of her lungs.

O'Callaghan smirked. "I told you not to do that."

"Don't kill him," Julian pleaded. "No one has to die today, please."

O'Callaghan pointed the gun again at the fat drug dealer, who was clutching at his bleeding calf, trying to stanch the bleeding. "He attacked you," he said, pressing the pistol against Chow's left temple. "I don't have any choice." He squeezed the trigger with a sick grin on his face.

Julian dropped the empty bottle and lunged forward, doing his best Raymond Lau impression. "*Toiiiiii,*" he grunted, punching O'Callaghan straight across the cheek. The sheer force of the blow knocked his sunglasses off, but there was no real damage.

"You hit me," O'Callaghan said calmly. He raised the gun and pressed it between Julian's eyes, the cold metal sending a shiver down his nose. "I don't care what Mr. Dayne says. No one hits me and lives to tell the story."

Julian stepped back. "I'm sorry, I—"

Without a word, a blunt red object came down over O'Callaghan's head, and he crumpled to the ground unconscious. Celeste stood in the doorway with *Dream of the Red Chamber* in her hands, breathing heavily. Her arms and legs were still vibrating from the force of the single blow she'd just delivered.

Julian exhaled. "Nice shot."

"What's going on here?" Celeste asked, dropping the book to the ground. "I heard a gunshot and—"

King Chow howled in pain. "*Yau mo yen ho yi dai ngo hui yi yun?*" The blonde-wigged woman sprang up and rushed to his side, helping the fat pimp to his feet.

"Oh my god," Celeste gasped. "What happened?"

King Chow rested his arm on the prostitute's shoulder. "*Koi gao jou ngo,*" he said to Celeste. "*Lei ge tzai yigeng wanjou.*" He and his consort hobbled together out of the room, the woman looking back at Julian as she stepped through the doorway.

"What did he say?" Julian asked.

Celeste replied simply: "The debt is paid."

Julian smiled. "Good."

"I don't understand," she said. "What are you doing here? I thought you were done with me."

"It's hard to explain. But it turns out that your boss and my boss are really the same person. And I made a deal with him for your life."

"You bought me," Celeste said frankly.

"Well, when you put it like that . . ."

She smirked. "How romantic."

1984 / Chapter 9: The Show Must Go On

Inspector Leung sat in the front seat of a black Mercedes Benz, speeding through the Cross-Harbor Tunnel on the road to Aberdeen. The car, which had belonged to Inspector Woo, handled quite well given the circumstance; Leung was driving so fast it felt like the wheels might fall off their axels, and the car was jolting and jerking constantly as he weaved through traffic. *Jianghu Studios*, he muttered to himself. *Ay, there's the rub. The hive of it all.*

He couldn't quite understand his fixation. Surely there were others who were more responsible for Leung's current misfortunes—people like Inspector Woo, Marshal Hong, Ricky Cheung, and even the commissioner. But three of them were dead already and getting to Dayne would be impossible. The second he stepped into the Wan Chai Headquarters, he would be arrested, killed, or worse.

But Leung knew he could slip into Jianghu Studios unnoticed. And if he got inside, he could track down Raymond Lau and Charlie Yip and let off two shots to the head. That was all Leung needed: one chance. That would be it for him. The guards would swarm in, and, if they didn't kill Leung, the police themselves would be in hot pursuit. The commissioner would send the best of the best: SDU, the Flying Tigers. And there would be no way for Leung to fight them off. They were trained to take down terrorists and notorious criminals, and he was just an old cop on his last legs.

Someone had to pay for Smithfield's death. Someone had to answer for the tar in his lungs and the bruises and gashes covering his body. Inspector Leung's hand trembled as he sped out of the tunnel. He hoped that Wong had gotten Smithfield's family to safety already. If Leung failed, maybe they could press their case from abroad—inform some Labour MP's and demand a thorough investigation of the whole matter—but the odds of success were slim at best. Maybe nonexistent. Leung's heart quaked, yearning for something lost but never real—the same feeling he had each night at the dockyard as he waited and waited for Little Chow's next fix. But Leung wasn't craving the opium anymore. He was addicted to something else.

Soon, he arrived at Jianghu Studios. There was just a single guardhouse between him and the parking lot, inside which sat a private security guard thumbing through the *South China Morning Post*— a thin man with rosy cheeks and bushy brown hair.

"Can I help you?" the guard asked in a thick Welsh accent, without even looking up from his magazine. "Employees only beyond this point. I'll need to see some ID."

"Of course," Leung replied. He reached out the window presented the ID and badge that he'd found in Inspector Woo's glove compartment. The guard set down his newspaper, which pictured Lady Thatcher and Deng Xiaoping shaking hands on its cover, under the headline SINO-BRITISH JOINT DECLARATION: HANDOVER AGREEMENT REACHED. The guard took the ID card and examined it closely, struggling to see the resemblance between the man in the picture and the man in front of him.

"Inspector Woo?" the guard asked skeptically.

"That's right. I'm here about Eddie Yang's suicide."

The guard raised an eyebrow. "Your boss assured us that the matter was settled."

"The commissioner himself sent me," Leung explained. "There's been a new development in the case, and Mr. Lau demanded a personal update on the situation."

"This is the first I'm hearing of this."

"If it wasn't, we'd be bad at our jobs. Mr. Lau asked that it be handled *discreetly.*"

"Hm," the guard grunted, squinting down again at the ID card. "That sounds like him, I guess." He pressed a small red button and the barrier arm rose into the sky.

British ignorance, Leung thought. *The one thing you can always count on.*

***

As he stepped inside the main building, Inspector Leung could see maybe a foot in front of him at most. The room was pitch black except for the few stage lights visible at the set far in the distance. Leung crept past the empty "police station," using the desks and walls for cover as he made his way across the room.

Leung spied a host of cameras, lights, and crew members at the end of the warehouse, where Eddie Yang had been found dead just days ago. It was like nothing had happened. Charlie Yip sat in his director's chair with his chin in one hand and a massive cup of coffee in the other.

"There's been some misunderstanding," Raymond Lau emoted unconvincingly. The handsome actor stood at the top of the stairs, dressed in an orange monk's robe. His hair was disheveled and he was sweating mightily, causing his normally smooth mullet to slick back. "I'm not the man you're looking for!"

At the base of the stairs, a young actress stepped forward, wearing a red cheongsam with white cranes sewn into the fabric. An older man in a black magisterial outfit stood beside her, pointing a long bamboo spear in Raymond Lau's direction.

"Don't listen to him," the woman said. "He pretended to be a monk, and then he tried to crawl under my sheets! He's the one who killed Uncle Zhou!"

"I'm not a monk!" Lau insisted.

"Then why are you dressed like one?" the minister yelled.

Raymond stepped backwards up the stairs, keeping both arms out in front of him. "I'm telling you," he said, "that bastard set me up. He sent me back in time to help you, but he didn't want revenge. He just wanted a scapegoat."

"Who?" the girl asked skeptically.

"The *real* monk," Lau said. "I told you: I'm a cop!"

"You liar!" the minister seethed. "All this talk of time travel and magic. What kind of policeman would act this way? I let you into my house and then you try to *shame my daughter!*" He thrust his spear at Lau, missing his throat by mere inches.

"Hey!" Lau protested. "She came onto me!"

The girl scowled at him. "He's lying, father! Kill him!"

"I'm telling you," Lau said, crouching into a battle stance. "I don't want to fight you, but I will."

The minister inched up the stairs, clutching the spear tight. "If you didn't kill Uncle Zhou, then who did?"

Inspector Leung removed the golden Beretta from his waistband and aimed directly at the center of the star actor's chest, imagining the character 怒 right in the middle of his sternum. He took a deep breath to steady his hands and waited until the orange robe was firmly in his sights. "I got you, you son of a bitch."

A stage light glinted off the barrel of the gun, catching Lau's eye. "Oh my god!" he yelled, startling the whole crew.

Leung pulled the trigger and a single shot rang out. It was aimed perfectly, but in the confusion, the minister lifted the spear so that its blade passed just in front of Raymond Lau's torso. The bullet deflected off its tip and landed in the foot of the teenage actress, who shrieked wildly in pain. From the force of the impact, the older man fell to the ground and the spear went flying into a porcelain urn, shattering it into pieces.

In frustration, Leung emptied the barrel of his gun, but Raymond Lau ducked behind the handrail and then took cover behind the upstairs door. The crew members all panicked and scattered for cover as Leung reloaded the weapon. The camera pointed right in his direction, but the director had scurried off, nowhere to be found. Leung ascended the staircase slowly, holding the pistol in front of him. "There's nowhere to hide!" Leung barked. "No one can protect you here!"

Leung kicked the door open, knocking Lau backwards into the wall behind it. The inspector pointed his gun at the star actor, who slunk to the floor in terror. A trail of yellow liquid seeped out from beneath his robe, smelling of coffee and baijiu. "Please," he pleaded, holding his arms out in front of him. "Please, don't . . . I'm scared!" His tears and sweat washed the layers of makeup off his cheeks, revealing the cuts and bruises that Eddie Yang had inflicted. "I'm sorry!"

It was his best performance all day.

As his index finger tensed, Inspector Leung felt a weight on his shoulders pulling him backwards.

Charlie Yip was on his back, wrestling Leung away from his star.

"Get off of me!" Leung scowled. He flailed wildly at the director, but the thin man pulled Leung backwards over the edge of the top stair until gravity took over. The two men rolled down the winding staircase, knocking their heads and bodies in the struggle. As they hit the bottom, the pistol dislodged from Leung's hand and slid toward the triptych screen at the center of the room.

Dizzied and bruised, Inspector Leung stood up slowly, trying to regain his footing. The director reached for the spear on the ground, but Leung kicked him in the stomach and pushed him hard against the wall, shattering yet another urn. He clasped his hands around Yip's thin neck, squeezing the life out of him. "You son of a bitch," Leung spat out. "You lied to me!"

"I had to . . ." Yip choked out in a whisper, his face quickly turning purple. "If I didn't, they were g-going to kill me!"

Leung squeezed harder and harder as if his hands were in rigor mortis, focusing all of his rage on the man in front of him. The director's eyes rolled backwards and the life exited his veins—until, suddenly, there was a sharp pain in Leung's abdomen, and he let go.

He looked down and saw the head of the spear protruding from the front of his stomach. He craned his neck around and saw Raymond Lau behind him, releasing the handle and scurrying off in fear.

"Now that's embarrassing," Leung said.

He fell to the ground, bleeding heavily. His vision grew dim, and he waited for the inevitable to come.

***

"Leung, Leung, Leung," a haughty British voice said, the pronunciation still slightly off. "What am I to do with you?"

Inspector Leung opened his eyes. He was still on the set of the Qing-era mansion, in a puddle of blood not far from where he'd found Eddie Yang's corpse. The whole room was now completely uninhabited, save for him and the fat, shadowy figure standing at his feet.

Slowly, the hazy image came into focus. A fat, bespectacled man stood over Leung, puffing on a filtered cigarette.

"It's *Leung*," the inspector choked out. "Not Lung."

"I apologize," Commissioner Dayne replied. "Even after all these years, Cantonese still sounds like gibberish to me. Nine different tones . . . I don't know how you can tell one word from another."

"You have to pay attention," Leung whispered, his voice losing strength.

"Me, I like things simple. When I say something, it's exactly what I mean." He took another puff from his cigarette and blew it out forcefully, fanning away the white smoke hanging in the air. "I told you not to pursue this case any further, *Leung*. But you did

283

and look what's happened to you. You deserve a better ending than this."

Inspector Leung groaned and rolled towards him. "C-cigarette," he whispered.

"Yes, of course. Where are my manners?" The commissioner removed a box of Lucky Strikes from his uniform pocket and handed one to the fallen inspector. Leung put it to his mouth, his hands jittering the whole while, and the commissioner helped him light it with a gleaming Zippo that had a white horse etched into its side.

Inspector Leung propped himself up against the broken triptych screen. The blood from his wound blotted out the character on the left fold, leaving only the character 力 on the right. Power was all that remained.

"So it was you the whole time," Leung coughed out.

"It wasn't just me," Dayne said. "All of the superintendents supported my decision. After all, your interference could have jeopardized the whole sale."

"Sale?" Leung asked. "What sale? What the hell are you talking about?"

"Don't you read the news? It's all over the papers."

Leung thought back to the guard's newspaper outside the studio—the picture of Deng Xiaoping and Lady Thatcher shaking hands on its front. It had all been right there in front of him, if only he'd just opened his eyes.

"You're selling Hong Kong," he said finally.

"It's unavoidable," Dayne replied. "Our lease on the New Territories expires in fifteen years. And without that, all of our power, water, and fertile lands fall into Chinese territory. To put it bluntly: Beijing has us by the balls. And they've threatened an invasion if we don't assent to their demands."

"So you cut a deal."

"Yes. We figured if we're going to lose the damn thing anyway, we might as well get something for it. And Beijing was more than willing to pay, as long as we kept this arrangement *private*. Officially, it's a total capitulation."

"This was all about money, then."

"Of course this is about money," Dayne said. "This is *Hong Kong*."

"Of course," Leung said wistfully. "I should have known."

The commissioner's brow furrowed. "But there were conditions."

"What conditions?"

"To ensure a smooth transition, they want to seize control of police authority, even before the territory is officially ceded. They're leery of any countermeasures our government could implement before the handover. So, for the next thirteen years, party loyalists will be placed in ranking positions on the police force. And, by 1992, they want a commissioner of their own."

"A steep price."

"But one I will gladly pay for our men."

"Please," Leung scoffed. "There's nothing worse than a self-righteous villain."

"And you think you're some kind of hero? If you'd succeeded in settling this personal vendetta, what would you have accomplished? The alternative was war. Corpses would have piled up in the streets."

"Now you're just being overdramatic. Raymond Lau is only an actor."

"No, Leung. He was our point of contact for this whole endeavor. *Canton Violence* was just a cover—an excuse to film scenes in the mainland. And while he was there, Raymond established meaningful connections with local officials, set up the necessary channels for our negotiations, even arranged the terms of sale himself . . . it's amazing what you can do with a smile and a bottle of *baijiu.*"

Leung sat in silence, awestruck. "He really was a secret agent."

"A cultural ambassador," Dayne said. "He has many fans in the mainland."

"But his films aren't even in Mandarin."

"Not yet," the commissioner said with a twinkle in his eye. "But they can be. Through these mainland co-productions, we'll be able to open many more doors with Chinese officials. Doors that will be far more profitable than this dinky little town alone. Raymond Lau is the face of Hong Kong, beloved by millions around the world. Beijing will jump at the chance to use his image to their ends. To smooth over this whole transition . . . and, of course, to help secure foreign investments."

"Propaganda," Leung said.

"Call it what you like," Dayne said. "I call it good business. And in exchange, Beijing has offered us a temporary reprieve: a policy of salutary neglect for fifty years and enough capital upfront to flood the market with Yulong. Fifty years to make the Yangtze River run white. Plenty of time to build a nest egg and cash out."

"A nest egg . . ."

"Financial stability for all our boys on the force."

"A retirement plan for the triads."

"If only you'd listened to me, I would have had a job for you too. I take care of all my dogs, Leung. But if they're disloyal, there's no choice but to put them down."

"Like Smithfield?"

Dayne grimaced. "The Smithfields and my family go back almost a century. Believe me, Leung. I didn't enjoy that nasty bit of business."

"And yet, you still did it."

"I had to," Dayne insisted. "He put the whole deal at risk. The Chinese have insisted on maintaining *stability*, so wildcards like Smithfield and Marshal Hong can no longer be tolerated. I thank you, by the way, for disposing of the latter. Saved me the trouble of doing it myself."

"You're no better than him," Leung said. "You're all criminals."

Dayne threw his cigarette to the ground and stomped it out. "There's no convincing a basset hound," he said. "You can't teach an old dog new tricks. But a new one . . ." The commissioner whistled sharply.

Inspector Leung expected the Flying Tigers to come swooping in through the windows, but, instead of a swarm, he heard only footsteps in the distance. A figure approached from the shadows, dressed entirely in black, the lights glinting off his dark sunglasses.

"Wong," Leung said simply.

"I'm sorry," Wong spoke softly, his eyes hidden from view.

"When we found him," Dayne said, "he was convulsing in the middle of the airport, trying to get through immigration with Smithfield's family. A seizure, brought on by withdrawal. He was very willing to share information in exchange for some chemical relief."

Leung's pain grew sharp. He coughed up blood, spitting his cigarette into the red pool below, then closed his eyes and felt himself sinking backwards into an endless darkness.

"I'm sorry," Wong repeated. "If I didn't, they were going to kill them both!"

Leung opened his eyes again. "Victoria and Julian . . ."

"It was an easy decision," Dayne said. "Say yes and be a hero. A young boy and his mother will live, and he'll be on the inside track to success: a featured role in Raymond Lau's new TV series."

"And mountains of Yulong," Leung said, staring intently at his partner. "When a white horse is not a horse . . ."

The commissioner smirked. "Every man has his price."

"Not me," Leung said. "You can't buy me."

"And that's why I can't let you live," Dayne said. He picked the golden Beretta up off the ground and handed it to Wong. "You should do it."

Wong pointed to himself incredulously. "Me?"

"I lost my most loyal dog today. Well, now's your chance to take his place."

Wong looked back at Leung, who was still just barely breathing. "But he's my *partner.*"

"Wong," Leung whispered, his eyelids already drooping closed. "It's okay. I'd rather it be you than that bastard Raymond Lau. Just make it quick."

The commissioner smiled. "Good boy."

Wong took a deep breath and pressed the gun to the center of his partner's forehead. The cold muzzle jolted Leung awake—his eyes opened wide, as piercing as the first day Wong had seen them.

"The boy," Leung whispered softly as he stared down the barrel of the gun. "Keep him safe."

The muzzle flashed silently.

Epilogue: Redology

Julian held a bundle of lit joss sticks as he knelt at his father's grave. Smoke billowed from the burnt embers, ascending into Julian's eyes, which were already filled with tears. He clasped his hands together as the images of his father and mother echoed in his mind. The palpitations in his chest were constant, as they had been since he set foot in this city, and he'd started to feel an almost static buzz in his fingertips, like a lightning bolt condensed. But now at least the wounds had begun to scab over. There would be a scar left, but he was still young. It would lighten over time.

Julian didn't believe in heaven or hell, never thought that life was anything more than a flash of light between the darkness, but still he said a prayer for his late parents, wishing them well wherever they were. Even if the words themselves were empty, they helped fill the gap between past and present. The tightness in his chest was still there, and it would be there for a long time, if it ever went away at all. But for now, Julian was content to live alongside it. To not fight the sensation, but to welcome it as a friend.

Julian reached down and deposited the joss sticks into the fresh mound of dirt on his father's grave. The short grass beside it swayed gently with the wind, which blew scented embers just past Julian's nose. He stood up and took a deep breath, savoring the smell of sandalwood as he looked down at Tai O Village far in the distance. He could see Celeste and Flora down below, looking like mere ants from this height. Beads of sweat began to form on his skin as he glared at the gorgeous ex-hostess in her lime-green bikini.

I couldn't save my parents, he thought, *but I could save her.* Whatever else had happened in this city, whatever compromises he'd been forced to make, he took solace in the knowledge that Celeste, at least, was free. Maybe he couldn't help everyone, he realized, but if he could save just one person then his was a life well spent. Mission success, as far as he was concerned. Both of his parents would have been proud.

As he stared down, the beads of sweat that had gathered on his arms deformed into thin streams running off his fingertips. A stifling heat had started to grow behind him, and he could hear the sound of rustling grass swirling into a typhoon. He turned around and dropped into a battle stance, finding himself face-to-face with Wong, who was holding a bamboo firestopper over his head.

"*Hiyyyah!*" Wong shrieked as he swung the pole down. Julian dodged, but it didn't matter; the tassels landed several feet to his left, where a small fire was now blazing. The joss sticks had blown over and ignited the surrounding grass into a near inferno, but Wong beat the flames repeatedly until the last ember was put out.

Julian exhaled. "I thought you were going to kill me."

"Quite the contrary," the monk huffed, dropping the pole to the ground.

"I appreciate it. That could have been a real mess."

"It's the least I could do," Wong said. "I saw what happened in the papers. Raymond Lau, dead by suicide. I imagine that was your doing."

"Not me," Julian said. "Not directly. But Mr. Dayne made me an offer I couldn't refuse."

"I can relate," the monk said. "Years ago, his father offered me the same choice."

"To kill your own partner?"

"Yes," Wong replied. "That's right."

"So you were the one who killed my father."

Wong shook his head. "No, Julian. A different partner."

"Then who did it? Who pulled the trigger?"

"Those are two different questions."

"So give me two answers."

"I'm afraid I'm out of those at the moment. But I can promise you this: If they're not dead yet, they will be soon. We all will."

"My father was no saint," Julian said. "I know that. And maybe I'm not any better. But he didn't deserve what happened to him."

"There is no better or worse, Julian. Everyone is just the same."

"You were going to betray me, weren't you? When we got to London, you were going to turn around and trade that tape for Celeste."

"Maybe I was," Wong said. "But in the end, we both got what we wanted."

"She told me what you did to her—leaving her there with her mother in that brothel. Letting her pay off your debts while you smoked your pipe in that den. She's never going to forgive you for that."

"Will you?"

Julian said nothing, gazing into the deep blue water in the distance—at two spotted islands that marked the border between China and Hong Kong. "I'm working on it," he said in a voice so frail it was almost blown off-course by the wind.

"Well, I hope you get there eventually," Wong replied, but he didn't sound like he believed it. "I came here to say goodbye."

"Goodbye?"

"Yes. Next week I'm flying out to Singapore."

Julian's eyebrow rose. "Why, you have family out there or something?"

"Celeste's mother. She went missing ten years ago, about the same time as her daughter. Word is, she might still be out in that direction."

Julian stepped forward. "Do you need any help?"

The old monk smiled warmly. "Maybe you are a better man than he was. Or at least a better inspector."

"Maybe," Julian said. "Maybe not."

"Before I left, I wanted to give you something." He opened up a small satchel draped over his shoulder and removed a thick black tome with distinctive hints of vanillin and benzaldehyde, like the scent of an old library. The words ROMANCE OF THE THREE KINGDOMS were etched in gold on its spine. "Your great-grandfather's diary," he said, handing it to Julian. "I should have given this to you long ago."

It was heavy, but the paper was so brittle it felt like it might crumble in his hands. "I'm not sure whether to thank you. Is this a blessing or a curse?"

"Can't it be both?"

***

As Julian walked back into the village, he passed a wilting flower on the road, just beside a shrine to Kwan Yu. He knelt down and picked the shriveled bud, depositing it in the hands of the bearded idol.

"Here's one for you," he said.

Because it was Sunday, Tai O was especially packed with tourists, and the shopkeepers had their hands full trying to keep up with the demand. Most of the week, Julian might have been the only *gweilo* in the whole village, but today the village looked more like New York than Hong Kong. The crowd was a model of diversity: mainland tourists, Americans, even domestic workers enjoying their only day off. Children snaked through the crowd, playing tag and squirting each other with old Super Soakers.

They smiled gleefully even as their parents stood apart.

Down at the edge of the river, Flora and Celeste sat with their feet in the water just beside the replica of Julian's old stilt house. Celeste wore a green bikini with a pair of fake Prada sunglasses resting on the bridge of her nose. She was so enraptured by the denouement of her book that she was oblivious to the lurid gazes of the villagers and tourists walking up and down the pier. Flora sat beside her wearing a blue one-piece swimsuit with her hair tied up in a bun, holding a long fishing pole in the water.

"It's dead out there," Flora complained. "I'm never gonna catch one."

"Not with that attitude," Celeste replied, barely paying attention.

"It's not about attitude. The water's polluted!" In frustration, she stood up and kicked the crude fishing pole into the river. "I'm going for a swim," she declared, doing a cannonball straight off the pier. "I'll catch those bastards with my bare hands!" Pale greenish water splashed onto Celeste and her novel, but she merely brushed the beads of saltwater off and continued reading to the end.

"I'm done," Julian said simply as he approached her, sitting down with his legs dangling off the pier.

"Me too," she said as she finally closed the book.

"How was the ending? Did they stick the landing?"

"There wasn't really an ending," she said. "After eighty chapters, it just *ends*."

"That's too bad."

"I heard there's another version out there with the final forty chapters. But they weren't written by the original author."

"Well, someone has to end it. Don't they?"

"What's that book you got there?" Celeste asked, pointing to the diary under his arms. "Is it any good?"

"It's just an old story," Julian replied. "Who knows how much of it is true?"

Flora bobbed her head out of the water, shaking the moisture off like a dog. "The water's great," she said. "You guys want to join me?"

"We're okay," Julian said, laughing at the sight.

"Come on," Flora insisted, beckoning with her grin. "It's nice and warm. Once you get back to London, you'll be stuck on dry land all year."

"Who said I'm going back to London?"

Flora's eyebrow shot up. "You're not?"

"I like it here," Julian declared. "I'm thinking of buying one of these houses."

"*Aiyyya*. What would you want one of these tourist traps for?"

"There's just something about this place," Julian said as he closed his eyes and squeezed Celeste tight, taking in the fresh ocean breeze. She wasn't the girl of his dreams and maybe they wouldn't have a storybook ending, but for now, at least, she was here and so was he.

As Julian leaned in to kiss her, a pink dolphin protruded from the water, squawking as it launched itself through the air. "There!" Flora shouted. "Did you see it?"

"No," Julian said, but it didn't matter. He was home.

About the Author

Ethan James Kaplan is a playwright and novelist from New York City. He has a BA in English and Creative Writing from Northwestern University and an MFA in Creative Writing from Queens College. Ethan has taught courses on writing, public speaking, and international affairs at Queens College and Hong Kong Polytechnic University. Ethan's play *Imitatio* was the winner of the 2017 Birdhouse Prize and was published by Ghostbird Press in 2018, and his play *Speculation* was performed as a staged reading at the Flea Theater in June 2016.

About the Press

Unsolicited Press isn't a fan of conformity. Founded in 2012, the small press has consistently sought to produce outstanding fiction, poetry, and creative nonfiction that breaks standards. Learn more at www.unsolicitedpress.com.

9 781947 021686